The House of Cthulhu

TOR BOOKS BY BRIAN LUMLEY

THE NECROSCOPE SERIES

Necroscope	*The Last Aerie*
Necroscope: Vamphyri!	*Bloodwars*
Necroscope: The Source	*Necroscope: The Lost Years*
Necroscope: Deadspeak	*Necroscope: Resurgence*
Necroscope: Deadspawn	*Necroscope: Invaders*
Blood Brothers	*Necroscope: Defilers*

Necroscope: Avengers

THE TITUS CROW SERIES

Titus Crow, Volume One: The Burrowers Beneath & The Transition of Titus Crow
Titus Crow, Volume Two: The Clock of Dreams & Spawn of the Winds
Titus Crow, Volume Three: In the Moons of Borea & Elysia

THE PSYCHOMECH TRILOGY

Psychomech
Psychosphere
Psychamok

OTHER NOVELS

Demogorgon	*Maze of Worlds*
The House of Doors	*Khai of Khem*

SHORT STORY COLLECTIONS

Fruiting Bodies and Other Fungi
The Whisperer and Other Voices
Beneath the Moors and Darker Places
Harry Keogh: Necroscope and Other Weird Heroes!

The House of Cthulhu

TALES OF THE PRIMAL LAND, VOLUME I

BRIAN LUMLEY

A TOM DOHERTY ASSOCIATES BOOK
NEW YORK

This is a work of fiction. All the characters and events portrayed
in this novel are either fictitious or are used fictitiously.

THE HOUSE OF CTHULHU: TALES OF THE PRIMAL LAND, VOLUME I

Copyright © 1991 by Brian Lumley

Introduction, "The Sorcerer's Book," "Lords of the Morass,"
"The Wine of the Wizard," copyright © 1984 by Brian Lumley for
The House of Cthulhu, Weirdbook Press. "How Kank Thad Returned to Bhur-Esh,"
copyright © 1977 by Ultimate Publishing Co., Inc., for *Fantastic*. "The House of Cthulhu,"
copyright © 1973 by Stuart Schiff for *Whispers* No. 1. "Tharquest and the Lamia
Orbiquita," copyright © 1976 by Ultimate Publishing Co., Inc., for *Fantastic*.
"Mylakhrion the Immortal," from *Fantasy Tales* No. 1. "Cryptically Yours,"
copyright © 1977 by Charles Melvin for *Escape*. "The Sorcerer's Dream,"
copyright © 1979 by Stuart Schiff for *Whispers* No. 13/14. "To Kill a Wizard!"
copyright © 1988 by W. Paul Ganley for *The Weirdbook
Sampler*. All stories collected in this edition, copyright © 1991 by Brian Lumley.

Originally published in 1991 by Headline Book Publishing PLC, London, England.

This book is printed on acid-free paper.

Map by Dave Kendall

A Tor Book
Published by Tom Doherty Associates, LLC
175 Fifth Avenue
New York, NY 10010

www.tor.com

Tor® is a registered trademark of Tom Doherty Associates, LLC.

Library of Congress Cataloging-in-Publication Data

Lumley, Brian.
    The house of Cthulhu / Brian Lumley.
        p.   cm. — (Tales of the primal land; v. 1)
    "A Tom Doherty Associates book."
    ISBN 0-765-31073-2
    EAN 978-0-765-31073-6
        1. Cthulhu (Fictitious character)—Fiction.   2. Monsters—Fiction.   I. Title.

PR6062.U45H59 2005
823'.914—dc22

                                                                    2005040580

First Tor Edition: September 2005

Printed in the United States of America

0   9   8   7   6   5   4   3   2   1

FOR MALYGRIS

CONTENTS

THEEM'HDRA

The Primal Continent

The Chill Sea

Here Be
Monsters

Reef of Great Whales

Teeth of Yib

Mammoth
Plains

Greater Marl

Hjarpon
Settlement

Fjords & Lochs

K

Ruined Keeps
of The
First Race

Unknown
Ocean

River Thand

Great Depths

Inner
Isles

Black
Isle

Mars
Of Slu

Thandopolis

Great Roc Pass

N

Secondary Cone(Active)

Volcano
Isle

Bhur-Esh

Gr

Scrublands

Wood & Grass Lands

Paps of Mam

Plains

Thinhla

S Southern Ocean

INTRODUCTION

Of Teh Atht, White Sorcerer of the Great Primal Continent of Theem'hdra, and of Sundry Matters Concerning an Age Forgotten Except in his Prehistoric Document, *Legends of the Olden Runes*.

by Brian Lumley [based on the original notes of Thelred Gustau, whose introduction follows]:

L ONG BEFORE ATLANTIS, before Uthmal and Mu, so distant in time past that a very great majority of today's scientists might never be persuaded of its existence, there *was* in primal Theem'hdra an hitherto unknown, unguessed Age of Man. How long ago exactly? I could say that this mighty continent existed twenty millions of years ago, but that would be pure guesswork. Perhaps it was forty millions, a hundred . . . I do not know.

I only know that in 1963, while observing at comparatively close range the fantastic eruptions of Surtsey as that island rose up from the sea off Iceland, I fished aboard my boat a massive piece of volcanic flotsam whose fortunate recovery seemed destined to reshape the thinking of the entire anthropological world!

The thing was both astonishing and awesome. Astonishing in that, embedded in the mass of grey-white, foamlike rock, a ball of blue glass like an eye clearly showed through the wash of waves. Awesome in that this mass (whose glassy passenger was, even at first glance, quite obviously an artifact of some sort) had recently been ejected from the heart of a newborn volcano.

Once they had the thing on board, my men were quick to break away the still warm lava crusts about its large glass core, then to carefully carry that nucleus to my cabin. Grey droplets of sea water still clung to its surface, and the soapy scum of lava and volcanic dust obscured its true colour and . . . contents. But when I had cleaned it with a towel, then those of my crew with me gaped and gasped and for a moment the magic of Surtsey's fiery birth was almost entirely forgotten.

For here was something that surely could not be! Locked in the bluish glass was a box of dull yellow metal in the shape of a nine inch cube. It had hasps and hinges and was covered with mystic symbols and the grimacing faces of krakens and dragons, hybrid dwarves and giants, serpents and demons and other night-things from all four corners of myth and legend. Without opening that box—indeed, before ever I stole my first glance at its interior and contents—I knew that it was ancient . . . but I could never have guessed that it *predated the very dinosaurs,* at least those sorrily defunct creatures whose bones decorate today's museums. "But," you are thinking, "the very earliest of men had not yet evolved, would not for ten millions of years after the dinosaurs had disappeared . . ." Oh? Well, I once thought so, too.

We put into port in Reykjavik and I took the glass ball with me to an hotel. It was solid, this sphere, and yet curiously light, made of glass unknown to modern science. After I had taken many photographs and shown the thing to a number of friends and colleagues—all evidence to support any claims I might later wish to make—then I sat down to determine a way to get at the golden box within.

Had the sphere been hollow, then a simple shattering of the glass might suffice, but it was not, and I had no wish to damage the box. In the end, nine frustrated days later in London, I procured a jeweller's diamond-tipped drill and commenced what I thought must prove an almost intolerably long process of drilling. In this I was mistaken.

I had drilled no more than two holes into the sphere, each to within an inch or so of its box nucleus, when there began to flow from the second hole an oily blue substance that smoked on contact with the air. Patently in drilling the second hole fractionally deeper than the first, I had broken through to this previously invisible agent which must surround the golden box. It must, too, be under some pressure, for it bubbled up the drilled hole and bled thinly down the outside of the sphere— and wherever it flowed the glass melted away like butter!

So acrid were the fumes that rose up ever thicker, I was soon driven to desert the house and had to abide in ignorance the passing of whatever catalytic reaction was taking place within. When the smoke had cleared some minutes later, on rushing to my work table, there I saw the golden box lying in a few slivers of evaporating glass. Even these rounded ice-like chips I tried to save, washing them under cold water; but to no avail, the catalyst had an unbreakable hold on them. And so finally I turned my attention to the box . . .

How my fingers trembled when, having wiped down the work-bench top and removed the box to my study proper, I eased back the hasps and lifted the lid on hinges which were as well oiled as if attended to only yesterday! For a long moment I could only stand and stare, all atremble and breaking out in a sweat of fevered anticipation, but then I forced myself to a semblance of calmness and set about to take more photographs . . . and more yet as I lifted each item from the box to spread across the table.

There was a tiny silver whistle whose mouth was sealed with hardened wax; several small dark bottles of thick liquid, each marked in redly glowing hieroglyphs on a sort of leathery label; a magnifying glass in a square golden frame delicately filigreed with intriguing arabesques and inlaid at the corners with iridescent mother-of-pearl; a tiny skull, as of a monkey, but with only one eyesocket central in the forehead, all covered in gold leaf except for the eye, which was a ruby big as my small fingernail; a folded map of sorts on a type of parchment which began to disintegrate as soon as I attempted to spread it (mercifully, I was able to get a photograph, though not a good one, before the thing had completely crumbled away to a fine dust, and merciful too that this was the only item in the box to be wasted in this manner); a set of silver dividers in perfect working condition; a beautiful bamboo flute of exquisite workmanship, carved with miniature mountains and forests, and with seascapes where boats bore curiously rigged sails whose like are elsewhere unknown in all Man's history; a lead pendant in the shape of a lizard devouring its own tail; the great, needle-sharp, curved ivory tooth of some beast of prey, with a hardwood handle set into its root end making of it a deadly dagger; and finally, beneath all of these lesser treasures, runebooks and scrolls and documents, all of fine skins no thicker than paper but lubricated in a way which left them supple after God-only-knows how vast a stretch of time.

Several loose leaves there were, too, finely hieroglyphed in figures completely new to me and almost certainly beyond the talents of any of today's cryptographers or runic interpreters; and as I laid these carefully on my table a draught disturbed them, threatening to blow them onto the floor. I used the first thing to hand—the ancient glass in its square frame—to pin them down, and so accidentally stumbled across a most fantastic revelation.

Whoever had stocked this golden box and sealed it within its now completely disappeared shell, had not only wisely and deliberately protected it against its journey into future aeons but had also forseen certain of the difficulties its discoverer must eventually face. Beyond doubt he had been a scientist of sorts, this man, but this was surely much more than mere science!

My head swam dizzily and I clutched at the table's edge, steadying myself. I blinked my eyes and looked again . . . then stared . . . And finally, rubbing furiously at my eyes, I shakily pulled up a chair and sat down to peer yet again, unbelievingly (or at least believing myself to be suffering the most astonishing delusions) at the hieroglyphs that now swam up large through the blue-tinged glass of the magnifier.

They were hieroglyphs no longer!

Now I could read those immemorial minuscules as easily as if I had written them myself, for now—or so it appeared through the impossible lens of the magnifier—they were in German, the language of my youth! Eagerly I read a page, two, three, unbelievingly copying the words down in scratchy English as I scanned them through that incredible glass, watching the blurred, alien and unknown characters and symbols writhing into clearly discernible words, phrases, sentences and paragraphs as I slowly slid the magnifier over them where they lay.

Then a tragedy. My hand was so a-shake, my eyes watering with the strain of staring at this continual, mesmerising metamorphosis, that I dropped the glass and gasped horrified as it cracked sharply against a corner of the golden box. Instantly a thin trickle of oily blue liquid seeped out from the interior of the lens—and need I relate what next took place? Less than twenty seconds later no trace remained of that miraculous lens, only its square golden frame and a rapidly dispersing mist of acrid smoke . . .

For a moment I despaired, cursing myself for a clumsy fool and almost crying out loud in my frustration; but then I snatched up my scribbled notes, three pages of them, and realised that all was not lost! In these few scraps of paper I had a key, one which would unlock the secrets of the manuscripts just as surely as any magical magnifier—but much more slowly. Oh, so very slowly.

For nine long years I have laboured—not only over my translations but also to gain recognition of an Age of Man predating prehistory!—but while I have successfully translated a good third of Teh Atht's runebooks and manuscripts, I have failed dismally to impress any real authority with the enormity of the treasure I found in a lava bomb hurled from the throat of a volcano.

Perhaps if my find had been less spectacular . . . if I had told no one of the disappearing sphere and lens of glass . . . and certainly had I made no mention of the magnifier's wondrous powers of translation, things might have been different. As it is: still I am irked considerably to be looked upon as "somewhat peculiar," or as "quaintly eccentric," and this despite my previous reputation and the fact that I have photographic evidence and friends who will vouchsafe the truth of what I say. My photographs must of course be "fakes," and all of my good friends mere "dupes."

And so what more can I say or do? Well, if I cannot tell the world of Theem'hdra, the Primal Continent at Earth's Dawn, in the way it should be told—as by a scientist above the lowly japes and deceptions of which I stand accused—then I am obliged to tell of it in some other manner. If I cannot present Teh Atht's words as statements of fact or at very least fragments of myth or fable from a time beyond time, then I must present them as modern fiction.

In this my good friend and collaborator Brian Lumley has been of tremendous assistance, colouring the legends as I unfold them and preparing them one by one for popular publication. If this was not Teh Atht's purpose, that this tomorrow-world of ours know of his own dimly fabulous time, then I am at a loss to say what his purpose was. Surely he had some such in mind when, placing his treasures in the golden box, he sealed it in its glassy sphere, and taking whatever other precautions were necessary for its aeon-lasting protection he sent it winging down all the ages of time from dim and distant but no longer forgotten Theem'hdra!

Thelred Gustau

What shall we say of that continent at the dawn of time, in the first "civilised" Age of Man? Its inhabitants called it

Theem'hdra, which is a name beyond translation; but how may we, looking back into the bottomless abyss of the past, name or classify a landmass which must, by now, have been above and below great oceans many times, returning in the main to its individual rocks and pebbles, and those in their cycle to finely sifted sands? Atlantis by comparison was yesterday . . .

We might perhaps think of Theem'hdra as Pangaea, but *not* the Pangaea visualised by today's experts. And that is not to castigate or belittle in any way those authorities whose choice it has been to turn blind eyes upon Thelred Gustau's work. No, I merely point out that their Pangaea, the "popular" Pangaea, was, in the grand scale of things, last week. In the same scale Theem'hdra was probably months ago.

And yet for me, as for Gustau, the Primal Continent no longer lies in the dim and fabulous past. Working as I have upon my colleague's translations, preparing them for publication as modern "fictions," I have grown to know Theem'hdra as I know my own England. It is a place to which I might journey simply by closing my eyes and sending my thoughts winging out on a mission of . . . race memory? I know the mammoth plains as well as I know the woods of my own childhood, the twisty alleys of Klühn as thoroughly as the steep streets of Durham City.

. . . Theem'hdra is of volcanic origin. Two volcanoes are mentioned in Teh Atht's manuscripts, both active in his time, but we base our claim in respect of the continent's origin mainly on what Thelred Gustau remembers of the map from his golden box; in that and in the photographs, however poor, which he managed to obtain before the parchment map disintegrated.

From Gustau's reproduction it can be seen that central Theem'hdra is a vast inland sea, almost circular, of about five hundred miles in diameter and ringed by the Great Circle Mountains. South-west of this inner ocean and within the surrounding range lies a mighty volcano which is in fact a secondary cone, still quietly active and now and then disturbingly grumbly. Surely the throat of the *original* volcano is now the mighty inner sea itself, and the crater walls, eroded by the winds, rains and tremors of a young planet, are now those same Great Circle Mountains?

But what a volcano that must have been! A fire-spewing cauldron five hundred miles across: Krakatoa itself would be the merest squib by comparison! Thus, in what was probably the most violent of all primal convulsions, Theem'hdra was born. And as the ages ticked by there were men . . .

On a line due west of the inner sea's centre lies the continent's second active volcano, an island cone standing off in the Unknown Ocean. This volcano, in its birthing, brought down and destroyed and buried beneath a lava plain the city of Bhur-Esh, which knew its heyday when Klühn, the modern capital on the eastern coast almost three thousand miles away, was merely a fishing village. Nevertheless, and while Bhur-Esh is to Klühn what Ur is to, say, modern Cairo, legends of Bhur-Esh came down to Teh Atht in his wizardly apartments overlooking Klühn's great bay, and he dutifully recorded them in his runebooks. And so we know the story of Kank Thad the barbarian, who departed slowly from and returned quickly to Bhur-Esh all in the same day, and thereafter wandered no more . . .

To return to the eastern coast:

Almost eight hundred miles south of Klühn—across the

Lohr and several smaller rivers, surrounded by dense coastal forests—lies the city of Yhemnis. It is a splendidly barbaric city of gold, ivory and ironwood, home and citadel of swart Yhemni slavers and pirates. East again, across the stormy Straits of Yhem and eighty sea-miles distant, the jungle-island Shadarabar (with Shad, its capital, squarely facing Yhemnis on the mainland) is also home to Yhemni tribes. Mercifully these dark brown peoples are as often at each other's throats as at war with the rest of the Primal Continent's more civilised people. But from this it must not be reckoned that the Yhemni are Theem'hdra's only barbarians—no!

For diagonally across the continent, at its north-westerly extreme, is a land of fjords and lochs and chilly waters. Nomadic wooly mammoths wander the great plains to the west of this region, hunted by towering white savages who—while there are many individual tribes and families—generally go under the group name of Northmen. More commonly, however, they are known simply as Barbarians!

The true Northern Barbarian is easily recognised: by his massive strength, his lightly browned skin, his love of soft women and hard drink, his rapidly alternating moods (between soaring high spirits and deepest, darkest depressions), his dread of sorcery, and by the distinctive mane of hair he wears, short and bristly, from nape of neck to base of spine.

Fishermen famed for their hunting of the great whales, sailors crafted in boat-building, warriors dreaded for the sheer madness of their berserker rages—yes, and traders, too, whose pelts and ivory are valued highly in Khrissa and Thandopolis—the Northmen are colourful, heroic characters, with a whole-hearted love of piratical adventurings and tall-tale telling and song-singing. They are also wanderers who may be found far from their chill homeland, in almost every part of Theem'hdra.

Of Khrissa (mentioned above, a cold and lonely city of basalt slabs at the mouth of the Greater Marl River four hundred miles east of the Mammoth Plains): its gaunt, sparsley-clad priest-inhabitants are a race aside from the majority of Theem'hdra's peoples. Tall and thin they are, bald-pated and shaven of all bodily hair; and equally austere their lives. Aye, for their sole task in life would seem to be the sending of prayers to their many gods that the ice barrier to the north might encroach no closer to the northern shores of Theem'hdra.

In the Year of the White Whales—when the ice only stopped after mounting the thousand mile reef, while to the east it even cast its creeping frosty-silver cloak about the feet of Tharamoon—Khrissa's priests sacrificed no less than three hundred of their women in order to still the deadly white advance. Woe betide any stranger in Khrissa when the ice crackles out of the north and the winter snows drift deep and ominous!

North-east of Khrissa, indeed, at the most northerly point of the mainland, there, ten miles out in the Chill Sea, Tharamoon the Mountain Island rises silent, forbidding and forbidden. Atop the highest needle peak a massive castle of grey stone glooms against greyer skies, and even though its one-time wizard inhabitant, Mylakhrion the Elder, is long dead and blown as dust in the wind, still the island lies vacant; for no man would tempt the monstrous magicks and curses Mylakhrion doubtless called down upon that blasted rock in his last days. No, not for all the wizard's treasures, fabled to rest with his bones, broken at the base of the castle's walls . . .

But while Mylakhrion, ancestor of Teh Atht himself, was old in Theem'hdra's youth (he had been dead eleven hundred years when Teh Atht dreamed his dreams of the BEGINNING and the END), nevertheless other, darker magicks had survived the centuries, creeping down the years to modern Theem'hdra.

Until recently the most hideous of all of these dark forces was chained, by rune and spell of Elder God, in a bottomless crypt upon Arlyeh, island of nameless ruins mid-ocean between the Frostlands and Klühn. And it was the reaver Zar-Thule who, together with the men of his dragonships, sailed in unto and landed upon the island, seeking out the priceless treasures of the House of Cthulhu . . . But that is another story.

Of the Frostlands, bitter regions to the east of the Great Ice Barrier:

Yaht Haal was the only city beyond the confines of the Primal Continent proper known to Theem'hdra's peoples: Yaht Haal, the Silver City at the edge of the Frostlands, which Zar-Thule sacked before his ill-omened landing upon Arlyeh. He sacked Yaht Haal and burned it down, torturing and killing all of the city's priests and doing worse things to its gentle, fur-clad snow-folk. And following the rape of the Silver City, the very next winter, the Great Ice Barrier came down and buried its desecrated temples and houses deep beneath crystal glaciers; for there were no longer priests and wizardlings to keep the ice away with their chants and spell-spinnings.

Now, I may seem to be making a lot of Theem'hdra's magicians and wizards and sorcerers, and I know that in our 20th Century such are frowned upon as the stuff of fairy tales and fables. But I repeat that Theem'hdra was *millions* of years ago, when this world of ours was still a very young one, whereon Nature experimented and created and did myriads of strange and nightmarish things. After all, Nature herself was in her youth, and she had not yet decided which talents men should have and which should be forbidden, discontinued.

In some men, in certain women, too, the wild workings of capricious Nature wrought weird wonders, giving them senses and powers additional to the usual five. Often these powers were carried down through many generations; aye, and occasionally such a man would mate with just such a woman, and then, eventually, through genealogical patterns and permutations long forgotten to 20th-Century scientists, along would come the seventh son of a seventh son, or the ninth daughter of a ninth daughter . . . and then?

Oh, yes, there was certainly magick in those times, though perhaps today, in our "enlightened" age, we would find different names for such as wizards, lamias, weirdlings and warlocks. For Nature has never truly ceased her dabbling, and now we casually acknowledge such words as telepathy, telekinesis, teleportation, and so on. And was not Einstein himself a magician, whose runes were just as powerful as any wizard's in old Theem'hdra?

But that is to labour a point . . . And so let us now return to the topography and anthropology of Theem'hdra:

North of the Bay of Monsters, between the mighty River Luhr and the Great Eastern Peaks, lie the Steppes of Hrossa where dwell the fierce Hrossaks. Tremendously skilled riders of fearsome lizard mounts, warriors almost without peer, the Hrossaks feud intermittently with the armies of massive-walled Grypha at the mouth of the Luhr, and with the Yhemni in their coastal forests. Other than the occasional raid or skirmish, however, the bronze Hrossaks are content to live at peace in their steppes where they farm and pride themselves in practicing the arts of war, and where they breed their lizard herds, providing leather and meat and sport a-plenty. The River Luhr is sacred to them and they will not cross it, and the peaks of the eastern range are much too high for them; generally, they are not good climbers.

Across the Luhr to the west, two hundred and fifty miles away rise the foothills of the Great Circle Mountains, within which, to the east of the inner sea, oozes the slimy Marsh of Slugs. Even the wildest, loudest adventurers dare only mention this vast and boggy nightmare of a region in the merest whispers, for that's the sort of place the Marsh of Slugs is—all forty thousand square miles of it! And so we'll linger there no longer but move on west across the great crater sea to the Inner Isles.

Central in that enclosed sea which was once the throat of a vast volcano, like green jewels strewn on a mantle of beautiful blue, the Inner Isles reach up their lava mountains to touch the sky. Here, rumour has it, dwells a tall, slender, comb-headed race of silver-grey beings who are not entirely human. Their houses are wooden and nestle on the slopes of their mountains; their needs are simple and are all supplied by the islands themselves and the teeming sea; their ways are gentle, even though they have strengths not immediately apparent, and their lives are ones of quiet and peaceful contemplation.

Yes, and their minds are the finest in all Theem'hdra, with senses that reach beyond the normal range of those we know. They are called the Suhm-yi, which means "the Rarely Seen," and it is because they are so rarely seen that we can offer no real proof of their existence, only the tales of wandering barbarians whose travels have taken them over the high northern rim of the Great Circle Mountains and across the deep blue inner sea.

Thus the area enclosed by these volcanic mountains holds both terror and beauty . . . but it also holds mystery. Mystery in the shape of massive stone cubes, featureless blocks with sides hundreds of feet long, which stand amidst the inner foothills all along the western range and are fabled to be the long-vacated houses of the world's first race, which was not human but came down to Earth from the stars in Theem'hdra's prehistory. Great mystery there, aye, and mystery too in the Black Isle, standing dark and still in a subsidiary lake of the inner sea to the north-east; but of that place, so far, we know nothing except that it is there . . .

AND THAT IN the main is Theem'hdra. From the bay of Klühn in the north-east to the Paps of Mam, Mother of Gods, at the continent's south-westerly extreme, and from the grim Teeth of Yib and the fjords of the north-west to Shadarabar off the south-east coast. In all, the continent is about 2400 miles east to west and 2000 miles north to south, with a total land area of about 3,750,000 square miles.

Including the peoples of Yaht Haal (if any remain alive) Theem'hdra houses six distinct races: the Northern Barbarians, the scattered white settlers of the coastal cities, the fabled Suhm-yi of the Inner Isles, the Hrossaks of the steppes, the swart and fiery Yhemni, and a pigmy race fabled to dwell in the Marsh of Slugs. Its gods are many, and some of them are in no way gods for prayers, rather for cursing by. Gleeth, blind Moon God, is believed to be benevolent, as is Shoosh, Goddess of the Still Slumbers, and Mam, Mother of Gods; but Ghatanothoa is a dark and doomful god—and even more so Cthulhu, though His worship is mercifully restricted to small, secret sects—Yib-Tstll, too. Then there are the Ice-Gods, whose names are kept secret by the priests of cold Khrissa, except for Baroom, God of the Avalanche, whose name is often invoked at the great drinking festivals of the Northmen.

And so little more remains to be told of Theem'hdra. Oh, there are rivers and lakes, towns and cities and other places that I have not mentioned; yes, and others I myself do not yet know, will not until Thelred Gustau translates more of Teh Atht's runebooks—but that lies in the future.

Thus I welcome you to the fables and legends of a time long dead and hitherto forgotten. If you choose to think of them as "fictions" in the modern vein, well, that is your choice. For myself: I have come to know Theem'hdra quite intimately and can go there simply by closing my eyes and sending my mind winging back across the aeons. Why not join me there, now, in that raw adventurous world in an age before all other ages of man, in the Primal Continent at the dawn of time?

POSTSCRIPT

. . . Since penning the above, for use as an introduction to an original book of Thelred Gustau's translations, the fantastic, the inexplicable has occurred. No, on second thought perhaps the occurrence was not entirely inexplicable; but if my guess is correct, certainly it was fantastic.

I had known for weeks that Thelred was excited about

something, and, in respect of his age, I had warned him against the excessive amount of work he was putting in on Teh Atht's *Legends of the Olden Runes*. It had seemed to me that he was neither eating nor sleeping normally and that something—some aspect of his work of which he had made no mention—had become an obsession with him.

On the day in question his housekeeper, Mrs. Petersen, prepared a breakfast which he no more than glanced at before hurrying to his study. There, as the morning grew towards noon, he sat at his desk with scratchily moving pen in hand and all the paraphernalia of his golden box within easy reach.

All through the forenoon he sat, disposing of a continuous supply of coffee, climbing from one level of high excitement to the next, until noon when he left the study and retired to his bedroom. The look on his face as he passed by Mrs. Petersen was: "wild, flushed, exultant!—but he was also plainly very tired." He asked that she rouse him at 7 P.M. and place coffee and sandwiches in his study before going home.

She followed his instructions to a point, but was so concerned by her employer's behaviour that she did not immediately go home. Instead she sat in her little kitchen and listened to the muffled sounds of the professor stirring in his study . . . to those, and to his frequent, excited exclamations.

She must have drowsed, for her next memory is of a terrific blast of sound, of a triumphant cry in the professor's voice, of a deeper, bass booming which could only barely be described as a voice, and finally of a splintering, crashing impact that shook the very house.

Rushing to his study she threw open the door on a scene of chaotic disorder. In the ceiling the chandelier swung on its chain and cast flickering shadows from light-bulbs made faulty by whatever blast had wrecked the room. Books and documents lay scattered all about; loose leaves still fluttered to the carpeted floor; the great bay window had been forced outwards from its frame into the garden, where even now a great shadow stirred black against the night.

Mrs. Petersen staggered to that unnaturally shattered window in time to see . . . a shape! A shape like that of a monstrous bird or bat that loomed up massive before rising into darkness to the whirring thrum of great wings, a black silhouette bearing upon its back the lesser shape of . . . a man!

I WAS AMONG the few, called upon by the police early the next day, to go along and make what I could of Mrs. Petersen's story. Did I have any idea exactly what the professor was working on?—they wanted to know—and had I known that he was experimenting with explosives? And what *sort* of explosives might they have been? These and many other questions, all of which I could only answer by shaking my head in utter bafflement. Plainly it had been an explosion of some sort that caused the damage to the professor's study, particularly the window, but that did not explain his total absence.

Surely there should be a body, or at least—traces of one! But no, there was nothing like that, no sign of any harm done to his person. What then had happened? And if he lived, where was Thelred Gustau now?

Later I was allowed to gather all of his scattered notes, documents, books and miscellaneous curiosa together, examining each item for damage . . . and then the puzzle began to piece itself into a pattern. Some weeks were to pass, however, before my conclusions were concrete, and even then they were not such as I might pass on to the police.

The clues were in Thelred's notes, in those copious if disjointed scribblings formed partly of translated fragments from Teh Atht, mainly of his own excitement at some tremendous breakthrough which he was sure was coming. And of course that breakthrough had come, on the night of the blasted study, the bass alien "voice," and the bat-bird shape that bore a triumphant manlike figure away into unknown dimensions.

For Thelred had written of the strange properties he believed to lie hidden in the stopped-up silver whistle, and of the potent energies locked in a tiny bottle of golden-yellow liquid from Teh Atht's box. He had likened these items to certain things hinted at in the peculiar, almost esoteric works of Dr. Laban Schrewsbury, and at the same time had jotted down notes concerning gigantic flying creatures called "Byakhee" and a tentacled, immemorially worshipped God-thing named Hastur.

Tenuous clues, all of them; and yet had he not recently complained bitterly of the ever-increasing scorn with which erstwhile colleagues now greeted his work? And had he not often stated his desire to be "away from all this . . .?" Never at peace with the hustle and bustle of our 20th Century, always seeking the solitude of vast ocean vistas and the lure of distant desert places, what was there to hold him here? And by "here" I mean in this world of men, at least in the present-day world of here and now.

Often he had declared his admiration for those tales of olden Arabia, where djinni might be found in magic lamps and brave men sought adventure high above the world on arabesqued, gravity-defying carpets. And now . . . has he discovered a magic carpet of his own, astride the back of a trans-dimensional Byakhee, which might fly him to those worlds of wonder he so admired?

Deny me if you will, but in my mind's eye I see him working at his desk, see him leap to his feet with an astounded exclamation to tremulously sip of the golden mead. I hear him hoarsely chant the invocation to Hastur and blow on the whistle so recently unstoppered. Aye, and then the blast of energy that heralds the coming of the Byakhee, tumbling the contents of the study and blowing out the windows while yet the summoner stands unharmed.

I see it all and know that it must have been so, for of all the incunabula of the golden box only the silver whistle—that and one of the tiny bottles—were absent upon my investigation . . .

AND NOW I alone am executor to the estate, and I know that soon I shall have mastered the legends writ so many aeons ago in alien cyphers upon the fine skins of Teh Atht's runebooks. What Thelred Gustau started I shall finish, but until then there are those fables already translated which, as I have said before, you may accept for what they are or, if you so desire, name "fictions" in the modern vein. The choice is yours.

The House of Cthulhu

Hoω KanK Tḟad Retürɲed to Bḟür-Esḟ

FOREWORD

W HEN THELRED GUSTAU originally invited me to read
what was then his latest translation from Teh Atht's
Legends of the Olden Runes, with an eye to my preparation of
the work for publication, he also placed in my hands some as-
sociational information about the locale of the story and certain of its participants. This information follows:

Long before Klühn ever became the capital city of
Theem'hdra—indeed, at a time when Klühn was little more
than a fishing village—then, to the extreme west of the continent at the edge of the vast Unknown Ocean, in a valley girt
round by the Ghost Cliffs of Shildakor, lay the city of Bhur-Esh.
Two thousand years later when Klühn had grown up, Bhur-
Esh, its valley, and the Ghost Cliffs too were long gone, buried
beneath a lava desert, and out in the Unknown Ocean a new
volcanic island stood grey, forbidding and still silently smok-
ing . . . But we are only interested in Bhur-Esh in its heyday.

For then the streets of the city were crowded and narrow
and crooked so as to be almost labyrinthine. They were lined

with shops and bazaars and brothels where merchants from all over the known world thronged to barter, buy and vend any and everything that could possibly be vended, bought or bartered. And in Bhur-Esh such merchants could carry on their businesses in almost perfect safety; because of its topography the city had very few thieves—it will be seen that they had nowhere to run!

As a self-supporting seaport and city (the inhabitants considered themselves collectively as a "nation" in their own right), Bhur-Esh was and had ever been neutral, neither attacking its neighbours nor being attacked. The pincerlike arms of the bay reaching out to the Unknown Ocean were high and sheer oceanward and well fortified within, with turrets, ramparts, arrowslits, and quarters for hundreds of soldiers; a regiment was kept there permanently. Too, in strategic places, ballistae loomed in impregnable rock-cut bastions on top of those arms, with hundreds of heavy boulders ready for the hurling.

That was one of the reasons why Bhur-Esh was neutral; the other, apparently, was the Ghost Cliffs of Shildakor. As Teh Atht himself has written: "What army except an army of wizards might broach such insurmountable barriers?" But these same barriers also worked in another way, explaining Bhur-Esh's deficiency of criminals and why, once discovered, there was no sanctuary to which they could flee. The cliffs were unscalable, the narrow mouth of the bay constantly guarded and equipped with a toll bridge.

The bay was wide at the landside and the cliff-enclosed valley was by no account small, so that while Bhur-Esh itself was a sizeable city with suburbs sprawling eastward almost to the very feet of the sheltering Ghost Cliffs themselves, nevertheless it occupied only a twentieth part of the "king-dom."

Between the calm waters of the bay and the city's west wall, fields stretched in green expanse, with farmhouses and barns scattered here and there and cattle enclosures and patchworks of growing crops; and lining these fertile fields at north and south hard-packed roads lay beneath the beetling rocks. These roads led from the barracks and quarters of King Vilthod's soldiers, on the outskirts of Bhur-Esh, to the battle-ments of the rocky bay arms.

The King's palace stood magnificent and serene, "a pinna-cled splendour to the eye of the beholder," at the city's hub. Its walls were surrounded by cropped, luscious-green grass imported from the barbarous North, and archers sat atop the walls with crossbows of eastern design to ensure that no man walked, sat or stood upon King Vilthod's grass. For the King's grass was his pride and joy—its seed paid for grain by pre-cious grain, nurtured to lush life and maintained by a bevy of gardeners—and the like of its northern green was unheard of elsewhere on the shores of the Unknown Ocean. Teh Atht tells us that: "Many an unwary stranger, perhaps fancying a juicy blade of grass to chew, had discovered a flighted bolt growing in his chest or throat before the grass could dangle from his lips . . ."

Likewise prized by the King, for its architecture and yellow-walled beauty (not to mention the money it doubtless pro-vided his coffers, which was probably why he had built it directly behind the palace), was the High-Court of Bhur-Esh. The High-Court stood tall and golden, but not nearly so splen-did as the palace, in a plaza of white-walled gardens and wind-ing pebble paths, "between delicate fountains and airy marble statues of gods and heroes long gone." Within its spacious halls the worst members of Bhur-Esh's criminal element—few, as explained—were tried by Thamiel, Chief Seeker of Truth to the King.

Normally the main courtroom was sparsely attended; a few chroniclers with their styli and tablets; a bard or two to sing Woes or Delights after the passing of sentence or declaration of innocence; the provost guard; a smattering of out-of-work city types, and the family and friends of the sinned-against and sometimes of the transgressor. On the day of which Teh Atht tells in the following legend, however, things were very different . . .

I

Never before had a man the like of Kank Thad the barbarian been brought to trial at the High-Court. His crimes had been many and varied and all sorts of imputations had been brought against him in the hour or so during which his case had been heard. In fact, no case *had* been heard, merely the basic facts: that Kank Thad was accused of Murder most foul and that, among other sundry offences, he had spat and done worse things on the palace-encircling grass of King Vilthod.

At the time of the latter blasphemies, some days earlier, the archer who had seen these acts had been nonplussed as to what action to take. There were edicts for sitters on the grass, and for standers or walkers upon it, but Kank Thad had done none of these things—he had merely extruded a gob of saliva grassward from the road where he stood admiring the palace. A passer-by, shocked and thinking to see the barabarian cut down at any instant, had whispered to him from a safe distance of what he did, advising him to move quickly along; whereupon Kank Thad had hailed the archer who still pondered his course of action atop the wall:

"Hey, archer on the wall!"

"Move on . . . get on with you!" the flabbergasted archer had returned.

"Archer," cried Kank Thad unperturbed. "I am told that one may neither sit nor stand nor walk on the grass. Is this true?"

"Aye."

"And spitting?"

"There are no orders. No one has—spat—before, on the grass!"

"And being a good archer of the King," the Northman grinned evilly up at the flustered man above, "you may only act on written or spoken instructions?"

"That . . . is true. Now move on!"

"Not yet, my friend archer," answered the barbarian, whipping up his clout and wetting with a loud guffaw on Vilthod's beloved grass.

Then, before the mortified archer had time to aim his crossbow, the hairy great white savage had turned to stride drunkenly off down a winding street in whose tortuous coils he was soon lost to sight. That archer, a dull fellow as witness the tale, was employed atop the palace walls no longer; for having reported the occurrence to his commander he had been stripped of rank and sent to the High-Court wherein slavish, menial tasks might be found more suited to his talents. There this day he had spotted Kank Thad and brought his charge against him—one of many.

The barbarian's debts were legion. He owed taverners for

ale by the gallon and meat by the platter, and a hosteler two weeks' rent for the kennel wherein he'd slept. These were among his heavier debts; his lesser ones were far more numerous.

Having at length been kicked out by the irate hosteler, he was charged with vagrancy too, and finally he was accused of murder. This being the most heinous of his deeds—barely, remembering the episode of the grass-wetting—it was the murder for which he found himself eventually called to answer.

"You have heard all against you. How say you then, barbarian? Are you innocent—or guilty of vile murder?" Thamiel asked his all-important question of the huge, chained savage before him.

Kank Thad, scarred horribly from cheek- to chin-bone down one side of his face, his left eye forever half-closed in a scar-tissue grimace, leaned against one of the carven basalt pillars to which he was manacled and grinned. His grin was evil as his aspect, square yellow teeth leering from behind hard, thin lips. A towering hulk of a man, he spat on the mosaic floor of the courtroom, tossing back his mane of jet hair—which grew, like that of all his race, in a narrow band right down to the base of his spine—before answering.

"Murder?" he scoffed. "That's a word I didn't know before I was washed up on your piddling beach when my good ship sank in the bay. And I'd never have come here if that storm hadn't forced me to seek safe harbour. Listen: in my homeland to the north, when two men fight and one wins, the victor is no murderer! Aboard my ship, if a man got spitted in a fair fight, his body went to feed the fishes and the one who lived was left to tend his scars! Murder? Of what do you speak, baggy one?"

Thamiel winced at the barbarian's words. The heavily-jowled, flabbily-bodied Seeker of Truth had put up with the iron-thewed Northman's insults all through his trial, and Thamiel's patience was running low. Still, he was a man renowned for the Perfection of his Justice, and he could be just even now—before this sea-rat died!

"You will say nothing in your defence, then?"

"I wanted a woman," the scarface answered with a shrug of his powerful shoulders, "and that one—" he pointed a shackled hand across the courtroom at a brightly daubed slut in the stalls, "was the one I wanted. I'd had her before when my money was good, and what's wrong with a bit on account, I ask you? She makes a good cushion for a boozed-up body. And I'll tell you something, you pallid sack of a man: a night with that one—why!—it would add ten years to your miserable life!" He grinned again, reconsidering that last. "—or finish you off for good!"

Fatty folds of flesh trembling in rage, Thamiel gawped and spluttered, then remembered the Faultlessness of his Justice and brought himself under control. "Wench," he spoke to the girl, "you have heard all that has gone . . . have you any last words for or against Kank Thad the Northman?"

Here the barbarian believed himself to be on firm ground. Had he not praised the girl, in his way, and had he not also given her a good night that time?—and paid for it too, by Yib! He had not taken into account the fact that he was now destitute, with only a battle-notched blade to his name; and of what use to a tavern-whore is an ugly barbarian with an insatiable lust, an empty pocket and a too-ready sword?

"That I have!" Lila the whore shrilled, her hair hanging down over her more than ample, passionately heaving bosom.

"I was bought and paid for by Theen of King Vilthod's Guard, aye, and on our way upstairs in the tavern of Hethica Nid, when this—this latrine slime—took me from him!"

"*Took* you from him?" Sitting at Thamiel's right hand, Veth Nuss the Mousey spoke up in his squeaky, tremulous voice. "Took you from an Officer of the King's Guard! Didn't Theen have his sword?"

"He did, Lord," Lila answered, "but the barbarian came up behind us and plucked it from his side!"

"This was not told before," Thamiel frowned, interested despite himself and his desire to get the thing over with.

"The questions were not asked, Lord," Lila protested. "I was asked only if Kank Thad *killed* Theen—and he did!"

"Well, go on . . . go on, girl, tell it now," Thamiel urged.

"Well, the barbarian took Theen's sword and flipped it point up into the ceiling of the tavern. Theen attacked him, but—" she glanced grudgingly at Kank Thad, "the northman is—*big*, Lord. He shrugged Theen off and laughed at him. And then—"

"So it is true then," Thamiel broke in, "that Theen was weaponless when the barbarian struck him down?"

"Aye!" Kank Thad suddenly shouted from between his pillars, "that's true enough. Tell them, Lila, you ungrateful ratbag—tell them just how 'weaponless' the guardsman was—and may your paps rot in the telling!" He hung in his chains and roared with berserk laughter.

"As Theen—" Lila hesitantly continued when finally the giant's laughter subsided, "—as he leapt to try to regain his blade stuck high in the ceiling, Kank Thad, he—he . . ."

"Yes, girl, what did the barbarian do?" Thamiel impatiently pressed.

"He—he struck Theen a very low blow."

"Eh?" Veth Nuss the Mousey frowned and shook his head. "Can you not be plainer, wench?" he squeaked.

"I lopped away his manhood with Gutrip, my once-true sword!" Kank Thad screamed in hellish derision. "Ripped it away and flipped it to the tavern dogs from Gutrip's tip. Murder, you say? Why!—I did the man a favour in putting him out of his misery. What good's a man who can't—"

"*Silence!*" Thamiel thundered, hoisting himself pudding-like to his feet. Even the low muttering and chattering from the galleries had stopped, and white faces peered in awe and horror at the hulking, manacled barbarian in his chains. Thamiel, shaken to his soul at the loathsomeness conjured by the Northman's admission, his composure utterly shattered now, stood with his finger pointing, trembling. "By your own words—" he finally managed, "you are *guilty*!—and now I pass sentence . . ." He drew himself up to his full height of five feet three inches and, barely remembering the Unimpeachability of his Justice, said: "Let thy sword be sundered!"

II

"Let the sword Gutrip be sundered!" The words of the Seeker of Truth were echoed to a hall outside the courtroom proper and a man, a minor court attendant but once an archer of the palace walls, clad now in a shift of mean cloth, laboured in under Gutrip's weight. He was grimly smiling for all his workworn appearance. He placed the weapon on tall marble blocks, its plain-guarded pommel on one, its point on another, its chipped middle suspended. The ex-archer raised a great iron hammer, at which Kank Thad—perhaps remembering better days before swinish habits sank him low—hauled on his chains and roared in an agony as if he himself were being tortured.

"By Yib, *no,* the blade is not to blame! Gutrip—" His anguished cry tapered off as the grinning court attendant, also remembering better days, brought down his hammer and shivered the scarred sword into a dozen flying shards.

"Gutrip—" the great prisoner groaned low in his throat. "Oh, Gutrip . . ."

"Let the spinning of the Silver Decider commence!" cried Thamiel.

Again the fallen archer moved, climbing the steps of a dais in the centre of the courtroom where, on a block of faceted crystal, a silver arrow balanced within a ring of rune-inscribed iron.

"Know you, Kank Thad, of the choice to be made?" Veth Nuss squeaked in his mouse-voice.

"I have a choice of punishments?" the barbarian brightened. "Yib—but this sounds better! What choice do I have? Is one of them banishment? If so, then ban—"

"*Silence!*" Thamiel of the Meritorious Justice thundered again. "The choice is not yours but that of the Silver Decider. If, when the arrow stops its spinning, the point faces into the north . . . then you go north, to the Ghost Cliffs of Shildakor. If the point faces to the south—then you go south, to the Square of the Sundering!"

"Ghost Cliffs?" The barbarian shuddered ever so slightly and his mane bristled all down his back at this hint of thaumaturgy.

"Sundering? I like the sound of neither. Explain, O bulging bilge-barrel."

"Gladly," Thamiel whispered, actually smiling through the barbarian's irreverence as he thought on the Transcendence of his Justice. "The Ghost Cliffs of Shildakor stand a mile high, sheer and stark, often overhanging and reaching in certain seasons into the very clouds. On a clear day a man might see the top through a good glass, and some day a man might even climb to the top—but this has not happened yet. The bones and tatters of a thousand fallen climbers litter the lower slopes. You, too, Kank Thad, might try the climb, depending upon which way the Silver Decider points."

"And the Square of the Sundering?" Little of the Northman's hairy spirit remained, but he managed to retain an almost theatrical bluster even yet.

"Why, is it not obvious? The dust in the Square of the Sundering is brown with dried blood, barbarian, and yellow and white with the pounded bones of men quartered there between four great horses bred for the task . . ."

"Hah!" the prisoner snorted. "I've yet to see the horses that might rip a son of Kulik Thad in pieces." He flexed his mighty muscles and the heavy chains and thick manacles groaned.

"Aye," Thamiel nodded his head, "we have had such before. We don't like to see our horses tired, though, by powerful muscles. And why should such be allowed when a couple of sword thrusts in the right places can help the job along a bit? A hack at a tendon here, a thrust at a stubborn joint there—"

"Ahem . . ." Veth Nuss ahemmed, reminding Thamiel of the Utter Insurmountability of his Justice, telling him not to elaborate. The punishments were surely enough in themselves without graphic descriptions. Thamiel smiled fatly at the barbarian's new expression—then gave the man atop the dais a signal. With a metallic whisper the Silver Decider began to spin, and eventually its pointer slowed . . . and stopped!

The arrow balanced delicately, stationary on its pivot—pointing north. Kank Thad was for the cliffs!

"Away with him!" At Thamiel's command ten powerful blacks seated on a stone bench rose, split into two parties, released the chains from the pillars and dragged the struggling, cursing Northman out of the courtroom and down a passage from which his fading blasphemies echoed for a goodly while. Away they took him, away to the deepest cells in the deepest dungeons under the white walls, pebble paths, airy statues and delicate fountains of the surroundings of the High-Court of Bhur-Esh.

Thus came Kank Thad to the city's dungeons, and in particular to that deepest of deep cells wherein only death-sentenced criminals wait—or prowl, or howl, or pray to heathen gods or whatever—during the short, short hours of their last night on Earth. Kank Thad, however, was no howler but a son of Kulik Thad; nor was he a prowler, for he saw little sense in wearing himself out wandering to and fro in the confines of his cell when tomorrow he had a great cliff to climb; and the only god he knew was one Yib-Tstll, who is no god to pray to but whose name may fairly be used in cursing; and so, because there seemed little else to do, the barbarian simply lay down in his cell and slept—he slept the sleep of a babe in arms until the night guard came on duty.

As fortune would have it his watchman was a Northman like himself, who first came to Bhur-Esh as a stripling stolen by swart slavers from Shadarabar in the east. Thasik Haag was a slave and a youth no longer but a greybeard now, and trusted as one whose duty is his all and holy above all other things. Thus Kank Thad's pleas (he was never one to miss out on any kind of chance, no matter how slim, in a tight spot) for the sake of the memory of northern lands with barbarous names fell on stony ground, and while he did at least wrench a tear or two from Thasik Haag's one good eye with his tales of the Mammoth Plains and the great hunts of home, he could in no way conjure a desire in the heart of that worthy ancient to assist him.

Instead, and in return for the barbarian's tales of dim-remembered northern territories, his jailer told him all he knew of the Ghost Cliffs of Shildakor: how Shildakor had been a wizard in immemorial times whose adventurous son had attempted to climb the great walls surrounding Bhur-Esh and the valley—and of how the boy fell and died! The wizard had straightway ensorcelled the cliffs, laying down a curse upon them, that henceforward ghosts would ever inhabit their crevices and niches.

Too, Thasik Haag was willing to share his supper and a skin of sour wine, and later he brought out a trothyboard and counters that they might play a game or two through the bars. In this he made a fatal mistake for he was a good player, and the sons of Kulik Thad—Kank especially—were not known for sporting natures but rather for short and fiery tempers.

Towards morning, when the first light was creeping in wispy mists over the eastern cliffs of the valley, down in that deep cell the loser of many trothy games, holding to a mere snarl the bull yell of anger that had grown in his chest all night, reached through the bars and grasped his keeper's windpipe in both of his hands. This had been the barbarian's plan all along, but damn it—he had first wanted to win at least one game!

Hauling hard, Kank Thad flattened his victim to the bars so that the astonished watchman was unable to draw his short-sword; and then, so as to make a quick dispatch and offer the greybeard no opportunity to cry out, he dug his fingers in and hauled even harder until skin, flesh, cartilage, windpipe and all parted from the writhing neck of Thasik Haag in a crimson welter of blood and sinew. The watchman hardly knew what had happened, for he was well dead before his murderer let his corpse sink down to the floor to rest. Then Kank Thad set about to make a systematic search of the old man's body.

It was all of an hour later when the captain of the dungeon guard descended the nitre-sweating stone stairway down to that deepest cell . . . there to find the shattered shell of the good and faithful Thasik Haag, and, crouching behind the bars in a corner of his cell in a black and murderous rage of hate and frustration, the great scarfaced Northman. Even with the watchman's shortsword the barbarian had been un-able to force an escape. At first sight of this horror-fraught scene the captain's hand went straight to his belt—where dangled the great key Kank Thad had thought to find in Thasik Haag's pockets . . .

HALF THE CITY of Bhur-Esh, it is told, turned out to watch Kank Thad take his departure of this world, gathering in select groups according to status at the feet of the Ghost Cliffs of Shildakor. Thamiel was there, of course, ringed around by a dozen guardsmen with loaded crossbows. He had gained an odd respect for the barbarian since learning of the additional murder of Thasik Haag: the Northman was definitely a berserker and even more dangerous than first believed! But safe in his impregnable circle Thamiel was, as ever, puffed up in the contemplation of the Indefectibility of his Justice.

Kank Thad's thoughts were for once chaotic as his bonds were released and, at half-a-dozen spearpoints, he was forced to mount first the piled bones and stinking shreds of corpses long fallen from the Ghost Cliffs of Shildakor. Noisome and slimy to his sandaled feet were those carrion remains, and given to crumbling and pitching him down into their vileness. Nonetheless he made his way for some fifteen feet over this debris of malefactors gone and finally turned with his back to the bare rock face.

"Climb, barbarian," Veth Nuss squeaked from Thamiel's flabby side.

"Climb, O minuscule? And what if I choose simply to sit here on a comfortable skull and drink in this marvellously ripe air?" Kank Thad hated to be ordered to do anything, and especially by one tiny as Veth Nuss. At a sign from Thamiel there came the whistle of cleft air as a bolt buried itself deep in the sandy rock through the Northman's free-hanging hair between his left cheek and shoulder.

"Look a little to your right, savage—and be warned!" Thamiel hissed as the huge murderer threw up an arm in anticipation of further missiles. When he saw that no more bolts were forthcoming, Kank Thad lowered his arm and did as directed, staring along the cliff to his right—and then he swore.

"*Yib!*" His curse was a mere whisper. At a distance of no more than a few paces a grisly skeleton sat, skewered through the eyesocket to the cliff.

"Aye," Thamiel offered, just loud enough to be heard, "he was one, just like you, who thought not to climb but sit on a skull and drink in the ripeness of the air." His voice changed abruptly. *"Now get on—My nostrils rot with the stink!"*

So the climb commenced and at first the going was relatively easy, with plenty of protruberant stones and knobs of rock, gaping fissures, and ledges, so that soon Kank Thad was quite high above the breathless crowd gathered there expressly to watch him fall. He did not intend to fall, however, for back home as a youth he had used to climb the sea-cliffs for gull eggs with the best of them; and now, when he'd reached what he thought a sufficient elevation, he paused on a wide ledge and turned to peer down at the multitude of tiny, tiny faces beneath him. The Seeker of Truth in his scarlet turban stood out plainly, with Veth Nuss at his side in the now slowly scattering circle of guards.

"O landwhale," the barbarian called down. "Hey Thamiel. You—woman-bosom!"

"I hear you," Thamiel called back, his voice trembling with rage at the new insults and the disturbing and embarrassing titters of the thronging assembly. "I hear—but will not listen. Go on climbing, or . . ."

"Or what, spherical Lord? I'm already out of range of your weapons. Iron bolts are far too heavy to ever reach me up here."

For the next few minutes Kank Thad sat back on his wide ledge and roared with laughter as bolts clattered against and bounced from the face of the cliff below his position. The closest shot fell short by at least the length of his body. On his ledge, wide enough to walk two horses, a great boulder lay half embedded in the weathered sand. The Northman went to this rock and, out of sight of the crowd below, prised it loose and hoisted it slowly, muscles straining, to his chest.

Then he carefully put the boulder down again and stepped back to the ledge's rim.

When Thamiel saw him come back into view he called out: "We'll wait until you either resume climbing or attempt to come down, barbarian. The latter action, I may point out, will only hasten your inevitable death . . ."

Looking down, Kank Thad positioned the "landwhale" in his memory's eye, stepped quickly back and again hoisted the boulder, rushed forward and tossed it from him, barely maintaining his balance as the well aimed projectile sped out and down as truly as a shot from a hurling-engine handled by an officer of Vilthod's artillery.

Thamiel was quick for one his size, and well he needed to be, flinging himself like a mobile mountain to one side and taking two of his guards with him. Veth Nuss, however, had not been looking (he was prone enough to attacks of vertigo on the thick Tzulingen carpets of his chambers in the High-Court without peering at the fly-like human way up on the Ghost Cliff walls), and the boulder all but drove him into the earth. He emitted not a single squeak but crumpled like a wafer beneath the boulder and spread out in a scarlet stain on the stony ground. One uncrushed arm and hand protruded from the now shattered boulder's perimeter, and, as irony would have it, the hand was clenched and balanced on the thumb, which pointed down . . .

III

For a few seconds there was a silence broken only by Kank Thad's uproarious laughter from on high—and then a multitude of hushed "Oohs" and "Ahhs" of horror went up from the crowd and a scream of rage from Thamiel the Seeker of Truth. A few seconds more and bolts were whizzing, sent more zestfully than before and decidedly, Kank Thad thought, more dangerously.

Earlier, when first he'd paused upon this ledge, the barbarian had seen a runner dispatched in the direction of the palace guard's quarters. He knew that some of Vilthod's guardsmen were longbowmen, and that their flight arrows might easily end his sojourn in this lofty aerie forever; and so he decided it was time to move on, and there was only one way to go—

When the longbowmen arrived at the base of the cliffs a short while later, the barbarian was already out of range and climbing steadily. Nonetheless, at Thamiel's command and strictly to hasten the Northman on his way, an experimental arrow was loosed, fell short, and just missed cutting down a cotter on its return.

In another quarter-hour, when Kank Thad next thought to look down, the people were less than ants and the spread city was but a toy. Away to the south lay the Unknown Ocean—placid in the bay like a pond, tossed and wild without—sparkling in the sun and with gulls wheeling about like white midges on the horizon.

Again the barbarian found himself a ledge on which to rest, amusing himself by flinging great boulders from it and picturing in the eye of his imagination the chaos these missiles would create below. They did indeed cause chaos—and death—and soon the crowd, all bar Thamiel and his guards (and some few others who were there now to stay) went home. Thamiel was determined to remain till the very end, observing the spiderlike antics of the sentenced man through his powerful glass.

By now Kank Thad was almost half-way to the top, taking his time, making frequent pauses—though his muscles were far from tired—systematically checking and observing the cliffs above so that he might always choose the best route. In two shallow niches he had passed crouching skeletons, doubt-less remains of bygone climbers who had found themselves too tired or frightened to carry on or turn back. There they had starved and died, shivering in fear of their terrible predicament—and perhaps of something else . . .

For a while now, as he climbed, Kank Thad had been pon-dering the tale told him by Thasik Haag, of Shildakor and the legendary curse he'd brought down on these cliffs following the fall of his son from their heights. A mist had started to weave up from the rock-walled valley below, and the vertical slabs had quickly dampened and turned cold to his touch.

Now oddly enough (or remembering Shildakor's curse, naturally) this mist went unobserved by Thamiel, still watch-ing through his glass, but it was very real to the Northman and it cut his climbing speed by half. For this was a ghost-mist, raised up by the ancient sorcery of Shildakor, to worry and dismay would-be climbers . . . and Kank Thad was suit-ably worried and dismayed!

Still, he had carried out observations of the not quite sheer face up to a point some eighty feet or so immediately above him, and mist or none there had seemed plenty of good hand and footholds over that distance. He decided to push on—it would be bad should he find himself stuck here for the night—perhaps the mist would clear as quickly as it had come. But Kank Thad's previous visual reconnaissance proved of little use in the rising banks of fog now surrounding him and cutting down his field of vision to a few scant feet, and soon he found himself for the first time in trouble.

Below, through his glass, Thamiel could see how slow and tortured the barbarian's movements had become, and he chuckled to himself as he watched. Spreadeagled, the big man was, on the awful face, moving upwards inches at a time, and the Seeker of Truth expected to see him fall at any moment. No man—certainly none in Thamiel's time—had ever gone so high before, and the gross, red-turbaned judge did not want to miss this insolent murderer's inevitable slip. One slip was all it would take now.

Yet even as these exceedingly pleasant thoughts were passing through Thamiel's mind, Kank Thad had spotted a reprieve of sorts. Just when it seemed his hand and footholds had run out—when nothing but a flat, smooth surface loomed in front and an abyssal emptiness behind—he saw, just a little to his left, a concavity in the face of the cliff from which long ago a great stone must have fallen. A gentle slide, letting his body fall sideways and to the left, would allow him to put his head and shoulder over the lip of the hole before gravity claimed him completely. Kank Thad looked once at his sandaled feet, to make sure they were firmly seated, pushed himself to the left with his hands, and then, as his motion picked up speed, he saw the—*thing*—that awaited him in the misted darkness of the concavity!

The barbarian's first impulse was to fling himself away, which would of course prove fatal, but his horror of the thing in the hole froze him rigid—and it saved his life! It was Thasik Haag sat there—legs adangle from the hole, the pipes of his throat hanging out in threads of gristly red and yellow, his good eye bulging and his black tongue lolling—Thasik Haag, or rather his shade. But even as the barbarian's rigid fingers struck the corpse-thing it disappeared, vanishing into mist and leaving the hole empty and once more friendly.

Kank Thad unfroze in the very last instant of time, his hands shooting forward into the small cave and his shoulders hunching to take the strain as his arms spread wide and wedged. For a second the lower half of his body hung in space, and then he hauled himself up and into the hole.

"Ye Gods!" he whispered to himself, the short hairs of his mane rising on his spine as he thought of the thing he had seen. "Ye Gods—but they named these cliffs aright and no mistake!"

By the time the barbarian was over his initial terror the mist had cleared somewhat, and he could see what looked like a good wide ledge some three man-lengths higher. He levered himself from the hole backwards and began to traverse the next section of his climb. It was not easy: projections were slight and toeholds shallow, and for the first time he felt the strain on his powerful muscles. Eventually he was only an arm's length below the ledge, which was when he gave a huge thrust with his legs and threw his arms up and over—*and into a gory mess!*

With one leg cocked on the ledge he reared instinctively back . . . and barely managed to hang by his fingertips as his leg slipped and the full weight of his huge frame fell on his hands. A ghost, of course, he knew that even hanging there—a mass of blood and squashed guts and brain—and an arm, and a clenched hand with the thumb pointing down . . . There had been a flattened grin on the face of the lich, and for an instant Kank Thad had thought to hear a mouse-like squeak of disapproval. Veth Nuss!

Slowly, a monstrous fear clutching his heart, the great Northman pulled himself up and peeped over the lip of the ledge. Nothing! Just a hard shelf of rock with a few pebbles. Wearily the barbarian hauled himself up and lay full-length where the lich of Veth Nuss had stretched in ruptured loathsomeness only a few heartbeats earlier. Now Kank Thad had had two warnings, and he knew what to expect of the rest of his climb.

GHOSTS? . . . DAMN them all, for no lifeless ghost could ever harm a man of warm flesh and hot blood! What he must do was simply . . . *ignore* the things, should any more of them appear. If only they wouldn't come at such inopportune moments!

But try as he might the barbarian could not ignore them, and toward the end of his tremendous climb he came across at least a dozen more. Swart Yhemni slavers from the distant East; grisly, bearded Northmen, fathers of buxom daughters lost to Kank Thad's wiles and lusts; taverners who'd called time far too early for a barbarian's thirst, or denied him credit in the first place—many of them. And so there should be, for the scarfaced Northman was an old hand at murder and all of these ghosts had been his victims . . .

Far below, Thamiel's suspense was almost too great to bear. The afternoon was drawing out and his flabby neck ached with the strain of peering upwards through his glass. Even to that instrument the climbing savage was now only a fly, and

Thamiel gave a shrill cry of disbelief and frustrated rage as he saw that fly suddenly merge with the high horizon of the Ghost Cliffs of Shildakor. Kank Thad had done it!—the barbarian had climbed the mile-high cliffs!

He had indeed, and his great lungs banged away in his chest and his great muscles throbbed and ached as he rested his elbows atop the nightmare abyss. His eyes swam and the sweat stood hot on his forehead; but not for long, for here a cool wind constantly blew from the east, blowing sand and grit in his eyes and bringing a final curtain of fog from the unseen valleys and unknown places beyond.

"I, Kank Thad, have done it!" the savage roared to the world. "What no man ever did before, that I—" He opened and closed his mouth, hanging on his elbows, peering into the mist. Then he shook his head and with a worried grin recommenced his broken cries of victory and self-esteem. "That I have—"

His boasting finally gurgled into a choked silence and the wind keened into his bared teeth . . .

Eyes bugging, the barbarian saw the horror lurch from out of the mist, saw the thing that had been a man crumple to its knees while still advancing, saw it reach out for him with jerking, crooked fingers and heard the agonised, rasping rattle of its throat. Clad in a bronze and leather breastplate, in thonged sandals and a leaden kirtle, it came—and its green features were twisted in eternal agony and its eyes blazed with the red light of revenge.

"*Yib!*" the barbarian croaked, and then: "Get you gone, Theen of Vilthod's Guard! I know you, lich—and you're impotent to harm me in death even as you were in life. Aye, and for that matter impotent of all else!"

Yet still the shade came on, shuffling on its knees before the Northman who fell back until once again he was hanging by his fingertips only. Blood flowed freely from between the horror's thighs, ghost-blood that yet splashed Kank Thad's face and ran scarlet down his straining arms, lich-blood that yet wetted the smooth rock of the cliff and made it slippery to the barbarian's fingers. In his mind's eye the terrified Northman saw himself once more in the tavern of Hethica Nid, and for the first time he recognised the monstrousness of the drunken atrocity he had perpetrated there. More freely yet ran the blood from the apparition's violated loins, wetter the rocks and slimier still.

"Oh, Gutrip!" the barbarian moaned once. "Why did you let me use you so?"—with which his fingers slipped in the blood and his great back arched in a death-embracing rigor and his eyes closed to shut out forever that ancient world.

And his body fell with the speed of one of those stars that slide down the heavens at night . . .

A mile below, Thamiel broke into a little dance and chortled and slapped his fat thighs, flinging his glass away in his complete exuberance and finally giggling hysterically. It had looked like the barbarian had won, and then, for no reason apparent in his glass, the great savage had fallen. Oh, how he laughed and stamped his feet.

Then, remembering his Imperishable and Immaculate Justice, he puffed himself up, set his scarlet turban a trifle more correctly upon his head—and quickly got out of the way.

And a few seconds later Kank Thad returned to Bhur-Esh.

The Sorcerer's Book

I TEH ATHT of Klühn, having ofttimes conversed with my , wizard ancestor, Mylakhrion of Tharamoon (dead these eleven hundred years), now tell the tale of how that mighty mage was usurped by his apprentice, Exior K'mool. At least, history has always supposed that he was usurped.

The story begins some fifty-three years before Mylakhrion's demise, at the fortress city Humquass on Theem'hdra's eastern strand, where that oldest and craftiest of sorcerers was the then resident mage, answerable only to the King himself. Humquass is no more, swept away by tides of time and war and Nature, but the legends live on.

I

Now in that day Humquass was a warrior city and its King, Morgath, was a warrior King; and the walls of the city were high and wide, with great towers where the soldiers were garrisoned; and the King's territories extended to the south, even to the Hrossak border which Morgath would push back if he had his way. For the King hungered for those southern lands and his warrior's heart ached for a kingdom which would enclose not only Hrossa to the River Luhr, but Yhemnis too. And Morgath would send ships across the Straits of Yhem to annex even Shadarabar, the island stronghold of savage black pirates.

As for Mylakhrion: he had served the King for fifteen years, since that time when first he came out of the west and across the mountains into Morgath's fierce kingdom. Aye, and in his way Mylakhrion had been a faithful servant, though truth to tell there were those who wondered who served whom.

For Mylakhrion's palace was greater than the King's—though far less opulent—and where Morgath received common men, Mylakhrion would receive none at all. The mage's familiars gave audience in his stead, speaking with Mylakhrion's voice and in his manner, but any emergence of the sorcerer himself was a singularly rare thing. Indeed, the very sight of Mylakhrion abroad and active in the topmost turrets of his palace tower—no less than the passing of comets across the sky or eclipses of the sun and moon—was almost invariably taken as portent of great wonders . . . and sometimes of dooms and disasters. And lesser mages seized upon such sightings, reading strange weirds into the wizard's ways, what little was known of them.

One thing which was known for a certainty was Mylakhrion's great age; not his actual age in years, but the fact that he was far older than any other living man. So thin as to be skeletal—with wrinkles to number against his years upon a skin of veined parchment pale as moonbeams—and with a long, tapering beard almost uniformly white, the wizard *was* ancient. Grandfathers could remember their grandfathers whispering of sorcerous deeds ascribed to his hand or wand when they themselves were mere children; and it was known for a fact that a previous apprentice of Mylakhrion's, one Azatta Leet, had recently died in Chlangi at an estimated age of one hundred and eleven years!

But in general the sorcerer's astonishing longevity was not much mentioned. People were mindful of his magnitude—and of Morgath's dependence upon him—and it was deemed neither moot nor even wise to probe too deeply into the hows, whys and wherefores of his attainment to so great an age. For all that he was ancient, still the mage's mind was brilliantly clear, his eyes undimmed and his sorceries (benevolent or otherwise) marvellous and utterly unfathomable to adepts of lesser learning. Moreover, he might not take kindly to allegations of vampirism and the like, practised to extend to eternity his existence in the world of men.

And in their thinking and their muted whisperings, the wizard's would-be compeers came close to the truth; for in his long search for immortality Mylakhrion had indeed performed many morbid magicks, though mercifully vampirism was not numbered amongst them. That is not to say he would *not* be a vampire if in that way he might prolong his life or regain his lost youth, but he knew better than that. No, for vampires were far too restricted and their lives in constant danger from attendant perils. Besides which, they were not truly immortal, not as Mylakhrion desired to be. He wanted to live forever, not to be eternally undead—or if not eternally, at least until the stake should find his heart.

On many occasions that master of magick had believed himself close to hitting upon the correct formula for immortality, that at last his feet were set upon the right path, but in the hour of his supposed triumph always he had been frustrated. He had prolonged his life far beyond the normal span, most certainly, but still he had grown old and must eventually die. And in any case, who would wish to live forever in a defunct body?

Now, knowing that his years were narrowing down, his search was more desperate and his disappointments deeper as days passed into years and the solution drew no closer. Now, too, he saw his coming to Humquass as an error; for while Morgath protected him and provided for his purely physical needs, his demands upon him grew more and more tiresome and consumed far too much of his time. Of which he might not have a great deal left.

For being a warrior King and going often to war, Morgath was constantly in need of favourable forecasts for his battle plans. Too, he sought for dark omens against his enemies, and he was no less interested in their stars than in his own. What with prognostications and astrological readings, auguries and auspices, personal weirds and bodements in general, Mylakhrion had not the time he required for his own all-important interests and darkling devotions.

Nor could the King's business be kept waiting, for the Hrossaks and Yhemnis had their wizards too, and Mylakhrion was required to turn aside the monstrous maledictions and outrageous runes which these enemy mages were wont to cast against Humquass and its King. Black Yoppaloth of the Yhemnis, a sorcerer of no mean prowess, was particularly pernicious; likewise Loxzor of the Hrossaks; and so it can be seen that Mylakhrion was hard put to attend his many duties, let alone pursue his own ambitions. And perhaps that would explain, too, Mylakhrion's reasons for sticking so close to his apartments. Why, his duties were such as to make him virtually a prisoner there!

And yet Mylakhrion had prospered under Morgath and so felt a certain gratitude toward him. Moreover, he liked the King for his intelligence. Aye, for intelligent kings were singularly rare in that day, particularly warrior-kings. And so the sorcerer felt he must not simply desert Morgath and leave him to the mercies of his equally warlike neighbours, and his frustration continued to grow within him.

Until the dawning of a certain idea . . .

NOW AMONG THE city's common wizards—real and assumed—there dwelled one Exior K'mool, a talented apprentice of Phaithor Ull before that mage rendered himself as green dust in an ill-conceived thaumaturgical experiment. A seer whose betokenings showed promise despite the fact that as yet they remained undeveloped, essentially Exior was oneiromantic. His dreams were prophetic and generally accurate.

And it came to pass that Exior dreamed a dream in which Mylakhrion took an apprentice to assist him in his sorceries, and Exior himself was the chosen one and rose to great power in Theem'hdra in the service of Morgath, King of Humquass. Upon awakening he remembered the dream and smiled wryly to himself, for he believed his vision had been born of wishful thinking and was in no way a portent of any real or foreseeable future. But then, a day or two later, Mylakhrion made it known that indeed he sought a young assistant . . .

Exior's heart soared like a bird when first he heard this news; alas, for a little while only. For how could Exior—a ragged street-magician who sold charms and love potions for a living and divined the futile dreams of his penniless patrons for mere crusts of bread—possibly apply for a position as apprentice to Mylakhrion the Mighty? The idea was preposterous! And so, however reluctantly, he put aside the notion and forced himself to consider his vision as purely coincidental to Mylakhrion's requirement.

And as days passed into weeks so Mylakhrion gave audience to many young men who presented themselves as prospective employees. As usual, the interviews were carried out through his familiars (though many applicants got no farther than Mylakhrion's gate) while the wizard, unseen by those aspirants who were actually allowed to pass into his palace, busied himself with more pressing matters in hidden rooms. In this way, many who might have impressed quite favourably confronted by a merely human interviewer—even by so awe-inspiring a man as Mylakhrion—found themselves completely overwhelmed in the presence of his familiar creatures; for these were three great bats whose faces were those of men!

Indeed, they had once been men, those fearsome familiars; wizards who had formed a sorcerous triad to crush Mylakhrion when he refused to join them. Unfortunately for them, his talents had been greater than all of theirs combined, hence their hybridisation. That had been many years ago, however, before ever he came to Humquass, and Mylakhrion had all but forgotten the details of the thing. He trusted his familiars implicitly; and besides, they had only the faces of his old enemies. Their minds were their own, or Mylakhrion's when he chose to use them as he now used them.

Finally, when even the older, failed magicians of Morgath's

lands began to present themselves at Mylakhrion's gate, Exior K'mool dreamed again; and in his dream he saw the man-faced bats nodding to him in unison before bidding him enter Mylakhrion's inner sanctum, where that Master of Mages was waiting to hand him his robe of apprenticeship. That was enough.

At dawn of the next day Exior dressed himself in his finest jacket and breeches—the ones with only a few minor repairs—and made his way tortuously through the mazy streets of Humquass to the walls of Mylakhrion's palace. There, at the great gate, he timorously took his place behind three others and waited . . . but not for long. A small barred window opened in a door in the gate and each of the other aspirants was cursorily dismissed in his turn. Seeing this, Exior began to turn away, at which point a voice stopped him. It was the voice of the man whose face peered through the barred window, and it said:

"Young man, what is your name?"

"K'mool," said Exior stepping warily forward. "Exior K'mool."

"And do you seek employment with Mylakhrion?"

"I do," he answered, wondering at the echoing and sepulchral quality of the man's voice. "I desire to be . . . to be the mage's apprentice."

"You seem uncertain."

"I am certain enough," said Exior, "but I wonder—"

"If you are worthy?"

"Perhaps." He nodded nervously.

"My master likes humility in men," said the face at the window. "Aye, and honesty, too. Enter, Exior K'mool."

The door in the gate opened soundlessly and Exior took a

deep breath as he stepped over its sill. He expelled the air in a loud gasp as the door closed behind him, and glancing about wide-eyed he was almost startled into flight at sight of the things he now saw. But where to flee? Where a moment before the sky had been blue and the sun warm, now, seen from this grey courtyard, the heavens were dark with racing clouds and a chill wind ruffled the fur-covered body of . . . of the bat-thing whose man's face had spoken from the window in the gate!

"Do you fear Mylakhrion's familiar, Exior K'mool?" asked the great bat-thing. "Or are you alarmed at the season here, which is ever different to that outside."

"A little of both, sir, I fancy," Exior finally managed.

The bat-thing laughed a loud, baying laugh and flapped aloft. "Fear not," it boomed, hovering in the air, "but follow behind me and you shall see what you shall see."

Exior gritted his teeth, put his fear behind him and strode after the creature across the windswept courtyard to enter into the palace proper: a stark and massive building of huge basaltic blocks with openings like black mouths which seemed to grimace hideously. Following the flap of membranous wings, he mounted corkscrew stairs of stone within a tower whose base must surely be big as the tavern where Exior lodged; and soon, arriving at a landing, he found the freakish familiar waiting for him before an entrance whose arch was carved with all the signs of the zodiac. Now, as the creature hopped across the threshold, he followed into a vast room whose contents held him spellbound in a single instant of time.

Mylakhrion's familiar settled itself upon a high perch, where it hung upside down the better to observe Exior's astonished reactions. After a little while it said: "And are my master's possessions of interest to you, young man?"

"Indeed they are!" the youth gasped, his jaw ajar and his eyes gazing in ghastly fascination all about the room. Why, if the contents of this single room were his, even Exior K'mool could be a mighty magician!

For here were scattered all the appurtenances of Mylakhrion's art, every sort and description of occult apparatus. There were acromegalic skulls of monstrous men and shocking skeletons of things which never had been men; strangely shaped phials and bottles filled with quiescent or bubbling liquids of golden, green or dark hues, all of a usage utterly unknown to Exior; bagpipes made of ebony and ivory and the cured intestinal sacks of dragons, whose music was doubtless used in the propitiation of certain demons; shelf upon shelf of books bound in brown leathers and yellow skins, and at least one whose umber bindings bore—Exior would swear to it—the purplish mottlings of tattoos!

Here too were miniature spheres of alien worlds and moons, mapped out and inlaid with cryptic runes of gold and silver; and all slowly turning where they hung from the fretted ceiling on ropes of tiny cowries. And here pentacles of power adorning the mosaic walls and floor, glowing with the inner fire of the gem-chips from which they were constructed. And sigil-inscribed scrolls of vellum upon a marble table, together with a silver-framed magnifier, an astrolabe, calipers and tiny bronze weights. And central in the room and resting alone upon a small stand of carved chrysolite, a great ball of clouded crystal.

The workshop of Theem'hdra's greatest wizard, thought

Exior—his entire library too—and all in this one room! But as if divining his very thoughts, the perch-hung chiropteran shook its head. "Nay, lad," the creature said, "for this is only one tenth of a tenth part of all my master's mysteries. I am his most trusted familiar, and yet there are rooms here which I have never entered, and others I would not even dare to seek out! Nay, this is merely his room of repose."

"And am I . . . am I to see . . . *him?*" Exior asked.

"If you are so fortunate to be chosen as his apprentice, certainly you shall see him. Daily. Perhaps too often! He shall instruct you thus and thus, and you shall do so and so. And if you are quick to learn, one day you may even grow mighty as Mylakhrion himself."

"I meant," said Exior, "am I to see him . . . now?"

"That depends . . ." the creature answered, and went on: "But now there are things I must ask you, Exior K'mool, and you shall answer truthfully to each and every question."

Exior nodded and Mylakhrion's familiar demon continued: "Good! Then answer me this: why do you seek this position?"

"I would study under the greatest mage in all the land," Exior answered at once. "Also my master would know how best to employ my own minor talents."

"And what are those talents?"

"I scry the future in dreams," said Exior. "Aye, and my dreams have never lied to me."

"Never?" The sepulchral tones of the bat-thing seemed honed with a certain scepticism.

"I have common dreams like any man; but there are special dreams, too, and when they come to me I can usually recognise them."

"And is that all you are, a dreamer?"

The blood began to burn in Exior's face, but he felt less humbled than angry. "I also translate tongues, read runes and fathom cyphers," he snapped. "My seer's eyes scry the meanings of even the most obscure languages, glyphs and cryptograms."

"Is that all?" The creature's voice was cold as deep, dark oceans of ice, drawing all of the heat out of Exior in a moment.

"I . . . I mix potent potions, and—"

"Love potions?" The bat-thing seemed almost to sneer.

Exior knew when he was beaten. Furious, he turned on his heel to leave the room, the tower, Mylakhrion's palace, the whole ridiculous idea behind him—and found his way blocked by two more giant chiropters. They did not speak but merely stood as statues in the arched entrance, their men's faces observing through speculative eyes Exior where he paused in confusion.

Finally, from behind the youth, the inverted one spoke again: "He who acts in haste often acts foolishly—and regrets at leisure. How do you answer that?"

Exior turned sharply upon his examiner. "He who accepts insults and taunts from his inferiors is an even bigger fool!" he hotly retorted.

The bat-thing righted itself upon its perch. "And do you consider Mylakhrion's favourite familiar your . . . inferior?" Its voice was the merest whisper now—the *hiss* of a dry leaf blown across a graveyard slab—but its human eyes were bright, hard and unblinking.

"That face you wear," said Exior K'mool, his words coming cracked from a throat suddenly dry as dust, "once sat upon a man's shoulders. Fool I may be, but my life and limbs are my own and I speak with my own voice. In short, I am still a man—and better a foolish man than some hybrid horror spawned of a wizard's—" And there he broke off, for the three were laughing at him, baying dinningly where they faced him, their booming laughter echoing loudly in the great room.

Astonished, and because there seemed little else to do, Exior waited until they were done and the one on the perch once more addressed him. "Mylakhrion," the creature finally informed him with a strange smile, "likes humility and honesty in a man, as I believe I have mentioned aforetime. He also likes a little spunkiness, on occasion—but not too much, for that might be mistaken for audacity. Forwardness and fools he will not suffer, but cowardice he abhors! You have done well, Exior K'mool—and now my master will see you."

And all three familiars nodded as one creature, just as Exior had seen it in his dream.

"SEER, BE SEATED," said Mylakhrion, and the youth at once recognised his voice as being one and the same with that of the bat-thing.

Mylakhrion sat upon his night-black throne and studied Exior minutely, coldly, with no emotion whatever visible in his straight-backed mien. His silver eyebrows were thin and turned sharply upward at the temples, and beneath them his eyes were of that same palest blue as the Outer Immensities glimpsed ofttimes by Exior in his dreams. Strange those eyes and almost vacuous, but at the same time filled with terrible lore and a knowledge forbidden to common men and middling mages alike.

His hands, where they protruded from the bell-like cuffs of his robe and rested upon the arms of his throne, were long

and thin and their nails sharply pointed; their colour, as that
of his much wrinkled face and sandaled feet, was a pale umber like unto certain parchments. A cold old man, Mylakhrion, and his gaze even colder. He trained that gaze upon
Exior as the youth sat down upon a tiny stool close to the
somewhat raised dais where sat the sorcerer himself.

The apartment was starkly bare in comparison with that
"room of repose" wherefrom Exior had been guided to this
even loftier chamber. It had a balcony with a balustrade of
marble gargoyles, opening upon a frightfully vertiginous view
(a wintry vista, despite the true season) of some drear and
windswept desert where mounds of rubble hinted of exten-
sive ruins. Exior did not recognise the scene, and he was sure
that it lay not anywhere in the vicinity of Humquass.

Now there was no king in all Theem'hdra who would normally allow the house of a common man to overshadow his
own; but Mylakhrion was distinctly uncommon, and besides,
he required a place higher than any other to facilitate his far-
seeing, and for the propitiation of elementals of the air; and
so Morgath had never voiced complaint. But the plain fact of
the matter was that the sorcerer liked to be remote from
mundane men; and where better than high in this forbidding
and precipitous palace tower, this veritable aerie of a room?

Exior had been brought here by the three familiars, and
their spokesman had accompanied him into the room through
great brazen doors. Once Exior was safe inside, however, the
bat-thing had quickly departed; whereupon Mylakhrion had
appeared from the balcony to climb the three small steps of the
dais to his throne of polished jet.

Now in that dim and sparsely furnished place, with only the
light from the balcony to relieve the gloom—and that a dim

and dingy light—Exior K'mool and Mylakhrion the Mighty gazed each upon the other, would-be wizard and Supreme Sorcerer alike. And whatever the thoughts of the youth in the presence of this legended enchanter, they were soon cut short as Mylakhrion commenced his own examination.

"So, young man, and you would be my apprentice, would you? Well, then, there is more I must know about you; what suffices for my familiars may not satisfy me. First let me tell you of the work, and then you must say if you are still interested; after which and depending upon your decision, I may ask you to perform a small task for me. If you perform well— and *only* if the task is completed to my satisfaction—then you shall be my apprentice. That may be to look too far ahead, however, for you might not care much for the work."

Mylakhrion paused for long moments and turned his strange eyes to the grey, racing clouds beyond the gargoyle balusters. The sharp nail of one of his fingers tapped for a little while, thoughtfully, upon the hard arm of his throne. Then, without returning his gaze to Exior, finally the wizard said:

"The hours will be long, and when there are not enough of them for any one day I shall make more. Never have nothing to do. And you must put aside fear; I have no room for it. There will be liches here to take horrid advantage of one who is afraid, for I am a necromancer. But as well as the dead, I call up spirits black and white, demons and devils and saints alike. I hold intercourse with ghouls, gaunts and wraiths, with werewolves, gnomes and jinnees; aye, for there is much to be learned from them. And remember: just as idle hands wither, so slothful minds mortify. I converse at length with Demogorgon; from time to time I sleep with succubus and have fathered lamia, harpy, vampire and elf. And all of them—my wives, children and changelings—they occasionally visit me. They call me master, and so shall you, and I am a *hard* task-master. Tasks are not allowed to remain unperformed; nothing which may be done today is ever done tomorrow. And for all that I have done; still I am unchanged. Aged, yes, but a man still—and mortal! And I seek immortality, Exior K'mool, which is why you are here: to lessen the burden and save time for me. For once time is fled, who may recall it? And again I say to you, remember: stitches in time save myriads! You will assist me not alone in many small tasks—be my messenger, potwatcher, my sweeper, linguist, my rune-reader, seer—but in great works and experiments also. And of all my knowledge shall you partake, learning and growing wise in the ways of magick. BUT—" (and abruptly the wizard paused, leaving Exior breathless as if he himself had spoken all of these words) "a warning! Never *never* seek to subvert my cause, change my course or deliberately and maliciously do anything to cause me discomfort, neither of mind nor of body! And if you are a good apprentice, then, when I am no more—" And again he paused.

In a little while, as Exior sat and fought to still his trembling, Mylakhrion turned his eyes back to the youth. "And are you still interested?"

Unable to find words, Exior merely nodded.

II

As night drew on and the sun sank down behind the mountains, Exior smelled a great storm blowing up and hurriedly sought shelter. He tethered his yak just within the mouth of a small cave hidden in the lee of wind-carved crags, then carefully checked to ensure that this was not the lair of some wild beast. Grumbling as he worked and occasionally cursing, he lighted a fire in a hollow place and brewed himself a pot of tea.

Six months ago he had looked back from his tail-end position in an escorted caravan leaving Humquass and smiled as he watched the walls of the city slowly merging into the southern horizon; since when he had not smiled a great deal, had faced dangers galore and covered thousands of miles in the performance of Mylakhrion's "small task"—which still remained unperformed. Now Exior had reached the end of his ability to endure any more hardship, the end of his tether, and he ought also to have reached the end of his journey. But . . .

"Go west," Mylakhrion had instructed him. "Cross the Eastern Peaks, pass between the Nameless Desert and the Mountains of Lohmi, follow the sun over wide and rolling plains to the foothills of the Great Circle Mountains, and there turn your feet northward. Keeping the foothills on your left hand, follow the edge of the plain and in the space of two days you will find a city lost in the desert sands.

"At the edge of the city's ruins lying closest to the foothills, there you will spy the broken fang of a once great tower, and in its base a door. Now listen carefully, Exior K'mool, for this is most important. Deep beneath the tumbled tower, hidden in a catacomb of caves, there within a secret chamber you will find a Great Book. It is locked and lies upon a pedestal of onyx. Bring me that book, Exior K'mool, and thereafter be known as Mylakhrion's apprentice!

"But know too, young man, that the dangers will be many and the way long and hard . . . Now, how do you say?"

Once more, like a fool, Exior had agreed; and shortly

thereafter he joined a caravan heading north. After eight days he left the caravan and struck out over the eastern range, crossing in a week. Another month took him to the Nameless Desert, and another saw him in the long grasses of the central plains. There his horse was bitten by an adder and he was obliged to proceed on foot. Two more months and autumn was drawing to a close; and now along with winter the Great Circle Mountains loomed, in whose foothills Exior met with friendly nomads and bought from them his yak. Five more weeks took him to the borders of the Desert of Ell, and for three days now he had been wandering northwest between desert and foothills.

By now he should have sighted Mylakhrion's lost city, but so far it remained lost. Lost, too, Exior K'mool, if he continued for very much longer with his quest. His water was low, food down to crusts; there was little or no grass for his beast—which in any case was old and tired—and worst of all the days were growing shorter and the skies darker with the rapid approach of winter. Indeed, before finding his refuge for the night, Exior had recognised the bleak and wintry landscape as that seen from Mylakhrion's tower room, and the clouds which fled ever south were those same clouds he had thought peculiar to the sky over the sorcerer's palace. Obviously Mylakhrion had spied out the way for him; why, then, had he failed to find the lost city?

That night, dreaming, the youth saw a great fang of stone rising from drifted sand and tumbled blocks. His dream was recurrent, but each time his slumbering spirit approached the visioned pile so the howling gale would startle him to wakefulness in his blanket, that or the cry of his frightened beast where it stood trembling in the lightning-illumined door of the cave. Mercifully the storm's direction was away from Exior's refuge, for its fury was such that it moved a vast amount of sand and both man and beast might easily have been entombed.

As it was, rising cold, tired and hungry from his troubled and fitful slumbers, Exior saw that the storm had blown itself out; also that he had been presumptuous to doubt those directions given him by Mylakhrion. For now, where great waves of sand had stretched to the horizon, the scattered remnants of a once mighty city lay uncovered to his bleary gaze. And not far off, within a stone's throw, a certain shattered spire drew his eyes as a northstone draws a nail. Without doubt this was that tower of which Mylakhrion had foretold, beneath which Exior would find the maze of caves and eventually the secret chamber and volume of ancient magick!

The youth fed himself and his beast as best he could, drank a little from his leather bottle and dampened the yak's nose and mouth, then walked the animal beneath wintry morning skies to the base of the crumbling but still massive monument. Alas, in the sand drifted against its base he could find no door; but above, almost within reach, fallen blocks revealed a dark hole somewhat wider than his shoulders.

Now before proceeding any farther, Exior made a pause and gave some thought to one other thing Mylakhrion had told him. There might well be a "guard," the ancient magician had warned, a spirit or demon set to watch over the secret room and its book; for the book contained such powerful magick that whosoever possessed it could make himself mighty above all men. It had belonged to a great sorcerer and necromancer, that book, but in a war of wizardry he had been obliged to flee the city in the desert and the book had been left behind. Even as he fled, the city was brought to a great ruin by his enemies, and thus it had remained to this day.

That had all been more than five hundred years ago, however, and only recently, through his own thaumaturgies, had Mylakhrion discovered again the lost city and fathomed its ancient secrets. And by now the "guard," if indeed such existed, must be much diminished through time and disuse; and surely Exior should have no trouble with a magick grown so small and centuries-shrivelled . . .

Well, perhaps not; but nevertheless Exior frowned worriedly as he made torches, piled stones and finally climbed until he could squeeze in through the hole in the wall of the tower. Cobwebby gloom met his eyes, and dusty, spiralling steps that wound down into darkness. He took one last look out through the hole at the drear landscape of tumbled blocks and fallen, shattered pillars—a landscape which now seemed much more friendly than the gloomy bowels of this ages-old tower—lighted a torch and commenced his descent.

Round and down he went, brushing aside or burning cobwebs out of his way; and tiny scurrying things moved aside for him, and dust trickled from ledges where the centuries had piled it; and only the gloom and the winding steps descending ever deeper into bowels of fetid earth . . .

After what seemed an inordinately long time, Exior reached the bottom and found himself in a great cavern whose walls were honeycombed with tunnels and caves. On guard against whatever might be lurking down here, he was making to explore the largest of these passages when a great rumbling roar froze him in his tracks. A belch of animal fury, the warning had issued from that very tunnel he had been on the point of entering. Trembling in every limb, Exior lighted a second torch and stuck it in the sandy floor, then drew his sword and waited for whatever it was that prowled these eerie excavations: doubtless that "guard" of which Mylakhrion had forewarned.

In a little while the demon appeared and jerked forward on spindly legs into the central hall. Half-spider, half-bat that being, and twice as big as a man to boot. With curving fangs like white scythes, and eyes big as saucers, the thing loomed over Exior and glared down at him; and finally, with a voice that rumbled volcanically and brimstony breath, it spoke:

"What do ye here, little man? This is a forbidden place. Begone!"

Exior shook his head in dumb defiance and held out his torch and sword before him. And finding his voice, he said: "I run an errand for my master, and you shall not stop me."

"And what is the nature of your errand?" questioned the demon.

"To find a room and a runebook," said Exior with many a gulp. "Also, to take that book back to my master."

"I know room and book both!" the creature answered. "Aye, and I guard them well. Wherefore it is plainly my duty to eat ye . . . or would ye care to play a game with me?"

"A game?" replied Exior, who vastly preferred any alternative to being eaten.

"Ye shall have a choice," the demon explained. "Go now and I shall do ye no harm, but if ye stay ye must play my game. If ye win the game ye may take the book and I at last may rest—but if ye lose . . ."

"Then?" Exior prompted, his heart in his mouth.

"Why, then I shall eat ye!" answered the monster with a great coughing laugh.

"And what is the nature of this game?" asked Exior,

wondering where best to strike the beast to bring it down, and whether he had the strength for such a stroke.

"I shall say ye a riddle," the demon replied, "and ye must tell me its meaning."

Now Exior's mind grew alert as he readied it for the trial; for there never had been a riddle or rune whose meaning eluded him for long, and despite his great fear he could not refuse the demon's challenge. "So be it," he said, "let's hear your riddle."

The spider-bat laughed again, then very rapidly and in a loud, clear monotone said:

"TI DNAMMOC I . . . MOOR TERCES EHT OT EM DAEL DNA, ERA YLLAER UOY SA UOY EES EM TEL WON, EMAG EHT NOW GNIVAH . . . EM MRAH TON YAM DNA NOISULLI ERA UOY . . . SESSENKAEW RUOY DNA, NOMED UOY WONK I!"

To which Exior at once and excitedly replied, "My answer is: '*I know you demon, and your weaknesses. You are illusion and may not harm me. Having won the game, now let me see you as you really are, and lead me to the secret room. I command it!*' "

The demon gave a great cry (of relief, Exior suspected) and immediately shrank down into the shape of a tiny lizard which wriggled away into the mouth of one of the tunnels. It paused to look back, whereupon Exior lighted a third torch and followed on behind. In a little while the lizard led the way to a door of brass and squeezed beneath it. When Exior shoved the door open on squeaking hinges, the tiny creature had disappeared.

The room was circular, domed and starkly bare; except for

its pedestal of onyx and the Great Book which lay upon it, thick with the dust of five long centuries and more. Quickly Exior crossed to the pedestal and laid his trembling hands upon the great, jewel-crusted cover. He blew away the dust and gazed awestruck at old leather inlaid with ivory, jade, gold and fabulous gems; and at the hasps and lock, green with age and neglect; and last but not least at the weirdly-wrought key where it lay beside the priceless volume.

And he remembered what Mylakhrion had told him: that in this book were writ the secrets of suns and moons, times past and times as yet unborn, and all the wonders of wizards dead and gone and the lore of darkling dimensions beyond the familiar three. Knowledge enough to make a man mighty above all other men. And Exior picked up the key and turned it protestingly in the ancient lock.

Then, as he began to lift the heavy cover—

Runes graven in the onyx pedestal caught his eye, and he let the cover fall back upon pages unseen. The glyphs were rare, obscure as the ages, and writ in a cypher to bedazzle the mind of any but a master cryptographer born. Such was Exior K'mool.

Brows drawn together in concentration, lips moving silently as they traced strange words, by the light of his fitful torch he read the runes. Then, lighting yet another torch the better to see, he read them again—and snatched back his hand from where it rested upon the sorcerer's book. For the message was very clear: that without a certain protection, the essence of any man brash or foolish enough to read the book would be torn from him, leaving him empty and foolish and bereft of mind, will and soul!

The protection, however, was comparatively simple: it was

a moon-rune, rare but well enough known to Exior, designed to propitiate the protective power of Mnomquah, God of the Moon and of Madness, known commonly as Gleeth. And now the youth knew that indeed the book's secrets were marvellous and monstrous, for Gleeth is a god who from his celestial seat sees and therefore knows all; and his moon-runes are correspondingly powerful.

Without hesitation Exior said the rune out loud, and when the echoes of his voice had died away he opened the forbidden volume to the first page. There, in rubric pigments which yet glowed despite the inexorable trickle of time's sands, the warning was repeated: that Gleeth's protection be sought before reading. Since he had already availed himself of the necessary precaution, Exior turned the next page, which bore no signature but commenced straightway with words of baleful might, and with bated breath he began to read . . .

FOR LONG AND long Exior read the book, and when his torches were finished he carried it up to the light; and for two days he read on and for two nights he sat and considered and did not sleep. He gave the patient yak his last crust, the last of his water, and on the morning of the third day closed the book and locked it. Then he stood up beside the ruined tower and looked all about at the drear desert and the sand-sundered city.

His eyes were pale now and chill, with shadows beneath, which were dark above the parchment of his cheeks. And his hair, no longer jet but grey; and his entire mien that of an old man heavy-burdened with wisdom and knowledge and sin, while yet his back was straight and his limbs young.

For an hour he stood thus, then turned to his yak. Alas,

the poor beast lay dead and a vulture picked at its eye, which was torn by the bird's beak. Angered, Exior said a word—a single *word*—and the vulture gave a startled cry and sprang aloft, falling lifeless in the next instant. And the yak shook its head, got to its feet and gazed upon its master. It gazed with one dim old yak's eye, and one which was sharp and bright and that of a vulture.

Then Exior tied the book to his saddle and mounted himself upon his beast's back, and so he left the Desert of Ell and made for home . . .

III

Three months and three weeks later, a stranger in a cowled cloak and riding upon a blinkered yak arrived at the gates of Humquass beneath its beetling walls. Without any of the usual formalities (for which gross inefficiency he must later make blustered and only half-believed excuses) the Commander of the Guard raised the gate and let the stranger in; and Exior—for such it was, as well you know—went straight to the palace of Mylakhrion.

There the gate in the wall opened at his approach and he passed through without hindrance, tethering his beast in the wizard's courtyard. And where beyond the city's walls all was early spring and the trees budding and flowers burgeoning into bloom, here a midsummer sun blazed down and the heat was stifling where lizards lazed atop white walled gardens of gardenias.

Exior paused not before this wonder nor even considered it, but entered the main tower where waited Mylakhrion's familiars. They gazed upon them, and he upon them; and then they bowed down low before him and let him pass. And so he mounted the stone-hewn stairs to seek out Mylakhrion in his lofty lair.

On this occasion, however, he had no need of ascending to so great a height, for Mylakhrion pottered in his room of repose. There Exior found him, and there the mage gave him greeting of a sort.

"Ho, Exior K'mool! So, you are returned to me at last, and just as I began to suspect that some ill had befallen you. And do you bring me the fruits of your quest?"

Exior said nothing but merely stared at the master mage, observing him curiously and with mixed emotions through his changed eyes. He threw back his cowl to show locks grey as Arctic oceans above a face almost pale as that of Mylakhrion himself. Then he approached a table and brushed its surface free from clutter, placing his linen-wrapped parcel centrally and untying its fastenings. And laying back the coverings he displayed the Great Book, and as Mylakhrion drew nigh he gave him the key.

Now the sorcerer's silver eyebrows rose a little; and without questioning Exior's silence or his strangely altered appearance, he took the key, opened the book and turned back its jewel-crusted cover. Then—

Mylakhrion frowned and his briefly risen eyebrows fell down low again over suddenly narrowed eyes. He turned his gaze to Exior and gloomed upon him, saying: "Youth, the first page is torn out! Do you see the broken edge, the riven vellum?"

And now, in a voice fully frosty as that of his master, Exior answered, "Aye, I have noted it."

"Hmph!" The enchanter seemed disgruntled and a little disappointed, but in another moment his curiosity returned. "So be it," he said, "for what is one leaf on the tree of all dark knowledge?"

Now during his journey home Exior had made a diabolic decision. As can be seen, he had determined to be done with Mylakhrion and so had torn out from the book the opening admonition. He reasoned thus: that having read the book he now had power to become mighty above all men, even above Mylakhrion himself. There would be no room for two such sorcerers in Humquass, wherefore the greybeard must go. And what better instrument of an abrupt assassination than this fearful, ruin-recovered volume of morbid magicks?

Unsuspecting and unprotected, Mylakhrion would read, and the book would bind him in its spell, crush him, destroy him utterly. For if the power of the thing were such as to seize upon Exior's spirit, sap the colour from his hair and flesh and sear his very soul—and him *protected!*—how then would the venerable Mylakhrion fare, all frail with age and weighted down with the burden of his unguessed years?

Well, he had lived long enough, and his release would be a kindness of a sort. And anyway, the awakened Exior would make a poor apprentice, who possessed power at least the equal of his supposed master. So let Mylakhrion read and bid him farewell, and then announce to the city the presence of a new and still more powerful mage in the palace of the sorcerer.

Thus had Exior plotted and now he stood upon the threshold of his destiny; and the book was open and Mylakhrion sat before it at the table; and as that self-confessed necromancer began to read out loud, so Exior shuddered as were he dead and felt the furtive tread of ghouls on the soft earth above.

An icy fist seemed closed around his heart and a question burned in his brain. How then was he brought to this? A murderer most foul, Exior K'mool, who once was a dreamer and mixed love potions for pennies? Even as Mylakhrion's voice made its sepulchral booming and rolled the work's rare words, so Exior gave a little cry and started forward; at which the sorcerer looked up.

"Is aught amiss, Exior?" There seemed a certain slyness in his question. "Do you fear to hear these marvels and monstrosities? Shall I read them to myself then, in silence?"

Exior shook his head. Was he afraid? Nay, for he had said again Gleeth's moon-rune and feared not. Not for himself. "Read on, master," he answered; but there was a catch in his voice which he had believed extinct.

Mylakhrion nodded. "So be it," he said, his voice fallen to the merest whisper. For a little while, in silence, the two gazed into each other's eyes; and those of the elder were narrowed now and very bright. Finally they fell once more to the written page.

And so that master of mages read on until he reached the bottom of a certain leaf, and as his fingers went to turn the page Exior once more gave a start. He knew the revelations overleaf were such as must surely sear any mere mortal, which Mylakhrion was of his own admittance. And again that fist tightened upon Exior's heart as he knew himself for a traitor.

"Stop!" he cried as the page began to turn. "Look no more, Mylakhrion! If you would save your sight, your mind, your very soul, *be still*! . . . For I have deceived you—"

Slowly Mylakhrion looked up and smiled. Even Mylakhrion, he smiled! And it was a real smile, banishing much of his customary coldness as the morning sun lifts rime from spring flowers. Exior saw that smile but did not understand; and Mylakhrion asked, "Do you fear for me, Exior K'mool, or for yourself? For your conscience, perhaps?"

"For both of us, if you will," answered the other harshly. "Whichever way you would have it—only read no more. There is a protection, lacking which the book's blasphemies will blast you! The warning was writ on the first page, which I tore out . . ."

"Oh?" Mylakhrion's smile diminished somewhat. Deliberately he turned the page, and when Exior made to snatch the book from him he held up a hand of caution. "Peace, young man. Watch—and learn!" And without further pause he read the page to its end.

During the reading Exior saw shadows gather in the room as with the approach of night. There commenced a strange tremor and a muted thunder which had their sources in the air of the room itself. Crystals splintered and phials flew into fragments; finely wrought mirrors shivered into shards and liquids boiled up and overflowed their crucibles; aye, and cracks appeared in the very walls while dust and debris rained down from the ceiling, ere Mylakhrion was done. Then he closed the book and looked up, and still he smiled. Nor was his mien changed at all, and the reading had done him no ill whatever.

"I . . . I—"

"Be silent and listen," Mylakhrion commanded. "You have done well, Exior K'mool, as I suspected you would. And you will make a fitting mage for Morgath, given time. As for me: now I up and get me gone to Tharamoon. And on that bleak and northern isle I shall build me a tower, as is my wont, and there seek that immortality which ever confounds me. This palace here in Humquass: it is yours. You have earned it, every last stone."

"I have earned it?" Exior was amazed. "But I am a traitor, and—"

"You were *almost* a traitor," Mylakhrion answered, "and that is the difference. You could not know that I am ever protected against dark forces, and that the book would not harm me. Therefore, when you would have stopped me from reading, you showed mercy. I like that quality in a man, Exior K'mool! And you have many qualities. Some humility, a deal of honesty, a little daring—and now, too, wisdom and mercy! All to the good, young man, for without them you could never succeed.

"Moreover, your talents are of the sort Morgath needs above all others. Myself, I was never much of a one for such minor magicks and studied them not extensively. But you? You are a seer and read runes and portents. You reckon well the auspices and faithfully foretell the future. Aye, and the King will be well pleased with you."

Mylakhrion stood up and took hold of Exior's shoulders. "Tomorrow you meet him, Morgath the King, and the day after that I leave for Tharamoon. How do you say to that?"

"But—" Exior began. And again: "How . . . why—?"

"Enough!" Mylakhrion lifted his hand. "It is finished."

"But all of this," and Exior gazed all about, "mine? I cannot believe it! Will you take nothing with you?"

Mylakhrion shook his head. "All is yours—except I shall take my wand with me, and my familiars three. And the book . . ."

"The book, of course!" Exior nodded. "And with it make yourself mighty above all men. Yes, naturally."

"No," Mylakhrion smiled again, "for I am that already. I will tell you why I take these things. My wand because it suits my hand, and my familiars because I am grown used to them. Their faces remind me of my youth, when I defeated them in a wizardly war. As for what I leave behind: these things were never really mine. They were gifted to me, or I purchased them, or won them by use of my magick. They are as nothing. But the book—that is mine." His eyes gazed searchingly into the other's face.

And now Exior gasped and his own changeling eyes went wide.

"Ah! I see the truth dawns on you at last," said Mylakhrion. "Your face grows gaunt with a great wonder and your jaw falls open. Rightly so—" and he nodded. "You are of course correct, Exior K'mool, and now you know all. The rune book is an old friend of mine and I would never leave without it. Not unless my leaving was enforced, as happened to me once long ago in the Desert of Ell . . .

"No, the book goes with me. For who can say when I shall have the time to write another?"

The House of Cthulhu

Where weirdly angled ramparts loom,
Gaunt sentinels whose shadows gloom
Upon an undead hell-beast's tomb—
And gods and mortals fear to tread.
Where gateways to forbidden spheres
And times are closed, but monstrous fears
Await the passing of strange years—
When that will wake which is not dead . . .

"ARLYEH"—A FRAGMENT FROM TEH ATHT'S *LEGENDS
OF THE OLDEN RUNES*. AS TRANSLATED BY THELRED
GUSTAU FROM THE THEEM'HDRA MANUSCRIPTS.

NOW IT HAPPENED aforetime that Zar-thule the Conqueror, who is called Reaver of Reavers, Seeker of Treasures and Sacker of Cities, swam out of the East with his dragon-ships; aye, even beneath the snapping sails of his dragon-ships. The wind was but lately turned favorable, and now the weary rowers nodded over their shipped oars while sleepy steersmen held the course. And there Zar-thule descried him in the sea the island Arlyeh, whereon loomed tall towers builded of black stone whose tortuous twinings were of angles unknown and utterly beyond the ken of men; and this island was redly lit by the sun sinking down over its awesome black crags and burning behind the aeries and spires carved therefrom by other than human hands.

And though Zar-thule felt a great hunger and stood sore weary of the wide sea's expanse behind the lolling dragon's tail of his ship Redfire, and even though he gazed with red and rapacious eyes upon the black island, still he held off his reavers, bidding them that they ride at anchor well out to sea until the sun was deeply down and gone unto the Realm of Cthon; even unto Cthon, who sits in silence to snare the sun in his net beyond the edge of the world. Indeed, such were Zar-thule's raiders as their deeds were best done by night, for then Gleeth the blind Moon God saw them not, nor heard in his celestial deafness the horrible cries which ever attended unto such deeds.

For notwithstanding his cruelty, which was beyond words, Zar-thule was no fool. He knew him that his wolves must rest before a whelming, that if the treasures of the House of Cthulhu were truly such as he imagined them—then that they must likewise be well guarded by fighting men who would not give them up easily. And his reavers were fatigued even as Zar-thule himself, so that he rested them all down behind the painted bucklers lining the decks, and furled him up the great dragon-dyed sails. And he set a watch that in the middle of the night he might be roused, when, rousing in turn the men of his twenty ships, he would sail in unto and sack the island of Arlyeh.

Far had Zar-thule's reavers rowed before the fair winds found them, far from the rape of the Yaht Haal, the Silver City at the edge of the frostlands. Their provisions were all but eaten, their swords all ocean rot in rusting sheaths; but now they ate all of their remaining regimen and drank of the liquors thereof, and they cleansed and sharpened their dire blades before taking themselves into the arms of Shoosh, Goddess of the Still Slumbers. They well knew them, one and all, that soon they would be at the sack, each for himself and loot to that sword's wielder whose blade drank long and deep.

And Zar-thule had promised them great treasures from the House of Cthulhu; for back there in the sacked and seared city at the edge of the frostlands, he had heard from the bubbling, anguished lips of Voth Vehm the name of the so-called "forbidden" isle of Arlyeh. Voth Vehm, in the throes of terrible tortures, had called out the name of his brother-priest, Hath Vehm, who guarded the House of Cthulhu in Arlyeh. And even in the hour of his dying Voth Vehm had answered to Zar-thule's additional tortures, crying out that Arlyeh was indeed forbidden and held in thrall by the sleeping but yet dark and terrible god Cthulhu, the gate to whose House his brother-priest guarded.

Then had Zar-thule reasoned that Arlyeh must contain riches indeed, for he knew it was not meet that brother-priests betray one another; and aye, surely had Voth Vehm spoken exceedingly fearfully of this dark and terrible god Cthulhu only that he might thus divert Zar-thule's avarice from the ocean sanctuary of his brother-priest, Hath Vehm. Thus reckoned Zar-thule, even brooding on the dead and disfigured hierophant's words, until he bethought him to leave the sacked city. Then, with the flames leaping brightly and reflected in his red wake, Zar-thule put to sea in his dragonships. All loaded down with silver booty he put to sea, in search of Arlyeh and the treasures of the House of Cthulhu. And thus came he to this place.

SHORTLY BEFORE THE midnight hour the watch roused Zar-thule up from the arms of Shoosh, aye, and all the freshened men of the dragonships; and then beneath Gleeth the blind Moon God's pitted silver face, seeing that the wind had fallen, they muffled their oars and dipped them deep and so closed in with the shoreline. A dozen fathoms from beaching, out rang Zar-thule's plunder cry, and his drummers took up a stern and steady beat by which the trained but yet rampageous reavers might advance to the sack.

Came the scrape of keel on grit, and down from his dragon's head leapt Zar-thule to the sullen shallow waters, and with him his captains and men, to wade ashore and stride the night-black strand and wave their swords . . . and all for naught! Lo, the island stood quiet and still and seemingly untended . . .

Only now did the Sacker of Cities take note of this isle's truly awesome aspect. Black piles of tumbled masonry festooned with weeds from the tides rose up from the dark wet sand, and there seemed inherent in these gaunt and immemorial relics a foreboding not alone of bygone times; great crabs scuttled in and about the archaic ruins and gazed with stalked ruby eyes upon the intruders; even the small waves broke with an eery *hush, hush, hush* upon the sand and pebbles and primordial exuviae of crumbled yet seemingly sentient towers and tabernacles. The drummers faltered, paused and finally silence reigned.

Now many of them among these reavers recognised rare

gods and supported strange superstitions, and Zar-thule knew this and had no liking for their silence. It was a silence that might yet yield to mutiny!

"Hah!" quoth he, who worshipped neither god nor demon nor yet lent ear to the gaunts of night. "See—the guards knew of our coming and are all fled to the far side of the island—or perhaps they gather ranks at the House of Cthulhu." So saying, he formed him up his men into a body and advanced into the island.

And as they marched they passed them by other prehuman piles not yet ocean-sundered, striding through silent streets whose fantastic façades gave back the beat of the drummers in a strangely muted monotone.

And lo, mummied faces of coeval antiquity seemed to leer from the empty and oddly-angled towers and craggy spires, fleet ghouls that flitted from shadow to shadow apace with the marching men, until some of those hardened reavers grew sore afraid and begged them of Zar-thule, "Master, let us get us gone from here, for it appears that there is no treasure, and this place is like unto no other. It stinks of death—even of death and of them that walk the shadow-lands."

But Zar-thule rounded on one who stood close to him muttering thus, crying, "Coward!—Out on you!" Whereupon he lifted up his sword and hacked the trembling reaver in two parts, so that the sundered man screamed once before falling with twin thuds to the black earth. But now Zar-thule perceived that indeed many of his men were sore afraid, and so he had him torches lighted and brought up, and they pressed on quickly into the island.

There, beyond low dark hills, they came to a great gathering of queerly carved and monolithic edifices, all of the same confused angles and surfaces and all with the stench of the pit, even the fetor of the *very* pit about them. And in the centre of these malodorous megaliths there stood the greatest tower of them all, a massive menhir that loomed and leaned window-less to a great height, about which at its base squat pedestals bore likenesses of blackly carven krakens of terrifying aspect.

"Hah!" quoth Zar-thule. "Plainly is this the House of Cthulhu, and see—its guards and priests have fled them all before us to escape the reaving!"

But a tremulous voice, old and mazed, answered from the shadows at the base of one great pedestal, saying, "No one has fled, O reaver, for there are none here to flee, save me—and I cannot flee for I guard the gate against those who may utter The Words."

At the sound of this old voice in the stillness the reavers started and peered nervously about at the leaping torch-cast shadows, but one stout captain stepped forward to drag from out the dark an old, old man. And lo, seeing the mien of this mage, all the reavers fell back at once. For he bore upon his face and hands, aye, and upon all visible parts of him, a grey and furry lichen that seemed to crawl upon him even as he stood crooked and trembling in his great age!

"Who are you?" demanded Zar-thule, aghast at the sight of so hideous a spectacle of afflicted infirmity; even Zar-thule, aghast!

"I am Hath Vehm, brother-priest of Voth Vehm who serves the gods in the temples of Yaht Haal; I am Hath Vehm, Keeper of the Gate at the House of Cthulhu, and I warn you that it is forbidden to touch me." And he gloomed with rheumy eyes at the captain who held him, until that raider took away his hands.

"And I am Zar-thule the Conqueror," quoth Zar-thule, less in awe now. "Reaver of Reavers, Seeker of Treasures and Sacker of Cities. I have plundered Yaht Haal, aye, plundered the Silver City and burned it low. And I have tortured Voth Vehm unto death. But in his dying, even with hot coals eating at his belly, he cried out a name. And it was *your* name! And he was truly a brother unto you, Hath Vehm, for he warned me of the terrible god Cthulhu and of this 'forbidden' isle of Arlyeh. But I knew he lied, that he sought him only to protect a great and holy treasure and the brother-priest who guards it, doubtless with strange runes to frighten away the superstitious reavers! But Zar-thule is neither afraid nor credulous, old one. Here I stand, and I say to you on your life that I'll know the way into this treasure house within the hour!"

And now, hearing their chief speak thus to the ancient priest of the island, and noting the old man's trembling infirmity and hideous disfigurement, Zar-thule's captains and men had taken heart. Some of them had gone about and about the beetling tower of obscure angles until they found a door. Now this door was great, tall, solid and in no way hidden from view; and yet at times it seemed very indistinct, as though misted and distant. It stood straight up in the wall of the House of Cthulhu, and yet looked as if to lean to one side . . . and then in one and the same moment to lean to the other! It bore leering, inhuman faces and horrid hieroglyphs, all carved into its surface, and these unknown characters seemed to writhe about the gorgon faces; and aye, those faces too moved and grimaced in the light of the flickering torches.

The ancient Hath Vehm came to them where they gathered in wonder of the great door, saying: "That is the gate of the House of Cthulhu, and I am its guardian."

"So," spake Zar-thule, who was also come there, "and is there a key to this gate? I see no means of entry."

"Aye, there is a key, but none such as you might readily imagine. It is not a key of metal, but of words . . ."

"Magic?" asked Zar-thule, undaunted. He had heard aforetime of similar thaumaturgies.

Zar-thule put the point of his sword to the old man's throat, observing as he did so the furry grey growth moving upon the elder's face and scrawny neck, saying: "Then say those words now and let's have done!"

"Nay, I cannot say The Words—I am sworn to guard the gate that The Words are *never* spoken, neither by myself nor by any other who would foolishly or mistakenly open the House of Cthulhu. You may kill me—even take my life with that very blade you now hold to my throat—but I will not utter The Words . . ."

"And I say that you will—eventually!" quoth Zar-thule in an exceedingly cold voice, in a voice even as cold as the northern sleet. Whereupon he put down his sword and ordered two of his men to come forward, commanding that they take the ancient and tie him down to thronged pegs made fast in the ground. And they tied him down until he was spread out flat upon his back, not far from the great and oddly fashioned door in the wall of the House of Cthulhu.

Then a fire was lighted of dry shrubs and of driftwood fetched from the shore; and others of Zar-thule's reavers went out and trapped certain great nocturnal birds that knew not the power of flight; and yet others found a spring of brackish water and filled them up the waterskins. And soon tasteless but satisfying meat turned on the spits above a fire; and in the same fire sword-points glowed red, then white. And after

Zar-thule and his captains and men had eaten their fill, then the Reaver of Reavers motioned to his torturers that they should attend to their task. These torturers had been trained by Zar-thule himself, so that they excelled in the arts of pincer and hot iron.

But then there came a diversion. For some little time a certain captain—his name was Cush-had, the man who first found the old priest in the shadow of the great pedestal and dragged him forth—had been peering most strangely at his hands in the firelight and rubbing them upon the hide of his jacket. Of a sudden he cursed and leapt to his feet, springing up from the remnants of his meal. He danced about in a frightened manner, beating wildly at the tumbled flat stones about with his hands.

Then of a sudden he stopped and cast sharp glances at his naked forearms. In the same second his eyes stood out in his face and he screamed as were he pierced through and through with a keen blade; and he rushed to the fire and thrust his hands into its heart, even to his elbows. Then he drew his arms from the flames, staggering and moaning and calling upon certain trusted gods. And he tottered away into the night, his ruined arms steaming and dripping redly upon the ground.

Amazed, Zar-thule sent a man after Cush-had with a torch, and this man soon returned trembling and with a very pale face in the firelight to tell how the madman had fallen or leapt to his death in a deep crevice. But before he fell there had been visible upon his face a creeping, furry greyness; and as he had fallen, aye, even as he crashed down to his death, he had screamed: "Unclean . . . unclean . . . unclean!"

Then, all and all when they heard this, they remembered

the old priest's words of warning when Cush-had dragged him out of hiding, and the way he had gloomed upon the unfortunate captain, and they looked at the ancient where he lay held fast to the earth. The two reavers whose task it had been to tie him down looked them one to the other with very wide eyes, their faces whitening perceptibly in the firelight, and they took up a quiet and secret examination of their persons; even a *minute* examination . . .

Zar-thule felt fear rising in his reavers like the east wind when it rises up fast and wild in the Desert of Sheb. He spat at the ground and lifted up his sword, crying: "Listen to me! You are all superstitious cowards, all and all of you, with your old wives' tales and fears and mumbo-jumbo. What's there to be frightened of? An old man, alone, on a black rock in the sea?"

"But I saw Cush-had's face—" began the man who had followed the demented captain.

"You only *thought* you saw something," Zar-thule cut him off. "It was only the flickering of your torch-fire and nothing more. Cush-had was a madman!"

"But—"

"Cush-had was a madman!" Zar-thule said again, and his voice turned very cold. "Are you, too, insane? Is there room for you, too, at the bottom of that crevice?" But the man shrank back and said no more, and yet again Zar-thule called his torturers forward that they should be about their work.

THE HOURS PASSED . . .

Blind and coldly deaf Gleeth the old Moon God surely was, and yet perhaps he had sensed something of the agonised screams and the stench of roasting human flesh drifting up from Arlyeh that night. Certainly he seemed to sink down in the sky very quickly.

Now, however, the tattered and blackened figure stretched out upon the ground before the door in the wall of the House of Cthulhu was no longer strong enough to cry out loudly, and Zar-thule despaired for he saw that soon the priest of the island would sink into the last and longest of slumbers. And still The Words were not spoken. Too, the reaver king was perplexed by the ancient's stubborn refusal to admit that the door in the looming menhir concealed treasure; but in the end he put this down to the effect of certain vows Hath Vehm had no doubt taken in his inauguration to priesthood.

The torturers had not done their work well. They had been loth to touch the elder with anything but their hot swords; they *would not*—not even when threatened most direly—lay their hands upon him, or approach him more closely than absolutely necessary to the application of their agonising art. The two reavers responsible for tying the ancient down were dead, slain by former comrades upon whom they had inadvertently lain hands of friendship; and those they had touched, their slayers, they too were shunned by their companions and stood apart from the other reavers.

As the first grey light of dawn began to show beyond the eastern sea, Zar-thule finally lost all patience and turned upon the dying priest in a veritable fury. He took up his sword, raising it over his head in two hands . . . and then Hath Vehm spoke:

"Wait!" he whispered, his voice a low, tortured croak, "wait, O reaver—I will say The Words."

"What?" cried Zar-thule, lowering his blade. "You will open the door?"

"Aye," the cracked whisper came, "I will open the Gate. But first, tell me; did you truly sack Yaht Haal, the Silver City? Did you truly raze it down with fire, and torture my brother-priest to death?"

"I did all that," Zar-thule callously nodded.

"Then come you close," Hath Vehm's voice sank low. "Closer, O reaver king, that you may hear me in my final hour."

Eagerly the Seeker of Treasures bent him down his ear to the lips of the ancient, kneeling down beside him where he lay—and Hath Vehm immediately lifted up his head from the earth and spat upon Zar-thule!

Then, before the Sacker of Cities could think or make a move to wipe the slimy spittle from his brow, Hath Vehm said The Words. Aye, even in a loud and clear voice he said them—words of terrible import and alien cadence that only an adept might repeat—and at once there came a great rumble from the door in the beetling wall of weird angles.

Forgetting for the moment the tainted insult of the ancient priest, Zar-thule turned to see the huge and evilly carven door tremble and waver and then, by some unknown power, move or slide away until only a great black hole yawned where it had been. And lo, in the early dawn light, the reaver horde pressed forward to seek them out the treasure with their eyes; even to seek out the treasure beyond the open door. Likewise Zar-thule made to enter the House of Cthulhu, but again the dying heirophant cried out to him:

"Hold! There are more words, O reaver king!"

"More words?" Zar-thule turned with a frown. The old priest, his life quickly ebbing, grinned mirthlessly at the sight of the furry grey blemish that crawled upon the barbarian's forehead over his left eye.

"Aye, more words. Listen: long and long ago, when the world was very young, before Arlyeh and the House of Cthulhu were first sunken into the sea, wise elder gods devised a rune that should Cthulhu's House ever rise and be opened by foolish men, it might be sent down again—even Arlyeh itself, sunken deep once more beneath the salt waters. *Now I say those other words!*"

Swiftly the king reaver leapt, his sword lifting, but ere that blade could fall Hath Vehm cried out those other strange and dreadful words; and lo, the whole island shook in the grip of a great earthquake. Now in awful anger Zar-thule's sword fell and hacked off the ancient's whistling and spurting head from his ravened body; but even as the head rolled free, so the island shook itself again, and the ground rumbled and began to break open.

From the open door in the House of Cthulhu, whereinto the host of greedy reavers had rushed to discover the treasure, there now came loud and singularly hideous cries of fear and torment, and of a sudden an even more hideous stench. And now Zar-thule knew truly indeed that there was no treasure.

Great ebony clouds gathered swiftly and livid lightning crashed; winds rose up that blew Zar-thule's long black hair over his face as he crouched in horror before the open door of the House of Cthulhu. Wide and wide were his eyes as he tried to peer beyond the reeking blackness of that nameless, ancient aperture—but a moment later he dropped his great sword to the ground and screamed; even the Reaver of Reavers, screamed most terribly.

For two of his wolves had appeared from out the darkness, more in the manner of whipped puppies than true wolves, shrieking and babbling and scrambling frantically over the queer angles of the orifice's mouth . . . but they had emerged only to be snatched up and squashed like grapes by titanic tentacles that lashed after them from the dark depths beyond! And these rubbery appendages drew the crushed bodies back into the inky blackness, from which there instantly issued forth the most monstrously nauseating slobberings and suckings before the writhing members once more snaked forth into the dawn light. This time they caught at the edges of the opening, and from behind them pushed forward—*a face*!

Zar-thule gazed upon the enormously bloated visage of Cthulhu, and he screamed again as that terrible Being's awful eyes found him where he crouched—found him and lit with an hideous light!

The reaver king paused, frozen, petrified, for but a moment, and yet long enough that the ultimate horror of the thing framed in the titan threshold seared itself upon his brain forever. Then his legs found their strength. He turned and fled, speeding away and over the low black hills, and down to the shore and into his ship, which he somehow managed, even single-handed and in his frantic terror, to cast off. And all the time in his mind's eye there burned that fearful sight—the awful *Visage* and *Being* of Lord Cthulhu.

There had been the tentacles, springing from a greenly pulpy head about which they sprouted like lethiferous petals about the heart of an obscenely hybrid orchid, a scaled and amorphously elastic body of immense proportions, with clawed feet fore and hind; long, narrow wings ill-fitting the horror that bore them in that it seemed patently impossible for *any* wings to lift so fantastic a bulk—and then there had been the eyes! Never before had Zar-thule seen such evil, rampant and expressed, as in the ultimately leering malignancy of Cthulhu's eyes!

And Cthulhu was not finished with Zar-thule, for even as the king reaver struggled madly with his sail the monster came across the low hills in the dawn light, slobbering and groping down to the very water's edge. Then, when Zar-thule saw against the morning the mountain that was Cthulhu, he went mad for a period; flinging himself from side to side of his ship so that he was like to fall into the sea, frothing at the mouth and babbling horribly in pitiful prayer—aye, even Zar-thule, whose lips never before uttered prayers—to certain benevolent gods of which he had heard. And it seems that these kind gods, if indeed they exist, must have heard him.

With a roar and a blast greater than any before, there came the final shattering that saved Zar-thule for a cruel future, and the entire island split asunder; even the bulk of Arlyeh breaking into many parts and settling into the sea. And with a piercing scream of frustrated rage and lust—a scream which Zar-thule heard with his mind as well as his ears—the monster Cthulhu sank Him down also with the island and His House beneath the frothing waves.

A great storm raged then such as might attend the end of the world. Banshee winds howled and demon waves crashed over and about Zar-thule's dragonship, and for two days he gibbered and moaned in the rolling, shuddering scuppers of crippled Redfire before the mighty storm wore itself out.

Eventually, close to starvation, the one-time Reaver of Reavers was discovered becalmed upon a flat sea not far from

the fair strands of bright Theem'hdra; and then, in the spicy
hold of a rich merchant's ship, he was borne in unto the
wharves of the city of Klühn, Theem'hdra's capital.

With long oars he was prodded ashore, stumbling and
weak and crying out in his horror of living—for he had gazed
upon Cthulhu! The use of the oars had much to do with his
appearance, for now Zar-thule was changed indeed, into
something which in less tolerant parts of that primal land
might certainly have expected to be burned. But the people
of Klühn were kindly folk; they burned him not but lowered
him in a basket into a deep dungeon cell with torches to light
the place, and daily bread and water that he might live until
his life was rightly done. And when he was recovered to partial health and sanity, learned men and physicians went to talk
with him from above and ask him of his strange affliction, of
which all and all stood in awe.

I, Teh Atht, was one of them that went to him, and that
was how I came to hear this tale. And I know it to be true, for
oft and again over the years I have heard of this Loathly Lord
Cthulhu that seeped down from the stars when the world
was an inchoate infant. There are legends and there are legends, and one of them is that when times have passed and
the stars are right Cthulhu shall slobber forth from His House
in Arlyeh again, and the world shall tremble to His tread and
erupt in madness at His touch.

I leave this record for men as yet unborn, a record and a
warning; leave well enough alone, for that is not dead which
deeply dreams, and while perhaps the submarine tides have
removed forever the alien taint which touched Arlyeh—that
symptom of Cthulhu, which loathsome familiar grew upon
Hath Vehm and transferred itself upon certain of Zar-thule's

reavers—Cthulhu Himself yet lives on and waits upon those who would set Him free. I know it is so. In dreams . . . I myself have heard His call!

And when dreams such as these come in the night to sour the sweet embrace of Shoosh, I wake and tremble and pace the crystal-paved floors of my rooms above the Bay of Klühn, until Cthon releases the sun from his net to rise again, and ever and ever I recall the aspect of Zar-thule as last I saw him in the flickering torchlight of his deep dungeon cell:

A fumbling grey mushroom thing that moved not of its own volition but by reason of the parasite growth which lived upon and within it . . .

Tharquest and the Lamia Orbiquita

From Teh Atht's *Legends of the Olden Runes,* as translated by
Thelred Gustau from the Theem'hdra Manuscripts.

I

NOW THARQUEST THE wandering Klühnite, riding hard from
Eyphra in the West where he had angered the High
Priest of the Dark Temple of Ghatanothoa by getting his
lately-virgin daughter with child, came over the Mountains
of Lohmi and spied the once-gilded spires and great walls of
Chlangi. Even crumbling Chlangi, which is called the Shunned
City.

Not unfairly is Chlangi named, for indeed her approaches—
aye, and her walls, streets and deserted houses—they are
shunned. Even now, though many years are fled since the
olden runes were writ, still they are shunned . . .

In Chlangi a robber-king ruled over a rabble of yeggs and
sharpers, exacting taxation from the scabby whores and un-
scrupulous taverners in his protection and allowing such to

vend in peace those poisons peculiar to their trades. And Tharquest frowned when he saw the city; for some twenty years gone when scarce a child he had visited the place, which was then wondrous in its opulence and splendid in the colour and variety of visitors come to admire its wonders.

Then the city had been abustle with honest, thronging merchants, and the wineshops and taverns had sold vintages renowned throughout the known world—especially the pure clear wine pressed with skill from Chlangi's own glass-grapes. The domes and spires had been gilded over; the high walls white with fresh paint: the roofs red with tiles baked in the ovens of busy builders, and all in all Chlangi had been the jewel of Theem'hdra's cities.

But now the city was shunned by all good and honest men, had been so for ten years, since first the lamia Orbiquita builded her castle nine miles to the north on the fringe of the Desert of Sheb. In that time the gold had been stripped from all the rich roofs and the vines of the glass-grapes beyond the north wall had grown wild and barren and gross so as to flatten their rotting trellises. Arches and walls had fallen into disrepair, and the waters of the aquaducts were long grown stagnant and green with slime. Only the rabble horde and their robber-king now occupied the city within its great walls, and without those walls the ravenous beggars prowled and scavenged for whatever meager pickings there might be.

And yet Tharquest feared not as he rode his black mare down from the Mountains of Lohmi, for his departure from Eyphra had been of necessity swift and he carried little of value. Even his mare—which he had stolen—wore no saddle upon her back, and her rein was of rope and the bit in her mouth of hard wood.

Most disreputable, Tharquest looked, with his robes torn and dishevelled in the flight from Zothada's father, and his eyes all baggy from many a sleepless night's riding. Still, he had a friend in Chlangi: Dilquay Noth, once an adventurer like himself and now a pimp for the city's less loathsome whores. At Dilquay's place he knew he would find food and shelter for the night. Then, in the morning, he would press on for Klühn on the coast, where a rich widow-wife awaited his caresses. In any case, he doubted if the High Priest of Dark Ghatanothoa would follow him here—not into the supposed sphere of ensorcellment of the lamia Orbiquita.

Himself, Tharquest had small faith in spells and enchantments—what little he had seen of such had been the quackery of village tricksters and stage magicians—and yet indeed in those days such things were. As in all inchoate worlds, Nature had not yet decided which gifts and talents she should let her creatures keep. Or rather, she had experimented and decided that there were lines better not continued. Slowly these discarded strains were disappearing, but every now and then one would be born seventh son of a seventh son of a wizard. And he too, if he remembered the keys, might inherit in addition to the usual five Nature's tossed-aside talents. Aye, and there were strangely endowed women, too.

So Tharquest came to Chlangi, and seeing the encampments of beggars without the walls and the way their narrow, hungry eyes gleamed as they fastened on the black flanks of his mount, he quickened the mare's step until his torn cloak belled in the sun and dust behind him. But the beggars made no move to molest him and he passed them through.

Into the evening city rode Tharquest, through the rotting

wooden remnant of what had once been the mighty West Gate. Then, passing carelessly under a crumbling arch, he was knocked from the back of his mount by a robber who clung spiderlike to the high stonework. Down he went and into the dust, to be hauled dazedly to his feet and disarmed by two more brigands before being dragged before robber-king Fregg.

When Fregg heard Tharquest's tale of his escape from the raging Priest of Ghatanothoa he laughed, and his cutthroat courtiers with him. Why! This Klühnite was obviously a brigand no less then they! They liked him for it and directed him out of Fregg's sagging pile—which was once a most magnificent palace—and on his way to find his friend Dilquay Noth the pimp.

Dilquay, he soon discovered, was doing well, living in a house not far from the palace wherein he kept his girls. Well-fortified the place and seated atop a small hill, like a castle in its own right and necessarily so; for pimping is a dodgy business in any city, and surely more so in Chlangi the Shunned . . .

Tharquest approached the great stone house—once the High Court of the long fled King Terrathagon, now the brothel of Dilquay Noth—up a flight of winding, basalt steps, arriving at a great iron-studded door with a little gated window. A rap or two at the oaken panels with the pommel of his simple sword brought bright blue eyes that peered from within. A gasp of recognition . . . and the door was at once thrown open. There in the spacious doorway, the burly, bearded Dilquay Noth.

"Tharquest the Wanderer, by my beard!—and bruised and banged about to boot! By all the Dark Gods, but you look beaten, my friend. In and sit you down—and tell me how come your clothes are torn and your face unshaven, you who live by your pretty looks!"

But for all his words Dilquay was not overly surprised by Tharquest's sudden appearance in Chlangi. Some nine months gone, when he had heard from a wandering beggar how Tharquest had taken the Sacred Oath of Ghatanothoa to be admitted as a novice to the priesthood in Eyphra, he had straightway sent the same beggar with a note to the adventurer telling of his whereabouts and demanding an explanation. What on Earth was Tharquest—the hero of many a grand defloration—thinking of, Dilquay had wanted to know, binding himself to a Dark God and swearing continence for ever?

Thus, when Tharquest's troubles came to a head in Eyphra—or when they came to a belly, as it were—and when the Priestess Zothada's size had finally given way the Klühnite's real reasons for desiring a bed within the Temple of Ghatanothoa, then the wanderer had stolen a mare and made for Chlangi, to a friend who would succor him and see him on his way to Klühn and the bright blue sea . . .

Now, seated in Dilquay's spacious apartment—better appointed, Tharquest noted, than even Fregg's hall in the fast-falling palace—they swapped memories of olden adventures. Finally the bearded pimp told of how, after leaving Tharquest's side to settle with Titi the Whore, he had talked her into giving up her trade and opening a brothel of her own with Dilquay himself to protect her rights. That had been four years earlier, at a time when Chlangi's streets had still been fairly well filled, but now Dilquay was thinking of leaving the city. This was not, as he explained, for fear of the lamia Orbiquita, but simply for scarcity of trade.

It was at this juncture that Titi the ample entered; aye, even legendary Titi of a Thousand Delights. Straightway she fell on Tharquest and gave his neck a hug, crying: "Ah!—but I knew that our wanderer, who can sell his services to any hot-blooded woman in all the known world, could never settle to the servicing of a mere God! Why!—I've girls here would pay you, if they knew what I know—except you wouldn't look at them twice, not even for money!" She laughed.

"Titi," cried Tharquest, struggling from her grasp. "By Ghatanothoa's defiled temple, but you're more beautiful than ever!" He was lying, for Titi had never been beautiful, but there was a camaraderie between them and it was good to see the face—even the slightly pockmarked face—of so old a friend.

And so, after much drinking and chewing and chatting, came the night. Dilquay and Titi went off to organise their ladies and Tharquest, well feasted of meat and drunk of not unreasonable wine, found himself tucked up in a clean bed in a room of his own. In his reeling, boozy head before he slept, he kept hearing Dilquay's tales of the lamia Orbiquita, and in his lecherous soul there burned a drunken plan for yet an-other amorous adventure . . .

Dilquay had pointed out to Tharquest the fact that none of Chlangi's robber-men were handsome, and few of them young, and had then gone on to explain why. The lamia Orbiquita had taken all of the strong, young, good-looking men for herself and had left the city to the battle-scarred brig-ands and whore-poxed pirates who now inhabited her. This was why, Dilquay said, Tharquest himself must soon move on or attract Orbiquita's attention. For the lamia lusted like a succubus after handsome, strong-limbed men, and was not above stealing into Chlangi in the dead of night on bat wings to lure off the occasional handsome wanderer she might hear was staying there.

She was said, too, to be beautiful, this lamia—but evil as the pit itself. And it was known that the beauty men saw in her was only an illusion, that the real Orbiquita was a well-poxed horror saved from the rot of centuries only by her own magical machinations. Furthermore, it was told that should any man have strength of will enough to resist the lamia once she had set her black heart upon him, then he could carry off with him all of the hoarded treasures hidden away within her castle.

. . . Now *that* would be a real adventure!

II

In the morning, lying abed while he properly thought the thing out, finally Tharquest made his decision. He would visit this lamia and stay the night, and the following morn would leave her unsated taking her treasures with him. Dilquay and Titi paled on hearing of this brash scheme, but they could not deter Tharquest with even the direst tales.

When later that same day the robber-king also heard of the Klühnite's plans, he laughed and wished him luck and gave him back his twice-stolen mare. Thus, following a midday meal at Dilquay's, Tharquest set off through the fallen North Gate and pointed his mount's nose toward the Desert of Sheb. And in their encampments the beggars who saw him take his departure tittered and slapped lean thighs, debating upon how soon the wanderer's mare would come galloping back alone, lathered and red-eyed, and how then there would be meat again in the camps of the ragged starvelings . . .

AFTER EIGHT MILES, by which time the castle of Orbiquita was a dark-spired outline against the early horizon—an outline reflecting neither beam of sunlight nor, indeed, any light at all, standing magically shaded even in the hot sun—Tharquest came to a shepherd's cot. He was thirsty by then and so tethered his mare and knocked upon the door of the rude dwelling. Pleasantly surprised was he when the door was opened by a young and gorgeous girl of long limbs, raven hair and great green eyes that looked upon him coyly as their owner bade him enter.

So Tharquest entered and seated himself and was given water. Then, his thirst quenched, he asked of the girl her man's whereabouts. His question came of sheer habit, for in Tharquest's life men—particularly husbands—were hazards to be avoided wherever possible. But she only laughed (showing teeth like pearls) and twirled girlishly about (showing limbs like marble cut by a master sculptor) and told him that she had no man. She lived with her father who was out after strayed sheep and not expected back for two days at least.

Now any man would have been tempted, and Tharquest sorely so, but he wanted to get on and reach Orbiquita's castle and earn his fortune. Remembering this through the flesh-lust that suddenly gripped him, he stood up and begged the lady's pardon but he must be gone, at which she bowed low (displaying breasts curved and golden as the full moon) and inquired of his destination. On discovering Tharquest's intentions her great green eyes opened very wide and she all but burst into tears, deploring his plans for wealth and greatness and pleading with him thus:

"Oh, wanderer, you are surely handsome and strong and brave—but yet more surely are you mad! Know you not the *power* of this lamia?"

"I have heard," Tharquest answered, "how Orbiquita has the means to show herself as a great and ravishing beauty, when in truth she is ugly and ancient and loathsome. But I have also heard how, if a man resist her enticements—presented succubus-like in the night—he might walk off unscathed in the light of day with all the treasures he can carry, even with the wonderful treasures of her grim castle. This I intend to do, for the lamia can only take her victims during those hours when the sun is down, and I do not intend to sleep. I shall stay awake and keenly attentive, wary of all things within yon castle's walls."

"Oh, Tharquest, Tharquest," she pleaded, "I have seen so many such as you pass by here, though none so godly of form, and have given them water to succor them on their way. But—"

"Aye, go on, lass."

"Always it is the same. They go to the castle full of high inspiration and bravado, but only their horses—flanks lathered, eyes burning red in awful fear—ever return! For the lamia is never satisfied with a *piece* of a man but takes all of him, fuel for her fires of lust and horror. No, you must not go to the castle, fair Tharquest, but stay here with me and share my bed this night. I'm so lonely here and often afraid. And in the morning, then return you whole and happy to the Shunned

City; and perhaps, if I who have little experience of men please you, take me with you? . . ."

And again Tharquest was warmed and felt a great temptation. But here he had a novel thought: was he not yet to be tempted by the lamia Orbiquita herself? And must he not resist such temptation for his life? Why!—if a mere shepherd girl might so readily set his senses spinning, what chance would he have against the succubus-like creature of the castle? No, let the girl be criterion for his intended night's continence; and Tharquest, swinging himself athwart the black flanks of his mare, laughed as he offered up a blasphemous blessing to Dark Ghatanothoa.

"May your gods protect you then, Tharquest," the girl called after his belling, tattered cloak.

"I have no gods," he called back, "save perhaps Shub-Niggurath, black ram with a thousand ewes." And he laughed.

"I'll wait for you," she cried. "Then, should you win your riches, your continence need not be extended beyond endurance . . ."

A SHORT WHILE later Tharquest came to the lamia's castle. The brooding, shrouded pile was girt around with strangely motionless trees, and as the wanderer had noted from afar, even standing in the sun it was oddly shaded. Beneath the trees by a narrow, silent streamlet he tethered his mare, proceeding on foot across the moat to the massive door. With the castle's turreted spires looming darkly above, he felt more than a little afraid, and he peered cautiously in at the open door. All was gloom and cobwebby dimness within, but the thought of the great reward soon to be his and the knowledge that the lamia only took her lusty nourishment at night bore up the wandering Klühnite's spirits.

Slowly he explored each room of the place, cellars to lofty spires, and as he did so his eyes grew more accustomed to the dimness and showed him a weird and singular thing. Each of the castle's rooms contained a bed of the finest cushions and silks, and at the foot of each bed great piles of clothing lay. There were boots and sandals and buskins, cloaks and capes, jackets and jerkins; trews, kilts and breeches; turbans, hoods and fancy titfers; shirts and kerchiefs and gauntlets and every thinkable item of manly attire—but nothing suitable for a woman. Why!—here were wardrobes for a hundred, nay, two hundred men . . . But where were those men? Who had they been?

Again Tharquest became sore afraid, glancing nervously about him, holding tight to the pommel of his simple sword and thinking on what he knew of the queen of this shadowed and unpeopled pile, the lamia Orbiquita. Dilquay had told him how, though she only took her prey at night, she would often assume human form in the hours of daylight to forage about and spy out the land for suitable victims. Possibly that was what she was even now about, and, heartened by the thought that he was at least alone in the castle, Tharquest engaged upon a systematic search of the place for the treasure fabled to lie hidden therein.

. . . Long into the afternoon he searched, finding neither jewels, gold nor wealth of any sort; neither priceless miniatures nor gilt-framed masterpieces. Not a single solitary coin did he find, but he did come across a room in which a great table stood fresh prepared and laden as for a banquet. There were great platters of meat and smaller dishes containing toothsome morsels and sweetmeats; flagons of white, red and green wine, and one as pure and clear (or so the wanderer thought) as the glass-grape wine of olden Chlangi; exotic fruits of every size and shape and colour; oysters, shrimps, lobsters and crabs; cocktails of flowers served with the black honey of ocean-girt Ardlanthys—the sort of banquet a man might order prepared for his guests on the day of his wedding . . .

. . . Aye, and in certain parts, the night of his funeral!

And feeling hungry, Tharquest tasted of the foods and sipped of the wines, finding all delightful to the palate and very satisfying. Then, uplifted physically and relaxed mentally, he set to and bound him up some torches from turbans in the piles at the feet of the beds in the various rooms. These he dipped in tureens of scented oil at the banquet table, and for torch handles he used wooden legs broken from chairs in that same room. Night was coming on apace now, and the Klühnite, without having noticed how weary he had gradually grown since sipping of the various wines, suddenly found himself tired.

III

Soon the sun sank down into the realm of Cthon and Tharquest, for the nonce, gave up his torchlit searching and wandering through the castle's rooms. He found himself a high room with only one door and one slitlike window. The door he braced against opening with a rough wedge of wood at its bottom before lying back on his bed of cushions and silks, his simple sword within easy reach of his right hand. Thus, in the flickering light of a scented turban-torch, the adventurer closed his heavy eyes in reluctant sleep.

And a strange dream came to him, wherein Tharquest wandered amidst green forests and swam in blue and sparkling pools of winelike water. A nymph there was, too—of silken tresses, with eyes deeper than the unplumbed Pool of Xthyll, slim and with flesh of living marble—who led him to her orchid bower and held out her arms to him.

Dying, the torch sputtered and gave off oily fumes as the dreamer turned in his bed and reached out avid, hungry hands over the ruffled silks—

—Tharquest coughed as the fumes reached him, coughed and choked and his mind began to rise up from abysses of sleep. Desperately he stretched out his arms and his body to the fading, wavering nymph within her evaporating bower— *and contacted horror!*

Horned and warty skin, rough as bark to his touch! Protruding nodules and suppurating sores! Breasts flabby, slimy and writhing! Hands with nails like claws of great crabs, and panting breath in his face smelling worse than the effluvia of the Burial Catacombs of Hroon! This, then, was the lamia Orbiquita!

Tharquest leapt shrieking awake, simple sword in trembling right hand, his left hand thrusting out a fresh torch to catch the embers of its dying brother. Flaring light—and a *Thing* that grew bat-wings even as he gazed in morbid fascination, launching itself from the bed to the window, pausing there for a moment in the slitlike opening to glare lustfully at him, then sliding off into the night with a hideous cackle and rustle of leathern membranes!

For an hour then Tharquest busied himself, hanging

drapes of cloaks and capes at the window and strengthening the fortification of the door by forcing a second wedge in at its top. Eventually, satisfied that he had done all he could to ward off any further attempts at his seduction and destruction by the lamia, the Klühnite sat back upon his bed and surveyed the results of his work in the flickering torchlight. Now that the job was done, he gave thought to what had passed and how close he had been to unutterable horror.

But eventually Tharquest's trembling limbs and quaking soul calmed, until, as his heart slowed its wild beating and his eyes began to ache with the strain of glaring about the room at the leaping shadows, the drugged wine of the lamia again brought down the ramparts of his awareness. The lids of his eyes slowly lowered, his terror-taut muscles slackened and his breathing slowed, his head fell to his chest and his body toppled gently over backward until he lay flat on the bed with his simple sword close beside him.

Some time passed while Tharquest sank deeper into sleep, and the second coming of the lamia Orbiquita went completely unbeknown to the slumbering Klühnite. She came as a twist of smoke, issuing in at the crack of the door, forming . . . forming . . .

Again in his dream the wanderer chased his laughing nymph through exotic forests ribboned with sparkling winestreams and pools, and again she led him to her bower of orchids, reaching out to him and pouting prettily and moving her body most seductively.

Tossing and turning in his bed, moaning in his sleep and whispering words of love remembered of many an adventure of old, Tharquest reached out his hands and found the beautiful body of the nymph. And at this the lamia rejoiced greatly, for she had altered her form (an art at which she was greatly adept) to that of a young girl, that she might better fool the handsome young wanderer. Violently he pulled her toward him—and in so doing caused his sword to fall with a clatter from the bed to the floor.

Tharquest heard the sword fall—even through his dreaming flesh-lust he heard it—and his sleeping mind was distracted from its course. Too, in the semi-awareness of his disturbed dream, he now discovered peculiarities: that the flesh his hands had found was cold as the spaces between the stars, and that the breath issuing into his face carried the same carrion stench he had known before! And abruptly he remembered where he was and what he was about.

Again the Klühnite came awake, leaping from his suddenly repellent bed. In mid-leap he plucked up his fallen sword in barely articulate hand, snatching at the low-burning torch on the wall. There upon the bed as he held the torch out at trembling arm's length, lay the perfect form of the nymph of his dreams! One shaky yet resolute step took him to the bedside, but even as he gritted his teeth to thrust his sword into the girl's side her body turned to smoke, streaming swiftly out under the door and leaving only the echo of an awful chuckle behind—that and the memory of a horror that had seemed to rot even as its substance became smoke!

More weary than ever but determined now to fortify the room as fully as possible, Tharquest lit a third torch, then stumbled about stuffing linings torn from capes and jackets into the cracks of the door and blocking the window slit completely with other articles of clothing. By the time he had finished the drug in his blood had reached its peak of potency and it was as much as he could do to keep his eyes open. The room swam and seemed to blur before him as he mazedly sought his bed of silks and cushions . . .

As the adventurer fell once more asleep, the lamia was already on her way back to her castle. She had flown into the Desert of Sheb to certain caves she knew—caves that went down to the very pits at Earth's core, where red imps leap from one lava pool to the next—and there she had warmed her chill and loathly flesh by hell's own fires that the imitation of life thus imbibed might better fool the man come to seek her treasures.

Still hot from hell she burned when she flapped down atop her pile. Aye, even so hot as to leave cloven prints burning in the stones of those ramparts—but much of her heat was lost as she formed herself into a pool of water to seep into the cracks of the stone and down, down toward Tharquest's room.

Again he was oblivious of her coming, slumbering on as tiny droplets of lamia-formed moisture gathered on the ceiling and ran down the walls.

. . . Yet even sleeping and dreaming, the Klühnite was now cautious. Without truly remembering the reasons for his reticence, nevertheless he followed his laughing nymph carefully. Such caution could not last, however, for was he not Tharquest the Rake, known in seventeen cities for his audacity and impudence and banned forever from fourteen of them through those same improprieties? When the nymph held out her arms to him he went to her, whispering false words of love to a yet more faithless lover, courting her as the tiny male courts the bloated black widow spider, reaching out his hands for her . . .

Fortunately for Tharquest, the drug was now past its greatest strength and fast waning in potency, and the warnings of past, sleep-fogged encounters with this nymph lingered yet in the eye of his inner memory. Her flesh was warm, true, and her body smooth and having none of rough lumps or pustules—but as he moved his body towards her and made to kiss her lips . . .

That horrendous smell!

In the nick of time, with no instant to spare, again the adventurer leapt from the arms of that poisonous princess of passion, leapt from her to catch up his sword and smite again and again at the bed . . . which was suddenly wet with liquid so that his blade came away dripping. And the droplets from his sword mixed with the moisture soaked through the now empty bed to the stone floor beneath, and the entire living pool swiftly flowed away down a narrow crack in the stonework and was gone. Again an eerie chuckle floated back to the shuddering Klühnite.

Very frightened but clearer in his mind now that the drug was dead and absorbed into his system, Tharquest saw that while the torch in the wall burned so low as to give very little light, yet there was a secondary light in the room. Its source was the windowslit where his raiment barricade had started to settle and slip. He tore the piled garments away, and there in the east a golden glowing haze already showed on the horizon. The sun was not yet up, but it would not be long.

Only thinking to be out of the place, Tharquest ripped away the silken wadding and wooden wedges from the door. He passed with a shaky laugh out into the castle's corridors, showing a flash of his former impudence as he sought himself the most magnificent cloak and boots he could find in exchange for his own tatters. Down the stone steps he went, simple sword secure in its scabbard, and as he reached the great outer door—then came his reward!

IV

Even as he made to leave the pile, a stone flag in the wall near the door pivoted outward revealing an inner cavity, and out from the hole cascaded the most fantasic treasure the wanderer could ever have dreamed of.

Tourmaline, turquoise and topaz; onyx, opal and pearl; garnet, jade and emerald; rose quartz, zircon and lapis lazuli; ruby, sapphire and bloodstone; diamond, aquamarine and amethyst—jewels and precious stones of every sort and size! And gold! And silver! Coins of every realm on Earth, and some, Tharquest fancied—because of their shapes and the images graven upon them—from yet more distant places. Strings of black pearls big as marbles; crowns and tiaras and diadems of alien design; jeweled daggers and golden effigies of strange gods—an endless stream of untold wealth, all flowing out upon the floor!

And so Tharquest knew he had won, and it was a matter of only a few seconds to fill his pockets with some of the choicest pieces, a continent's ransom. Thus, well weighted down with fantastic jewels and priceless bric-a-brac, the wanderer passed from the castle of Orbiquita, and as the golden glow grew yet brighter beyond the far horizon he made his way quickly to his tethered mare. Freeing the animal's rope rein, he was about to mount when he heard his name called. Glancing about, he soon saw the shepherd girl approaching in a hooded cloak through the silent trees.

"Tharquest!" she gasped, peering fearfully about. "Oh, Tharquest, I feared you would be lost—that the lamia would devour you—and so I had to come here to know for certain. I thought never to see you again!"

He smiled his audacious smile and bowed low, doffing his hat and flicking his luxurious cloak. "The lamia is defeated," he cried, "and was there ever any doubt but that this was the way it must be? Did you truly believe that I might fail? And riches—" He dipped into a pocket and tossed the girl a glowing green gem even as green as her eyes and of a like size. "Why!—what could that bauble alone not buy?"

"Oh, Tharquest, Tharquest!" She clapped her hands in delight and glowed with pleasure, holding her prize up to the far dim light beyond the trees, and peering into its green-fire depths. Then, as she bowed low in acceptance of the gift, the Klühnite glimpsed once more those soft delights first viewed in her father's cot, and he remembered her parting words of the previous afternoon.

Aye, and she must have recognised that look in his eyes, for she laughed and twirled about, her hands to the fastenings of her cloak. And lo!—when next she faced him that cloak lay at her feet and she stood naked and coyly blushing there in the silent glade.

Yet ready as he ever was, the wanderer had learned things that night, and as he leaned forward as if to kiss her his hand secretly fondled the hilt of his simple sword. But no, her breath was sweet as honey, her lips warm with life, her flesh smooth and delightful to the wanderer's touch. And so Tharquest quickly threw off his robes and they fell together to the green grass in the glade of stirless trees—

—And the sun not yet up above the horizon!

And her breath (sweetened by an elixer of Djinni brewed deep in the Desert of Sheb) was sugar as her lips fastened upon him. And her flesh (again warmed by hell's own fires while red imps skipped across the lava pools) quivered warmly under him. And her body (shaped by that art of which she was adept) opened up beneath him and sucked him in, skin and blood and bone and all, fuel for her fires of lust and horror. And Tharquest gave but a single shriek as he went, hearing in his passing the shrill screaming of his suddenly terrified mare . . .

LATER, GLUTTED THE nonce and needful of rest, the lamia Orbiquita flapped off on leathern wings in the direction of her shepherd's cot, there to sleep through the morning and lie in waiting for the next adventurer to happen that way.

And later still there was tumult in the camps of the starvelings beneath Chlangi's walls—tumult and the preparation of cooking pots and pans—as a black mare, lathered about her flanks and red-eyed in a fearful and nameless dread, came galloping to her doom.

To Kill a Wizard!

Т HEY COME AND they go, these wizard-slayers," whispered
Mylakhrion to his currently favourite familiar, a one-
legged jackdaw of spiteful mien. "Some creep in the night like
thieves—" (the ancient mage stifled a yawn, of boredom perhaps) "—others bound boldly over the drawbridge, eyes flashing fire and swords aglint; and there are those who disguise
themselves as simple men seeking an old, fatherly magician's
advice." He chucked the bird gently under its curving beak.
"But then, I don't need to tell you these things, do I? You
yourself have slain a wizard or two, in your time."

"I have, I have," croaked the bird, his bright button eyes
unblinking, his head cocked to catch his master's words. "You
also, Mylakhrion, I would have slain, were your protections
less potent that time." And there was bitterness in the jackdaw's croaky voice.

"Come now, Gyriss," Mylakhrion softly chastened, his
voice like a fall of autumn leaves. "After all this time—how
many years?—is there still enmity between us? *You* came to
Tharamoon seeking to slay me, remember? And I wonder,
were our roles reversed, would I still live to talk to you? I

doubt it. As to your welfare: who else in all Theem'hdra would procure these good nuts, at today's prices, in order to pamper a balding, one-legged jackdaw?" He dangled his long fingers in a bowl of almonds.

"But once I had *two* good legs," croaked Gyriss. "And as for nuts—which you magick out of thin air, at no cost at all—why, I ate only the rarest viands and drank only the finest wines!"

"Wines!" the wizard chuckled. "Choice meats. Whoever heard of a jackdaw eating rare viands? You're an ingrate, Gyriss, and in a mood tonight, that's all. Was I ever unkind to you?"

"Only the once," came the answer, as sour a croak as ever Mylakhrion heard.

"Ah! But then it was you or me," he answered, adjusting the wide sleeves of his rune-embroidered robe. And his voice was colder now. "Anyway, it bores me to review all that. What use to open up old wounds, eh? Now let it be, Gyriss, and come tell me what you make of this." He nodded toward his great blue-green shewstone of crystal where it was set central at the flat apex of a tripod table all carved of black wood and inlaid with gold and ivory arabesques.

The jackdaw hopped from its perch to Mylakhrion's shoulder with scarce a flutter, peered with him at the shewstone which, as the wizard drew an intricate figure in the air with his forefinger, at once grew cloudy as from some eruption of internal aethers.

"See! See?" said Mylakhrion, as the mists in the crystal ball opened like ethereal curtains upon a bleak and wintry scene. "I've been watching him approach for days now, and at last he has reached Tharamoon itself. How say you? Is this not just such a wizard-slayer, come to try his luck?"

Gyriss craned his feathery neck and looked closer, his beady eyes agleam. He saw a man in a boat, sailing stormy waters on the approach to Tharamoon's crescent bay. "Aye," he croaked, "but no ordinary slayer by a mile. I know this one. He is Humbuss Ank, a Northman—and quite recklessly mad!"

"A Northman!" Mylakhrion narrowed his silver eyebrows, drew them close together over his sharp nose. "Mad, you say? *Hah*! But they are berserkers all, these men of the fjords! You, too, were a wild one, if memory serves . . ." And to himself he remarked the bird's keen eyesight, for he himself had discerned no clear detail of the figure in the boat except that it was a man.

The jackdaw's feathers stood up along his spine. He shook himself, sprang aloft, flew round the rim of the high tower room crying: "Berserkers all, berserkers all!"—and alighted again on Mylakhrion's hunched shoulder. "True, true," he croaked, "but even more so in the case of Humbuss Ank. And with good reason."

"Say on," commanded Mylakhrion, keenly interested. He had somehow guessed that Gyriss might be knowledgeable in the subject of wizard-slayers.

"This one's father, mother, and elder brother," the jackdaw explained, "were slain all three by the cold magicks of Khrissan ice-priests. It happened at a fording- and trading-place on the Great Marl River, and this is how it was:

"It was in the late autumn of the year and the coming winter would be a bad one; already the ice crept over the Reef of Great Whales, and the skies were ominously heavy with more than their fair share of snow and blizzard. Thull

Ank and his strapping wife Gubba had trapped well; their haul that year was of the highest quality. The trading went well—for a while, anyway. But Humbuss' brother, Guz, drank too much of the bitter wine of the ice-priests, and when he was drunk made much sport of their ice-gods and -goddesses.

"So they slew Guz and his father both with their magicks, and took Gubba back with them to Khrissa as a sacrifice to the very gods her son had scorned. Aye, and they stole all their pelts and goods, too—word of which eventually got back to Humbuss, a mere lad then in Hjarpon Settlement. Since when he is grown to a man and lives only to kill wizards and priests and all such purveyors of magick wherever he may find them. And now at last it seems he's come for you, Mylakhrion of Tharamoon . . ."

"My thanks, Gyriss," said Mylakhrion archly. "Though why I should detect accusation in your tone I cannot say! Towards myself? Because I, too, am a wizard? That is as it may be; but I am not one of Khrissa's cruel mages, nor indeed do I make human or any other sacrifice to strange gods. As for women, I respect them—the human sort, anyway. I forced myself upon a lamia or two in my youth, but only as ritual ingredients in my spells. So do not glare your beady accusations at me! Now then, let me look more closely at this berserker come to kill me . . ."

He narrowed his eyes at the bird, but deliberately refrained from asking how Gyriss knew so much about Humbuss Ank. Then without further pause he drew another figure with his finger, a shape which seemed to fall slowly from fingertip to shewstone and be absorbed by it. And lo!—the picture in the crystal ball swam up large as life, larger than the very crystal itself, until wizard and familiar both might fancy they were themselves integral in the frore and windswept scene.

And Mylakhrion seemed to stand upon Tharamoon's pebbly strand within the bay, with Gyriss flapping upon his shoulder; and they watched as the lone boat battled the breakers to finally shoot through the sharp volcanic rocks of the reef and into calmer water unscathed. The ragged sail was lowered as the boat swept on ashore, and down from his reeling craft sprang a man into the frothing surf even as the keel of his boat bit sand and grit; so that in a trice this northern adventurer was dragging his vessel ashore, hauling it up the beach with arms that looked utterly tireless.

Fingering his beard, Mylakhrion nodded thoughtfully. "A strong man, this one, Gyriss."

And his familiar—perhaps too eagerly, too gladly—agreed saying: "That he is, that he is! No wily warrior this, Mylakhrion, but merely strong. Brainy?—never! But brawny? As an ox, brawny! A man to laugh in the face of your magicks, this Humbuss—aye, even in the face of hell itself! He'll storm on through all your mirages and illusions, no matter how monstrous, and damn any demons you may conjure back to the dark where they're spawned. It is not so much that he is invincible, rather that he thinks he is. Mind over matter, O master—which is a sort of magick in itself!"

"Hmm!" mused the wizard darkly, a trifle surly now. "Let me look closer. I wish to see his face."

Meanwhile: the Northman had made his boat secure in the lee of the cliffs, which now he set about to scale. And Mylakhrion floated up light as a feather to where the invader swarmed up those sheer crags like a monkey. He looked into Humbuss' face, even into his blackly glittering eyes, and Humbuss saw him not. For of course this was only a picture in a shewstone, however real it might seem.

And Mylakhrion saw a man whose soul was empty, bereft of any last vestige of honour or decency. His black eyes were narrow, cruel and full of lust; his hard mouth was twisted in a sneer; his blunt nose and hollow left cheek were grimly scarred, and his squat nostrils sniffed the chill night air like those of a great bloodhound. His narrow black mane stood up stiffly down his back, like the risen hackles of a dog; and diagonally across that broad, muscled back he bore a mighty broadsword, strapped there in its leather scabbard, its blade notched from many a fierce affray.

Then Mylakhrion drew back and away into his tower retreat, and Gyriss flapping still where he clung to his shoulder. And the wizard snapped his fingers, at which the shewstone cleared and became simply a blue-green ball of crystal, quiescent and opaque.

"Gyriss," said Mylakhrion then, "this man is a brutal slayer, and yet I relish not the thought of killing him. Indeed killing is not my way at all, for it lacks sensitivity. So tell me, how may I stop this thing before it goes any further?"

Gyriss flew to his perch and sat preening, saying nothing.

"Well? Have you no ideas?"

"What can I say?" the jackdaw finally croaked. "He's a brute and a berserker on a lifelong quest for revenge."

"Revenge? I think not," said Mylakhrion. "No, there's more than that brings him here." At which the jackdaw gave a small start, glad that his master was looking the other way. "He may have *started* this life work of his out of some perverted sense of duty to his priest-slain kith and kin," Mylakhrion continued, "but since then it has got quite out of hand. Now I think he kills because he likes it, or for profit. So much I divined when I looked into his face. If it is the former, mayhap I'm in trouble. If the latter—"

"Then you can buy him off with a pouch of priceless gems," croaked Gyriss.

"Why not?" said Mylakhrion, bringing his pacing to an abrupt halt. "Indeed, why not? I have a vault full of jewels, and what use are they to me?"

"No use at all," said Gyriss, "when you can simply conjure them out of the air—as you conjure my nuts!"

"But that must be a last resort." Mylakhrion paced some more, holding up a finger. "For if I'm to give gems to this one, next year there'll be a dozen like him. First I shall attempt to deter him with magick!"

"But he scorns magick," answered Gyriss. "Many another mage has tried to frighten him off. And where are they now?"

"I do believe you're enjoying this!" said Mylakhrion with a glare. "Nathless, what you say is probably true. Still I shall *try* to frighten him away. It's that or kill him out of hand, and I won't spill blood if it can be avoided—as you are well aware." And he glowered pointedly at Gyriss, who for his part croaked:

"You could always transport him back whence he came . . ."

"In the last year or two I've transported—how many wizard-slayers?"

"Four, by my count," answered the bird at once, "plus a pirate ship and its motley crew."

"Correct!" snapped Mylakhrion. "A pair of dull brigands

back to Klühn; a black pirate princeling back to his jungled island, him and his ship and all his crew with him; and a deranged Hrossak hunter back to the steppes. I weary of transporting! Also, word may soon get out that transportation is my sole defence! What's more, if it's true that this Humbuss Ank has killed so many sorcerers, by now he may well have some small understanding of magick himself. The cancellation of the rune of transportation is easily achieved, if a man knows the words. And once one spell is broken, then other enchantments are checked that much easier. Spells are like building blocks which interlock: remove one and the entire wall is weakened. No, I'd not risk that with this one—except if I fail first to scare him off."

"So," said Gyriss, summing up, "you'll scare him, or transport him if he won't scare, or buy him off as a last resort. And is that the sum total of the measures you'll take against him?"

"It is!" snapped Mylakhrion. "And it must suffice, else I'll be left with no choice but to kill him."

"*If* you can," croaked Gyriss quietly, wickedly.

"What?" cried the wizard. "If I can? And how, pray, may he prevail, against a fortress of magicks and machineries such as this tower of mine? You try my patience, Gyriss!" And he stamped his foot on stone flags. "Perhaps you'd welcome my demise? And would you remain a jackdaw forever? For you surely will if some barbaric doom befalls me. Who then to open my runebook and read the words which alone may unspell you, ungrateful bird?"

And Gyriss was rightly cowed, and hunched down into himself upon his perch. "I meant only to say," he croaked, "that if you're to set guards and traps and such you'd best be about it. By now Humbuss Ank has scaled the cliffs and strides this way. Some twenty miles, as I gauge it. Rough country, but still he'll be here before morning."

"*Hmph!*" grunted Mylakhrion. And, "Calm yourself, Gyriss. There's time enough and more. As for his chances: a snowflake would stand more chance in hell! Methinks you make too much of him. Myself: I shall be fast asleep when—if—he gets here. I would not soil my hands on him but leave such servile chores to others far less sensitive. Attend me if you will, I go now to make the arrangements . . ."

Mylakhrion's tower was reached via a drawbridge across a chasm too wide for jumping, whose sheer sides went down endlessly into darkness. Beneath the tower itself were many mazy vaults whose contents were conjectural and at best dubious; above the ground stood six floors serving various purposes. Topmost consisted of a storeroom, pantry and kitchen, bath- and steam-room, small study, and observatory for astrological readings. Gyriss had never seen those rooms: they were forbidden to him, as was the wizard's bedchamber and orchid-decked conservatory on the penultimate level.

That left four floors with which the jackdaw was familiar. The great room with the shewstone was one of three interconnected rooms on the fourth level, beneath Mylakhrion's bedchamber, which also contained the vast majority and endless variety of his thaumaturgical books and experimental apparatus. The next floor down was a maze of storerooms, usually all but empty, for Mylakhrion conjured most of his supplies as required. But beneath that the two lower floors were dangerous places indeed for would-be intruders. For built into the rooms therein were certain mechanical devices so designed as to utterly incapacitate all unwary thieves and the like. They were veritable mantraps, which now

Mylakhrion would bait. But first he'd set his guards on the narrow and stony path beyond the drawbridge, by which route Humbuss Ank must needs approach.

So down he went to the vaults with Gyriss (who didn't much care for the dark) where he animated three stone statues and led them stiffly up out of darkness and across the drawbridge. On the far side he turned and faced them, and scowled his disgust at them. For they were—had been—favored familiars in their time, and he had placed some small trust in them. But many years agone they'd turned on him and deliberately lured a wizard-slayer here, for which Mylakhrion had punished them by turning them to stone. He'd punished the wizard-slayer, too—one Gyriss Kag—replacing them with him. But once in a while he'd bring them up and let them ease their joints, and at times he even had work for them. Now was such a time.

The three were chiropterans, great bats who wore the faces of men they'd once been. Now as they stumbled in Mylakhrion's wake he spoke to them, saying: "A man is coming who would kill me. You—" he pointed to the first man-bat, "—will remain here, at the drawbridge. If he comes this far you will offer him this for his trouble and tell him to turn aside." And he gave the chiropteran a fat pouch of gems. "Fail to turn him back," he answered, "and I'll stand you forever on the balcony of my tower observatory to weather in the wind and the rain."

Then he walked half a mile with the other two and paused again, speaking to the second of them: "You will remain here. If my would-be slayer comes this far, you will utter the rune of transportation and hurl him back whence he came. Failure to do so will see you broken in two halves upon this very spot, where time and nature will mold your pieces into small stones."

After a further half-mile he stopped again where the path wound down a steep cliff, and to the third bat-thing said: "You will astonish the man with illusions, and afraid for his life he'll flee. In the event he does *not* flee—you shall be dashed into small, small fragments. I, Mylakhrion, have spoken!"

And with Gyriss on his shoulder he returned to his tower, set his mechanical protections, proceeded up the winding central staircase to his bedchamber. At the door he took the jackdaw on his finger, saying: "There. And fear not for me, Gyriss. I shall sleep like a babe, and this Northman shall not disturb me. Begone!" At which the bird descended to the room of the shewstone, where for a while he sat in utter silence, waiting for his master to fall asleep . . .

WITHIN THE HALF-HOUR, unable to hold off any longer, Gyriss flapped silently to a balcony and across it into the fast approaching night, and flew up to peer into his master's bedchamber through the single great window there, which fortunately stood open. The room was all of mosaics, covering floor, walls and ceiling. Above flew ebony swallows in a lapis-lazuli sky; the walls were a jade forest with jewelled birds of paradise; and the floor was of chrysolite ferns, inlaid with an hundred marble monkeys.

There slept Mylakhrion, as his huddled form beneath the satin bedclothes testified. But to be absolutely certain, Gyriss passed through the window into the forbidden room and swooped once on silent wings around the bed to hear the wizard snoring. Satisfied then, he left the tower and sped across the drawbridge, following the path toward the distant Bay of Tharamoon. And beneath him he spied the three chiropteran guards where Mylakhrion had placed them. Eventually in the gloom he saw the Northman Humbuss Ank striding toward him and he descended, flying well over the other's head.

"Humbuss!" he croaked then. "Look up. It is I, Gyriss Kag."

The barbarian saw him, paused, guffawed and slapped his thigh. "What? And is it really you, Gyriss, who once swigged ale with me and slew the occasional wizard? Come down and speak to me, if you're one and the same, and explain why you've called me here to this cold and lonely crag."

Gyriss alighted on the other's mighty shoulder. "I'm him, all right!" he croaked. "Do you remember that ill-omened night each of us boasted how he'd be the first to breach Mylakhrion's protections and kill him? Drunk, we were, and me so drunk that I set out at once to be started on the quest. But you held back, saying you'd work your way up to him by degrees. Do you remember?"

"I do," said Humbuss, still mirthful. "And it seems I was right to be cautious. He was too much for you, eh?"

"Indeed he was, and too much for many another I've called here. But not, I pray, too much for you. For with my help, old friend, you'll surely slay him."

"Well, so far so good," growled Humbuss. "I followed the course you set me across the sea and through the ragged reef, and here I am. You mentioned a treasure, Gyriss, and I desire it. Also, I desire the great prestige of killing Mylakhrion the so-called 'immortal.' But what would you have out of this?"

"Only my human form once more returned to me," answered Gyriss. "And the satisfaction of seeing Mylakhrion die! For after you've killed him you'll read a certain rune of restoration from his great runebook and I'll be a man again. After which I'll show you his treasure house."

"Good enough!" Humbuss agreed. "And now: how may you help me, eh?"

And Gyriss told him all about the three guardians of the way, and something about the drawbridge, and more about Mylakhrion's tower itself. Following which he flapped aloft and returned the way he'd come, his heart filled with treacherous satisfaction . . .

MEANWHILE, BACK AT the tower: a tiny black spider surveyed her jackdaw-ruined web at Mylakhrion's window, and angered spun a silken thread and drifted on it to where the wizard slept. She alighted on his cheek and crept into his ear, and Mylakhrion awakened, listened, smiled and sat up. He waited for her to emerge, then carefully carried her back to her web, which he repaired at once with a word and a wave of his hand.

"My thanks, small friend," he whispered, and slowly descended to his room of many magicks—even to the room of the shewstone . . .

HUMBUSS ANK CAME upon the first man-bat and commanded him, "Stand aside!"

"Much as I would like to, I cannot," answered the chiropteran. And he conjured an illusion wherein he swelled up massive as a mountain. Humbuss laughed and pushed him off the cliff, and stiff from his stony sojourn in the vaults he could not fly but fell like an icicle in the melt—and like an icicle was dashed into small, small fragments, as Mylakhrion had decreed.

Half a mile later Humbuss came to the second guard and said, "Out of my way, bat-thing!"

To which the other answered: "*Sdrojf eht ot kcab—Kna Ssub-Muh, enogeb!*"—which was the rune of transportation.

But Gyriss had told him the rune's reversal, and before the spell could take effect Humbuss cried: "*Diputs, gnud tae!*"—and hacked the chiropteran in twain. Just as Mylakhrion had prescribed.

And finally, when he came to the drawbridge, Humbuss found the third guard waiting, who offered him the jewels and bade him turn aside. But the Northman merely snatched the jewels from him and scornfully shouldered him out of the way, then ignored him utterly and turned to face the drawbridge. And scattering small handfuls of jewels into the abyss as Gyriss had instructed, he commanded: "Drawbridge, show me where you really are!" And the jewels passed through the illusory drawbridge and into the abyss; but to one side they fell not, and Humbuss stepped out across what seemed thin air, letting jewels drop in front to guide him safely across. And so at last he entered in through the door in the tower's base.

Now Gyriss had warned him about the two lower levels, and so Humbuss was wary. But even as he glanced in through the main door of the lower level's complex, so the jackdaw came fluttering down from above to remind him of the dangers:

" 'Ware, Humbuss! These are not treasures you spy but illusions!"

Humbuss looked again. The floor of the room behind the open door was tiled with small hexagonal mirrors, so that all in the room seemed duplicated. What he saw, therefore, seemed doubly awesome. For in that room were heaped treasures beyond all human dreams of avarice, where every known gem—and many unknown—spilled from piles upon the mirror floor! And even as he stood there with the juices of greed making his mouth moist, so a mouse scampered across the threshold and ran in amazement, ogling his mouse-reflection, to and fro amidst the glitter and the wealth. But no harm befell the mouse.

"It is the floor!" cried Gyriss. "The mouse has no weight, but only place the tip of your great sword upon the floor beyond that door—"

Humbuss did so—and scarce had time to withdraw his blade before the scintillant illusion vanished! And in its place a brilliant flashing of silent, silver blades, a sieve of shimmering motion, a mesh of metallic teeth and shining scalpels. And all so silent! So that in a moment the room breathed out a fine damp mist of mouse-essence and closed its door gently in Humbuss' face.

And even Humbuss Ank was a little awed by the room's deadly efficiency, so that he needed no urging to climb the stone stairs to the next level. Gyriss flapped along behind him, but the bird seemed more anxious now. " 'Ware, Humbuss, 'ware! When I came to kill Mylakhrion, I stepped upon a floor of fine mosaics, all shaped like a flight of jackdaws—and see what became of me!"

Already the Northman had reached the next level and would not have paused a moment—had not his narrowed eyes glimpsed beyond a second open door such a harem as to send even a eunuch into a frenzy of passion! And no eunuch Humbuss Ank but hot-blooded Northman.

"*Stars!*" he gasped. And the ladies where they feasted at a circular table all glanced his way, and smiled, and wriggled, and beckoned him to come in.

"No!" cried Gyriss. "This, too, is a machine, and that door is a door to another place, not of this world. It is a place Mylakhrion knows. Look again: these are not women but succubi and lamias. And see what they're eating, Humbuss. *Only look at their repast!*"

Humbuss looked. Beneath the circular table, visible now that the mist of lust was off his eyes, the great fat body of a man writhed and twitched where it was bound to the table's central leg. But his head went up through the table, and was open at the top like an egg—into which the ladies dipped their silver spoons . . .

Shuddering, even Humbuss Ank, he drew back from the door and climbed again; and up past the third and fourth floors went barbarian and bird together, to the very door of Mylakhrion's bedchamber—which also stood open.

Now Gyriss grew excited indeed. "Only once have I been within," he croaked as quietly as possible, "and so cannot help you here. The chamber seems innocent enough, but from here you're on your own. I will not watch, for I admit to feeling faint from my own treachery."

"What?" hissed Humbuss in amazement. "He's a foul magician, is he not?"

"The mightiest," Gyriss agreed. "But his magicks are more nearly white than black. I will not watch."

"Faintheart!" said Humbuss. "He made of you a crippled bird!"

"Because I came to kill him," squawked Gyriss, but not loudly. "Since when . . . he has not been unkind to me. You still have time to go back, Humbuss . . ."

"Bah!" thundered the barbarian. And, "Have done!" And he strode across the mosaic floor to where the wizard's figure stirred as he came sluggishly awake beneath satin bedclothes. And as if mysteriously guided, Humbuss' booted feet stepped not once upon a capering marble monkey, but always on the spaces between. Up went his sword as the bedclothes were thrown back, and down in an arc of tarnished, notched steel—

—To strike in halves a squawking, treacherous jackdaw!

And from behind, where Gyriss had fluttered at the door, now came a low sad sigh, and a sombrous voice saying: "Welcome, Humbuss Ank, to the house of Mylakhrion!"

Humbuss whirled, saw the magician materialise there, whose night-black wings grew into a cloak of glowing runes; and gawping his astonishment he stepped forward. Alas, his left foot came down upon a scampering monkey.

Then, in an instant, the mosaics parted and up from below hissed an hundred silver scythes, striking once and returning below before the mosaics could close again. And all so quick that Humbuss did not see, or even feel, the blade which sheared his trunk-like left leg cleanly above the knee . . .

IN THE MORNING Mylakhrion buried Gyriss in a tiny grave in his garden behind the tower. And watching from the high balcony of his observatory, a lone chiropteran of stone stared blindly down and prayed only for good weather. And chained to the neck of the stony man-bat a tiny one-legged monkey gibbered and complained bitterly.

Mylakhrion heard his cries, looked up and smiled. "No, no," he cried, shaking his head. "There you stay for now, my friend. At least until your temper's improved. And even then you must be house-trained.

"Indeed, for the personal habits of Northmen are utterly notorious . . ."

Cryptically Yours

The following letters, numbered one to eight, are in the main self-explanatory. They will serve admirably to illustrate some of the many perils facing professional wizards in that bygone Age when the world was very young and magic was not merely a word in books for small children . . .

I

Domed Turret of Hreen Castle,
Eleventh Day of the Season of Mists,
Hour of the First Fluttering of Bats.

Esteemed Teh Atht—

You will doubtless recall that we were apprenticed to-gether (along with Dhor Nen, Tarth Soquallin, Ye-namat and Druth of Thandopolis) under Imhlat the Great; also how we vied, each against the others, in aspiring to greatness in our chosen profession. Though we were mere lads then (how many, many years ago?), still I remember being impressed by your own industry. Aye, even I, Hatr-ad of Thinhla, whose peer is not known east of the Inner isles, was *most* impressed by the sorcerous industry of Teh Atht. You were a likeable lad—friendly despite the ceaseless competition and bantering and occasional bickering—for which reason I now call upon you, in the name of the comradeship we shared in Imhlat's tutelage, for assistance in a matter of extreme urgency.

Mayhap it has come to your attention that of the six apprentices mentioned above only we two and one other, Tarth Soquallin, remain alive? The others are recently fallen foul of ill-omened, indeed *evil* fates, for all three have met with strange and terrible deaths! Not only Dhor, Ye-namat and Druth, but Imhlat the Teacher, too! Even Imhlat the Great—whose gnarled old hands instructed us in our first passes, weaving weird designs of power in the air—he, too, is gone, wasted away in a grey rot that descended upon him from the moon (they say) and took him all in the space of a single night.

Now I know not your thoughts in this matter, or even if you've considered it at all, but it seems to me that certain dark forces roam free and rapacious in Theem'hdra, and that their fell purpose is the destruction of her wizards one by one, thus plunging the entire continent into an age of darkness, when the light of sorcery will be extinguished forever! If I am correct then our lives, too, are in peril . . . for which reason I have set up every possible magickal barrier against these unknown agents of evil. This of course is the reason for my letter: to beg of you a certain rune (which I am given to believe may recently have come down to you from your long dead ancestor, Mylakhrion of Tharamoon?), that I might finalise the security of Hreen Castle.

I refer specifically to the Ninth Sathlatta, which—or so I am informed—is a protective device efficacious over all other magicks in the whole of Theem'hdra. Were it indeed your good fortune to be in possession of this spell, I would count myself ever in your debt upon safely receiving a copy of the same.

Take care, Teh Atht, and beware the nameless terror that surely lurks in Theem'hdra's shadows, threatening us all—

Yours for the Numberless Rites of Lythatroll—

Hatr-ad the Adept.

In addition—

Perhaps you know the whereabouts of that inveterate wanderer, Tarth Soquallin? If so, be so good as to advise me of the same that I may also warn him of the hovering horror . . .

Hatr-ad.

II

Topmost Tower of Klühn,
Eighteenth Night,
Hour of Clouds Wisping across the
Full Moon . . .

High-born Hierophant, O Hatr-ad!—

Honoured was I, Teh Atht, to receive your correspondence, even though it cost me the services of a most faithful retainer—and him his life! As to how this came about: I am myself at a loss to explain it.

I can only assume that those same dark forces of which your note so eloquently warns entrapped the bat to which you doubtless entrusted the missive, replacing that messenger with the great and winged Gaunt which assaulted my apartments over Klühn in the hour before dawn of the 12th day. Mercifully I myself was not to house, and so the monster took a manservant in my stead, almost obscuring with his blood the words you so carefully inscribed in cypher upon the parchment which I later found clenched in his lifeless fingers.

Thus it would seem that your warning was indeed most timely, and I thank you for it. As to your request for a copy of the 9th S., please find the same enclosed. Note that, remembering well your penchant for cyphers, I have couched the rune in just such a frame—albeit a simple one—the better to amuse and entertain you, however briefly, during your leisure hours.

Alas, I have no knowledge of Tarth Soquallin's whereabouts, but be sure I myself shall now take all precautions to avoid whichever evils befell our former colleagues, and that I remain, in eager anticipation of your next—

Yours for the Exorcism of Org the Awful,
Teh Atht of Klühn.

III

Hidden Vault beneath Hreen Castle;
Twenty-first Night;
Hour of the Tittering Without the Pentagram.

Brother in Blessed Sorceries, O Teh Atht—

A thousand thanks for your letter—and for the cypher-inscribed 9th S., which I shall duly translate as soon as I get five minutes to spare—both safely arrived yester-evening in their silver cylinder affixed to the leg of a great eagle. The bird itself, alas, fell prey to an over-zealous archer in my employ, whom I shall punish fittingly. Still and all, it were not entirely the man's fault, for he had strict instructions with regard to any alien invader of my keep, and was not to know that the bird was but a messenger of your esteemed self.

It was indeed a mercy, brother, that you were away upon the advent of the Gaunt which killed your retainer, and I shudder in contemplation of what might have taken place had you been present to receive so monstrous a visitor! My condolences at the loss of a faithful servant, and my joy that you yourself were spared so terrible an ordeal. Indeed you were correct in assuming that my messenger was but a bat, and I am filled with rage at the vileness of that agency which could so readily turn dumb, harmless minion into ravenous beast!

Now to a matter of even darker import: for we two are now the sole survivors of Imhlat's school for sorcerers, Tarth Soquallin having recently succumbed to the unknown doom! Aye, even Tarth the Hermit, gone forever from the world of men, for I have it on good authority that he is, alas, no more. It would seem that in the midst of magickal meditations he vanished from a cave—a hole in the face of a granite cliff, with no windows and only one stout door—after uttering but a single piercing scream. When finally his disciples broke down the door, they found only his wand and seven rings of gold and silver . . . those things, and a number of tiny golden nuggets which may once have filled certain of his teeth . . .

Oh, my brother, what is to be done? The very thought of the evils that surround us and the perils which daily press closer fills me with a nameless dread—or would, if I did not know that my old friend, Teh Atht, is at hand to assist me and offer his sound and unimpeachable advice in these darkest hours—

Yours for the Moaning Menhir,

Hatr-ad.

On afterthought—

Since I really have very little time to waste on riddles—however entertaining they may be—would you be so good as to forward with your next the key to the encyphered 9th S.?

Gratefully—

Hatr-ad.

IV

Sepulcher of Syphtar VI;
Thirty-eighth Evening;
Hour of the Unseen Howler.

Master of Mysteries, O Hatr-ad—

Confirmation of Tarth Soquallin's demise reached me almost simultaneous with your own doom-fraught epistle (I envy you your informants!), and not only his demise but those of several other sorcerers, too, though lesser known and further flung. Ikrish Sarn of Hubriss was one such, and Khrissa's Lord-High Ice-Priest another. Thus have I come down into the tomb of Syphtar VI to seek out his spirit and inquire of it, but lo—Syphtar answers not my call!

Indeed strangeness is abroad, Hatr-ad, even *great* strangeness! It would seem that some dark spell of thaumaturgic impotence is upon me, so that my sorceries are utterly without effect. Can I doubt but that the source of this new infamy is that same secret centre of evil whence ooze the poisonous spells which, one by one, drag down our fellow sorcerers to dreadful doom and death? Nay, I cannot doubt it; it must surely be so.

But with regard to these measures of yours for the protection of Hreen Castle against whichever evils theaten: I may be able to offer the very ultimate in protections, beside which even the ninth Sathlatta pales to insignificance! You were indeed correct in deducing that my ancestor Mylakhrion bequeathed to me certain of his secrets, and that these have recently come down to me across the centuries. Aye, and one of them is a rune of the greatest power, of which I would freely advise you if only I could be sure that my letter would not be intercepted!

Obviously a spell of this magnitude must never fall into the wrong hands, for . . .

My friend—*I have it!*

Upon a skin which I shall enclose, please peruse the characters of an unbreakable cypher to which I alone possess the key. When next you write, enclose some proof positive by which I may know that our correspondence is completely confidential and secure, and by return I shall forward the key to the cypher, thus placing the greatest of all protective runes in your hands.

Rest assured that I have already used the spell in my own defence—indeed, this very morning—wherefore I fear no evil in the length and breadth of Theem'hdra. (It dawns on me that this near-stultification of my other magicks, of which I have already made mention, must be a side-effect of the greater power, whose task is after all to dampen dangerous sorceries! This is a mere inconvenience as compared with my very life's safety, and doubtless the effect will soon wear off.)

But a warning: the only man who may break down the wall of this protection is one who understands its construction; and once this is done even the smallest spell will work against the one thus betrayed. Naturally I fear no such betrayal from my brother Hatr-ad the Illustrious, else I should not offer this information in the first instance. Be certain, too, that I have not studied the rune sufficiently to understand its reversal; and I trust you will likewise refrain from deliberately discovering the means by which the protection may be cancelled?

In all such matters I have the greatest faith in my brother-sorcerer, Hatr-ad, and thus, in eager anticipation of your next letter, I remain—

Yours for Enduring Enchantments,
Teh Atht of Klühn.

On Afterthought—

With regard to the encyphered 9th S.: It seems I've lost the key! I wrote the thing down on a scrap of parchment which I've since mislaid. There are several such cyphers I use but I have neither the time nor the inclination to divulge all of them. However, this should no longer present a problem, since the new rune supercedes and is far more powerful than the 9th S.. In any case, your own devices have been adequately efficacious to date, as witness (happily) your continued existence!

Sorcerously—
Teh Atht.

One other matter—

My fears over the confidentiality of our correspondence are not unfounded, I assure you, and I warn you to examine such carriers as we use most carefully. The pigeon that brought me your last missive had no sooner delivered up its cylinder than it flew asunder in a thousand searing fragments! I conjecture that it had been fed pellets of some agent, which, reacting with the bird's inner juices, produced this monstrous effect. Certainly the body fluids of the poor creature were become so mordant that the walls of the tower in which it exploded are now pitted and blackened most severely! Mercifully, I was not harmed, nor any retainer of mine.

Will this vileness never end?

Yours—

Teh Atht.

V

Aeries of Hreen Castle;
Nest of the Fanged Hawk;
First Day of the Season of the Sun;
Dawn—

Illustrious Engineer of Illusions,

Most happily I report my continued good health, despite all the spells doubtless cast against me by those unknown agencies of which every sorcerer in all Theem'hdra now goes in dread fear and loathing. Without a shadow of a doubt I owe my well-being in great part to you . . . for which reason I trust that you, too, are well and that no evil has befallen you?

Your tomb-bat messenger from Syphtar's sepulcher reached me safely, carrying its precious rune, and in the tenth day following my receipt of the same I at last translated the thing from the glyphs in which you had so cleverly enciphered it. Aye, for I am now familiar with your system, Teh Atht, and I marvel at the magnitude of a mind that could devise so mazy a cryptogram! It was not so very difficult, however, once I had broken the code that hid from my eager eyes the 9th S., for it would appear that all your codes are cast in pretty much the same mold. You may now rest easy in the knowledge that your spell shall not fall into alien hands, and that the need to supply me with a key to the code no longer exists . . .

Moreover, before I commenced the inscribing of this letter here in this high place, I made the necessary signs as the sun came up and I said the words of the rune, and lo!—now I am protected against all evils. All thanks to you, Teh Atht, who succored me in my hour of greatest need.

Yours in the Discovery of Mysteries—

Hatr-ad.

VI

Chamber of Infirmity—
Third Day of the Sun—
Hour of the Tide's Turning.

Honourable Hatr-ad,

Overjoyed as I am to hear of your own continuing good health, alas, I cannot report a similar condition in myself. Indeed no, for I am the victim of several severe disorders—which by their very nature I know to be most unnatural! Unnecessary to go into details, but sufficient to say that I am unwell. Even unto death am I, Teh Atht, unwell . . .

Only the most powerful of unguents and nostrums keep me alive (for my spells no longer work and I am obliged to rely upon merely common cures) so that even the writing of this letter is an ordeal to one whose hands tremble and jerk in unendurable agony as his body festers and rots! If you could see me, Hatr-ad, I believe you would shriek and run from the horror I am become—and I am completely at a loss to remedy the matter of my own free will.

Thus my letter is a plea, that you put aside whatever else engages you at this time and weave your most beneficent sorceries on my behalf—else I am done for! For without a shadow of a doubt those same fell forces of which you forewarned are upon me, and lo—I am at their mercy!

My decline commenced almost immediately upon receipt of your last—which, bat-borne and innocent in itself, was nevertheless like some harbinger of doom—and as it progresses so it accelerates. It would seem as though a combination of plagues, cankers and contagions are upon me, and without outside help I am doomed to an hideous death even within the space of ten days, possibly less. How this can possibly be when I am protected by the Rune of Power I am again at a loss to say. The evil which is abroad in Theem'hdra is powerful indeed!

I can write no longer. The pus that seeps from my body's pores threatens to foul the vellum upon which I scrawl this final plea: that you spare no single second but come immediately to the assistance of—

Thine in Ultimate Torment,
Teh Atht . . .

VII

Hreen Castle—Imperial Residence of:
Hatr-ad. Mightiest Magician in all Theem'hdra—
First Night of the Full Moon;
Hour of Gleeth's Blind Smiling on the Eastern Range.

Doom-Destined Teh Atht—

Not without a modicum of remorse do I, Highborn Hatr-ad, inscribe this final epistle—the last you shall ever read! Indeed, of all other sorcerers in Theem'hdra, you were the one I most respected: for if ever a man were sufficiently gifted to oppose me in my great ambition—of which I was often wont to boast during our apprenticeship in old Imhlat the Idiot's tutelage—then you were that man. Or so I thought . . .

Perhaps my words recall to your obviously age-enfeebled mind that ambition of mine? Aye, I'm sure they do, for oft and again I swore that one day I would make of myself the most powerful sorcerer in all the land. That day is now at hand, Teh Atht, and you above all other men have assisted me in the realization of my dream.

Now, too, it is plain to me that I ranked you o'er high among magicians, for who but a fool would give away a spell of ultimate protection?—and in so doing *rob himself of that very protection!* Aye, Teh Atht, for surely you have guessed by now that I am the origin and the source of the terror over Theem'hdra? Surely you are now aware whose spells they are that bring down the land's sorcerers in their prime, that rot you yourself in your bed, where even now you lie impotently awaiting death? Nor can that death be so very far away now; indeed, it amazes me that you survive, if you survive, to read this letter!

Even now I would not openly betray myself thus had not word reached me of your confinement, and of the fact that your throat has rotted so that you speak not, and that your body is so wasted that you are barely capable of the feeblest stirrings. Yet, if your very eyes are not utterly dissolved away, you will be able to read this, for I have written it in one of your own codes that no other may know of my triumph.

But what pleasure is there in an empty victory, Teh Atht? For surely my triumph would be empty if in the end none remained to know of it? Thus I now reveal all to you, that before you die you may know of Hatr-ad's victory, of his ambition fulfilled. For surely now I am indeed the greatest sorcerer in all Theem'hdra!

My thanks, Teh Atht, for your inestimable aid in this matter, without which I might yet be sorely pressed to bring about the desired result. Now you may rest your festering eyes, my old and foolish friend, in the final sleep. Go, and find peace in the arms of Shoosh, Goddess of the Still Slumbers . . .

Yours for the Dream of a New Age of Magickal Empire,
Hatr-ad the Mighty.

VIII

Room of Red Revenge;
Apartments over Klühn;
Day of Recovering,
Hour of Truth!

O Most Misguided, Miserable Hatr-ad—

Heartless one, I fear that your odious ambitions are come to an end—and better for Theem'hdra and all her more worthy wizards were that ending not protracted. Therefore let me linger not over the matter but get to its root with all dispatch.

For you were unmasked, o murderer, long before you chose to show your true face. Nathless it was deemed only fair and just that the truth be heard from your own lips before sentence was passed. The truth is now known . . . and I have been chosen to pass sentence.

Even now I can hardly ponder the enormity of your crimes without feeling within myself a gnawing nausea, that so vile and monstrous a man could guise himself as "friend" in order to go about his death-dealing devilments!

Murderer! I say it again, and the punishment shall fit the crime . . .

As to why I bother to write this when your fate will speak volumes of its own, there are reasons. Mayhap amongst your retainers, cronies and familiars there are those who, lusting after similar lordly stations, would carry on your fiendish business in your wake? To them, I, Teh Atht, address this warning—mazed in no cypher but writ in the clear, clean glyphs of Theem'hdra—that it suffice to set their feet upon more enlightened paths.

As for enlightenment: allow me now to unravel for you the more tangled threads of this skein, that you may see yourself as do we, whose sorceries are deemed white (or at worst grey) against your black!

To begin:

Throughout all Theem'hdra I have my informants, who

work under no duress but are all beholden to me in one way or another. From them, barely in advance of your first letter, I learned of the dissolution of Druth, the demise of devil-diseased Dhor, the eerie exanimation of Ye-namat, and even the terrible termination of old Imhlat the Teacher.

Now, it were perhaps no surprise had but one or even two of these old comrades gone the way of all flesh; it is not uncommon for sorcerous experiments to go sadly amiss, and the dead men were crafty sorcerers all. But *four* of them?

Moreover I found it a singularly suspicious circumstance that Hatr-ad—who never found reason to communicate with me before, and of whom I had heard precious little of merit in the long years since our mutual apprenticeship—should be so quick off the mark to recognise the advent of malevolent powers and warn me of them.

Then when I gave thought to all you had written, it dawned on me that indeed I had suffered certain discomforts of late; nothing serious but . . . headaches and creaking joints and bouts of dizziness now and then. Could they have been the residue of malicious spells sent against me and deflected by the protections which are ever present about my apartments?

If so, who had sent these spells and why? To my knowledge I had no dire enemies, though certain acquaintances might be trifling jealous of me. Indeed, such was my mode of life, and my days so free of troubles, that I had often thought me to relax the magickal barriers that surrounded me—it were such a bother to keep them renewed. Now I was glad I had not done so!

Then my thoughts returned to you, Hatr-ad; even to Hatr-ad, whose boasting in the Halls of Nirhath, where Imhlat the

Teacher instructed us, was not forgotten but sounded suddenly loud and ominous in the ears of memory. Your boasting, and your off-stated ambition . . .

Years by the score had gone by since then, but do ambitions such as yours ever really die?

Now Tarth Soquallin, even Tarth the Hermit, wandering wizard of the deserts and mountains, had always been a great and true friend of mine, and if it were true that some nameless terror was bent upon the destruction of Theem'hdra's sorcerers—particularly those who had studied under Imhlat—how then had Tarth fared in this monstrous coup?

Well, he and I had long since devised a means by which I might know of his approximate whereabouts at any given moment. In a cupboard unopened for seven years, after much searching, I found the device: a pebble, not unlike a northstone which, when dangled at the end of a thread, would always point out Tarth's direction. Discovering him to be in the west, and by the agitation of the pebble knowing him to be not too far removed, I reasoned he must be upon the Mount of the Ancients and to that region sent one of my eagles with a hastily inscribed message. (It seemed to me both easier and speedier to contact him directly than to inform you of his location that you yourself might then "warn" him of the so-called "nameless terror.")

Lo, the answer came back within a day and a night, saying that indeed he, too, had suffered minor pains and irritations, but pointing out that while he was not properly protected, as I was, nathless an evil agency would find it hard going to do him lasting harm, since he was so constantly on the move. A spell let loose to find its own way is far less potent than one directed to the known haunts of its recipient!

Furthermore, Tarth agreed to a little necessary deception. This was simply to let it be known that he was dead of strange sorceries, and to assist me in the speedy dissemination of this information by use of his disciples. Ah!—and how swiftly indeed word of Tarth's "demise" reached you, Hatr-ad (whose agents were doubtless on the lookout for just such news?), and how graphic the details of his disappearance, all bar his wand and rings and his teeth of gold!

Aye, and that was the end of Tarth's aches and pains—though this was not to be discovered for awhile—for what use to send out death-dealing spells against a man already dead? Eh, Hatr-ad?—

In the meantime I did several things. I worked swiftly, for I did not wish to delay o'erlong in answering your letter, but in the end my plan worked well enow. First, I sent off a request to an informant of mine in Thinhla, that he employ a certain system (in the use of which I also instructed him) to detect any hurtful magickal emanations from Hreen Castle. Second, I sent further messages of warning to Ikrish Sarn of Hubriss, to Khrissa's nameless Lord-High Ice-Priest, and to many another sorcerer, advising all to disengage quietly from their normal affairs and "disappear," and also to put about soft-muted tales of doom, disease and death. Third, I answered your letter, sending you an addled version of the Ninth Sathlatta and couching it in cyphers which I knew you would eventually break—but not too soon . . .

Still and all, my suspicions were as yet unfounded, the evidence against you all circumstantial—though I did deem it strange that the unknown Agency of Doom had not yet taken you yourself, when it had already accounted for men who were by far your sorcerous superiors!—and so I refrained from taking any premature action against you. After all, why should you write to me in the first place—and possibly alert me to your own dark hand in the horror—if indeed you yourself were not in mortal fear of the nameless thing? . . . Unless you were simply seeking some other way to do away with me, since patently the initial attack had done nothing more than discomfort me. Aye, and word had come to me by then that there were certain strangers in Klühn who daily made discreet inquiries in respect of my health. (Men of Thinhla, as it later became known!)

But then, simultaneous with your second letter, word arrived from Thinhla in respect of Hreen Castle, your own abode, and the *veritable miasma of morbid magicks emanating from it*! No protective thaumaturgies these, Hatr-ad, but lethal spells of the very blackest natures, and so at last I recognised beyond any further doubt that direful agency whose hand was set against Theem'hdra's wizards . . .

Had any such doubt remained in my mind, however, then were it most certainly removed by the mode of messenger you employed: the great Gaunt, the pyrotechnic pigeon and, with your third, my own bat whose wings I now found dusted with potent poisons. You may well have written the last in the aeries of your castle, but surely was it sent to me from some foul crypt beneath Thinhla's deepest foundations.

By then though I had already supplied you with My-lakhrion's most powerful protective spell and a means by which its code might be deciphered and its reversal discovered. Just so, Hatr-ad—and lo, you sent just such a vilely reversed spell against me, thus to weaken me and leave me defenceless in the face of your sly sorceries.

Well, evil one, the spell could not work against me, for

contrary to what you were made to believe, I myself had not used Mylakhrion's magick! Thus your casting was most easily deflected and *turned back upon its very author*!

... Aye, and you are utterly defenceless, Hatr-ad, while even now those sorcerers whose doom you plotted conjure spells to send against you; and no use to try Mylakhrion's rune a second time, for it will only work once for any single person. So you see, o wretch, that there is no avenue of escape from the sentence I now pass—which is: that you shall suffer, even unto death, all of the black magicks you yourself have used or attempted to use in your hideous reign of terror! The list is long:

From Tarth Soquallin and myself: The Skin-Cracks, Temple-Throbs and Multiple Joint Seizures; from Ikrish Sarn and Khrissa's Ice-Priest: the Inverted Eyes and the dreaded Bone-Dissolve; and from many another wizard various castings of greater or lesser measure. Moreover we have not forgotten the dead. On behalf of Imhlat, Dhor Nen, Ye-namat and Druth of Thandopolis, we send you the Green Growths, the Evaporating Membranes and, last but not least, the Grey Rot!

Sentence is passed. You are granted one full day upon receipt of this in which to put your affairs in order, but thereafter until you are no more you shall suffer, in ever-increasing doses, the forementioned afflictions. Waste not your remaining hours in further fruitless malevolencies; spells from all quarters have been cast about you that any such emanations shall only rebound upon you.

However, I am authorised to remind you that there is one way in which you may yet cheat us all, Hatr-ad; but if you do, at least do it gloriously! The towers of Hreen Castle are high,

I am told—indeed, they are almost as high as your frustrated, evil aspirations—and gravity is swifter and surer than the knife or pellet of poison . . .

The choice is yours.

Cryptically—
Teh Atht.

Mylaĥĥrion the Immortal

THERE WAS A time in my youth when I, Teh Atht, marvelling at certain thaumaturgical devices handed down to me from the days of my wizard ancestor, Mylakhrion of Tharamoon (dead these eleven hundred years), thought to question him with regard to the nature of his demise; with that, and with the reason for it. For Mylakhrion had been, according to all manner of myths and legends, the greatest wizard in all Theem'hdra, and it concerned me that he had not been immortal. Like many another wizard before me I, too, had long sought immortality, but if the great Mylakhrion himself had been merely mortal . . . surely my own chance for self-perpetuity must be slim indeed.

Thus I went up once more into the Mount of the Ancients, even to the very summit, and there smoked the Zha-weed and repeated rare words by use of which I might seek Mylakhrion in dreams. And lo!—he came to me. Hidden in a grey mist so that only the conical outline of his sorcerer's cap and the slow billowing of his dimly rune-inscribed gown were visible, he came, and in his doomful voice demanded to know why I had called him up from the land of shades, disturbing his centuried sleep.

"Faceless one, ancestor mine, o mighty and most omniscient sorcerer," I answered, mindful of Mylakhrion's magnitude. "I call you up that you may answer for me a question of ultimate importance. A question, aye, and a riddle."

"There is but one question of ultimate importance to men," gloomed Mylakhrion, "and its nature is such that they usually do not think to ask it until they draw close to the end of their days. For in their youth men cannot foresee the end, and in their middle span they dwell too much upon their lost youth; ah, but in their final days, when there is no future, then they give mind to this great question. And by then it is usually too late. For the question is one of life and death, and the answer is this: yes, Teh Atht, by great and sorcerous endeavour, a man might truly make himself immortal . . .

"As to your riddle, that is easy. The answer is that *I am indeed immortal*! Even as the Great Ones, as the mighty furnace stars, as Time itself, am I immortal. For ever and ever. Here you have called me up to answer your questions and riddles, knowing full well that I am eleven hundred years dead. But do I not take on the aspect of life? Do my lips not speak? And is this not immortality? Dead I am, but I say to you that I can never truly die."

Then Mylakhrion spread his arms wide, saying; "All is answered. Farewell . . ." And his outline, already misted and dim, began to recede deeper still into Zha-weed distances, departing from me. Then, greatly daring, I called out:

"Wait, Mylakhrion my ancestor, for our business is not yet done."

Slowly he came back, reluctantly, until his silhouette was firm once more; but still, as always, his visage was hidden by the swirling mists, and only his dark figure and the gold-glowing runes woven into his robes were visible. Silently he waited, as silently as the tomb of the universe at the end of time, until I spoke yet again:

"This immortality of yours is not the sort I seek, Mylakhrion, which I believe you know well enow. Fleshless, bodiless, except for that shape given you by my incantations and the smoke of the Zha-weed, voiceless other than when called up from the land of shades to answer my questions . . . what is that for immortality? No, ancestor mine, I desire much more from the future than that. I want my body and all of its sensations. I want volition and sensibility, and all normal lusts and passions. In short, I want to be eternal, remaining as I am now but incorruptible, indestructable! That is immortality!"

"There is no such future for you, Teh Atht!" he immediately gloomed, voice deeply sunken and ominous. "You expect too much. Even I, Mylakhrion of Tharamoon, could not—achieve—" And here he faltered and fell silent.

I perceived then a seeming agitation in the mist-wreathed phantom; he appeared to tremble, however slightly, and I sensed his eagerness to be gone. Thus I pressed him:

"Oh? And how much *did* you achieve, Mylakhrion? Is there more I should know? What were your experiments and how much did you discover in your great search for immortality? I believe you are hiding something from me, o mighty one, and if I must I'll smoke the Zha-weed again!—aye, and yet again—leaving you no rest or peace until you have answered me as I would be answered!"

Hearing me speak thus, Mylakhrion's figure stiffened and swelled momentarily massive, but then his shoulders drooped and he nodded slowly, saying: "Have I come to this? That the most meagre talents have power to command me? A sad day indeed for Mylakhrion of Tharamoon, when his own descendant uses him so sorely. What is it you wish to know, Teh Atht of Klühn?"

"While you were unable to achieve immortality in your lifetime, ancestor mine," I answered, "mayhap nathless you can assist me in the discovery of the secret in mine. Describe to me the magicks you used and discarded in your search, the runes you unravelled and put aside, the potions imbibed and unctions applied to no avail, and these I shall take note of that no further time be wasted with them. Then advise me of the paths which you might have explored had time and circumstance permitted. For I *will* be immortal, and no power shall stay me from it."

"Ah, youth, it is folly," quoth he, "but if you so command—"

"I do so command."

"Then hear me out and I will tell all, and perhaps you will understand when I tell you that you cannot have immortality . . . not of the sort you so fervently desire."

And so Mylakhrion told me of his search for immortality. He described for me the great journeys he undertook—leaving Tharamoon, his island-mountain aerie, in the care of watchdog familiars—to visit and confer with other sorcerers and wizards; even journeys across the entire length and breadth of Theem'hdra. Alone he went out into the deserts and plains, the hills and icy wastes in pursuit of this most elusive of mysteries. He visited and talked with Black Yoppaloth of Yhemnis, with the ghost of Shildakor in

lava-buried Bhur-Esh, with Ardatha Ell, a traveller in space
and time who lived for a while in the Great Circle Mountains and studied the featureless, vastly cubical houses of the
long-gone Ancients, and with Mellatiquel Thom, a cousin-
wizard fled to Yaht Haal when certain magicks turned against
him.

And always during these great wanderings he collected
runes and cantrips, spells and philtres, powders and potions
and other devices necessary to his thaumaturgical experiments. But never a one to set his feet on the road to immortality. Aye, and using vile necromancy he called up the dead from
their ashes, even the dead, for his purposes. And this is something I, Teh Atht, have never done, deeming it too loathsome
and danger-fraught a deed. For to talk to a dream-phantom is
one matter, but to hold intercourse with long-rotted liches . . .
that is a vile, vile thing.

But for all his industry Mylakhrion found only frustration.
He conversed with demons and lamias, hunted the legendary
phoenix in burning deserts, near-poisoned himself with strange
drugs and nameless potions and worried his throat raw with
the chanting of oddly cacophonic invocations. And only then
did he think to ask himself this question:

If a man desired immortality, what better way than to ask
the secret of one *already* immortal? Aye, and there was just
such a one . . .

Then, when Mylakhrion spoke the name of Cthulhu—the
tentacled Great One who seeped down from the stars with
his spawn in aeons past to build his cities in the steaming fens
of a young and inchoate Earth—I shuddered and made a certain sign over my heart. For while I had not yet had to do
with this Cthulhu, his legend was awful and I had heard

much of him. And I marvelled that Mylakhrion had dared seek out this Great One, even Mylakhrion, for above all other evils Cthulhu was legended to tower like a menhir above mere gravestones.

And having marvelled I listened most attentively to all that my ancestor had to say of Cthulhu and the other Great Ones, for since their nature was in the main obscure, and being my-self a sorcerer with a sorcerer's appetite for mysteries, I was most desirous of learning more of them.

"Aye, Teh Atht," Mylakhrion continued, "Cthulhu and his brethren: they must surely know the answer, for they are—"

"Immortal?"

For answer he shrugged, then said: "Their genesis lies in unthinkable abysses of the past, their end nowhere in sight. Like the cockroach they were here before man, and they will supersede man. Why, they were oozing like vile ichor be-tween the stars before the sun spewed out her molten chil-dren, of which this world is one; and they will live on when Sol is the merest cinder. Do not attempt to measure their life-spans in terms of human life, nor even geologically. Measure them rather in the births and deaths of planets, which to them are like the tickings of vast clocks. Immortal? As near immor-tal as matters not. From them I could either beg, borrow or steal the secret—but how to go about approaching them?"

I waited for the ghost of my dead ancestor to proceed, and when he did not immediately do so cried out: "Say on then, forebear mine! Say on and be done with beguiling me!"

He sighed for reply and answered very low: "As you com-mand . . .

"At length I sought me out a man rumoured to be well versed in the ways of the Great Ones; a hermit, dwelling in the peaks of the Eastern Range, whose visions and dreams were such as were best dreamed far removed from his fellow men. For he was wont to run amok in the passion of his nightmares, and was reckoned by many to have bathed in the blood of numerous innocents, 'to the greater glory of Loathly Lord Cthulhu!'

"I sought him out and questioned him in his high cave, and he showed me the herbs I must eat and whispered the words I must howl from the peaks into the storm. And he told me when I must do these things, that I might then sleep and meet with Cthulhu in my dreams. Thus he instructed me . . .

"But as night drew nigh in this lonely place my host became drowsy and fell into a fitful sleep. Aye, and his ravings soon became such, and his strugglings so wild, that I stayed not but ventured back out into the steep slopes and thus made away from him. Descending those perilous crags only by the silvery light of the Moon, I spied the madman above me, asleep yet rushing to and fro, howling like a dog and slashing with a great knife in the darkness of the shadows. And I was glad I had not stayed!

"Thus I returned to Tharamoon, taking a winding route and gathering of the herbs whereof the hermit had spoken, until upon my arrival I had with me all the elements required for the invocation, while locked in my mind I carried the Words of Power. And lo!—I called up a great storm and went out onto the balcony of my highest tower, and there I howled into the wind the Words, and I ate of the herbs mixed so and so, and a swoon came upon me so that I fell as though dead into a sleep deeper by far than the arms of Shoosh, Goddess of the Still Slumbers. Ah, but deep though this sleep was, it was by no means still!

"No, that sleep was—*unquiet!* I saw the sepulcher of Cthulhu in the Isle of Arlyeh, and I passed through the massive and oddly-angled walls of that alien stronghold into the presence of the Great One Himself!"

Here the outlines of my ancestor's ghost became strangely agitated, as if its owner trembled uncontrollably, and even the voice of Mylakhrion wavered and lost much of its doomful portent. I waited for a moment before crying: "Yes, go on—what did the awful Lord of Arlyeh tell you?"

". . . Many things, Teh Atht. He told me the secrets of space and time, the legends of lost universes out beyond the limits of man's imagination; he outlined the hideous truths behind the N'tang Tapestries, the lore of dimensions other than the familiar three. And at last he told me the secret of immortality!

"But the latter he would not reveal until I had made a pact with him. And this pact was that I would be his priest for ever and ever, even until his coming. And believing that I might later break free of any strictures Cthulhu could place upon me, I agreed to the pact and swore upon it. In this my fate was sealed, my doom ordained, for no man may escape the curse of Cthulhu once its seal is upon him . . .

"And lo, when I wakened I did all as I had been instructed to attain the promised immortality; and on the third night Cthulhu visited me in dreams, for he knew me now and how to find me, and commanded me as his servant and priest to set about certain tasks. Ah, but these were tasks which would assist the Great One and his prisoned brethren in breaking free of the chains placed upon them in aeons past by the wondrous Gods of Eld, and what use to be immortal forever more in the unholy service of Cthulhu?

"Thus, on the fourth day, instead of doing as bidden, I set about protecting myself as best I could from Cthulhu's wrath, working a veritable frenzy of magicks to keep him from me . . . to no avail! In the middle of the fifth night, wearied nigh unto death by my thaumaturgical labours, I slept, and again Cthulhu came to me. And he came in great anger— even *great* anger!

"For he had broken down all of my sorcerous barriers, destroying all spells and protective runes, discovering me for a traitor to his cause. And as I slept he drew me up from my couch and led me through the labryinth of my castle, even to the feet of those steps which climbed up to the topmost tower. He placed my feet upon those stone stairs and commanded me to climb, and when I would have fought him he applied monstrous pressures to my mind that numbed me and left me bereft of will. And so I climbed, slowly and like unto one of the risen dead, up to that high tower, where without pause I went out onto the balcony and threw myself down upon the needle rocks a thousand feet below . . .

"Thus was my body broken, Teh Atht, and thus Mylakhrion died."

As he finished speaking I stepped closer to the swirling wall of mist where Mylakhrion stood, black-robed and enigmatic in mystery. He did not seem so tall now, no taller than I myself, and for all the power he had wielded in life he no longer awed me. Should I, Teh Atht, fear a ghost? Even the ghost of the world's greatest sorcerer?

"Still you have not told me that which I most desire to know," I accused.

"Ah, you grow impatient," he answered. "Even as the smoke of the Zha-weed loses its potency and the waking world beckons to you, so your impatience grows. Very well, let me now repeat what Cthulhu told me of immortality:

"He told me that the only way a mere man, even the mightiest wizard among wizards, might perpetuate himself down all the ages was by means of reincarnation! But alas, such as my return would be it would not be complete; for I must needs inhabit another's body, another's mind, and unless I desired a weak body and mind I should certainly find resistance in the person of that as yet unborn other. In other words I must *share* that body, that mind! But surely, I reasoned, even partial immortality would be better than none at all. Would you not agree, descendant mine? . . .

"Of course, I would want a body—or part of one—close in appearance to my own, and a mind to suit. Aye, and it must be a keen mind and curious of mysteries great and small: that of a sorcerer! And indeed it were better if my own blood should flow in the veins of—"

"Wait!" I then cried, searching the mist with suddenly fearful eyes, seeking to penetrate its greyness that I might gaze upon Mylakhrion's unknown face. "I . . . I find your story most . . . disturbing . . . my ancestor, and—"

"—and yet you must surely hear it out, Teh Atht," he interrupted, doom once more echoing in his voice. And as he spoke he moved flowingly forward until at last I could see the death-lights in his shadowy eyes. Closer still he came, saying:

"To ensure that this as yet unborn one would be all the things I desired of him, I set a covenant upon my resurrection in him. And this condition was that his curiosity and sorcerous skill must be such that he would first call me up from the Land of Shades ten times, and that only then would I make myself manifest in his person . . . *And how many times have you called me up, Teh Atht?"*

"Ten times—fiend!" I choked. And feeling the chill of subterranean pools flowing in my bones, I rushed upon him to seize his shoulders in palsied hands, staring into a face now visible as a reflection in the clear glass of a mirror. A mirror? Aye! For though the face was that of an old, old man—*it was nonetheless my own*!

And without more ado I fled, waking to a cold, cold morn atop the Mount of the Ancients, where my tethered yak watched me with worried eyes and snorted a nervous greeting . . .

BUT THAT WAS long ago and in my youth, and now I no longer fear Mylakhrion, though I did fear him greatly for many a year. For in the end I was stronger than him, aye, and he got but a small part of me. In return I got all of his magicks, the lore of a lifetime spent in the discovery of dark secrets.

All of this and immortality, too, of a sort; and yet even now Mylakhrion is not beaten. For surely I will carry something of him with me down the ages. Occasionally I smile at the thought and feel laughter rising in me like a wind over the desert . . . but rarely. The laughter hardly sounds like mine at all and its echoes seem to linger o'erlong.

Lords of the Morass

NO GREATER GOLDSMITH in all Theem'hdra than Eythor Dreen, whose works in that wondrous metal, particularly his sculptures, were admired by all and sundry but only ever commissioned by kings, who alone could afford them. Kings, aye . . . and the occasional sorcerer.

Since I myself have always found transmutation tedious (while the alchemy is simplicity itself, the consumption of time and energy is enormous!), and because Eythor had guaranteed me a massive discount on his gold, I commissioned him to amass and fashion the required amount in a likeness of myself.

This was no act of vanity, but in those days I was often the target of lesser magicians whose malicious sorceries were ever disturbing my experiments and studies; and so I required an effigy of myself upon which all such injurious spells and curses might spend themselves in my stead. The scarred and pitted condition of that sculpture now—as if worked upon by mordant liquids and seared by weird energies— surely stands mute witness to my wisdom in this matter . . . but that is all aside.

In order to do the job justice, Dreen came to stay with me for some little time in my apartments over the Bay of Klühn; which was where he told me the following tale. I have no reason to doubt a single word of it, but the reader may judge for himself.

Teh Atht . . .

I

We were on the central plain, Phata Um and I, following a streamlet towards its source somewhere in the Great Circle Mountains. Far to the north lay the Desert of Ell, and to the south, not too far away, the Nameless Desert of dark repute. We panned for gold in the silty basins below gentle falls, wherever bends occurred in the stream, and whenever the surrounding formations looked auriferous to our prospectors' eyes.

Initially we had worked a middling vein in the Mountains of Lohmi, fleeing south empty-handed when a band of robbers out of Chlangi discovered our diggings, stole our gold and ran us out of camp. All was not lost, however, for we managed to retain a camel, two yaks and most of our equipment—not to mention our lives! And so we decided to wend our way to the Great Circle Mountains, follow them north to the River Marl and so up into Khrissa. From there a boat would take us home to Eyphra . . . if we could afford our passage on such a vessel.

Setting out across the plain, we prospected as we went and eventually came upon the streamlet, there finding a few small nuggets. Now gold has been, is now and always will be

a curse upon mankind. Men will kill for it; women sell themselves for it; its lure is irresistible. It brings dreams sweeter
than opium and its colour has trapped the warmth and lustre
of the very sun. It has a marvellous malleability all its own,
and its great *weight* is that of the pendulum of the world!
What could we do, Phata Um and I? We followed the stream,
of course, and we found more nuggets. And the farther west
we proceeded, the more and bigger nuggets we found.

Now for certain the stream flowed down out of the Great
Circle Range, and equally obvious the fact that it passed
through a vein rich beyond precedence. The nuggets and dust
we had taken from the stream already were sufficient to set
us up comfortably, but the *source* of this wealth, the mother
lode—ah!—that would make us rich beyond all dreams of
avarice; aye, and all our descendants after us. So it pleased us
to fancy.

But here let me tell you about Phata Um, my partner. He
was younger than me by ten years, Phata: big, blond, slow
moving, with the frame and supple limbs of a young god—
but quiet and generally resentful of people. They made fun of
his slow, easy-going ways—of his slow smile and his shyness.
But they made it behind his back. He could pull the head off
an ox, that one, and a single blow from his mighty fist would
surely crush and kill any lesser man.

That was why he was a prospector. There is no one to laugh
and poke fun at you in the mountains or along the great
rivers. Only other prospectors. And because I myself am not
much for company—a bit of a loner, you might say—why we
got along splendidly, Phata Um and I. I suppose I might put it
in a nutshell by stating quite simply that if I was the brain of

our partnership, then Phata was the brawn; but at the same time I hasten to impress that I was *not* his master but a true partner, and the split was always right down the middle. Phata was like a little brother to me and loved me dearly, and for my part I guarded his interests as were they my own.

Indeed, in country wild and uncharted as this, my partner's interests *were* my own; his senses of direction and survival were unexcelled, and I swear he was as great an outdoors man as any long-maned barbarian from the north-west. Where I could get lost and starve in a back-street in my own town (I exaggerate a little, you understand) Phata Um could happily navigate the stormy Teeth of Yib or dwell for a six-month in the heights of the Great Circle Mountains themselves; and all without the least discomfort!

Even before we met Phata had been a great traveller; he knew the mountains, plains and deserts, the rivers and the lochs—all of the places where a man would go to commune with himself, to find peace in utter loneliness. Which was why I listened to him whenever he had something to say about the dangers of the regions in which we travelled; and usually I would follow to the letter his advice in such matters—except where gold was concerned. Nor was I alone in my avarice, for Phata too would seek far beyond all wise or commonsense boundaries for sight of that heavy, yellow, precious stuff of dreams.

Such was now the case as, still following the stream, we entered the foothills of the Great Circle Mountains. As we went we still collected the occasional nugget and continued to fill our tiny leather sacks with dust; and the fact that already we were wealthy men served only to spur us on, despite Phata's warning that we rapidly approached a region of extreme hazard. For as my partner began to read signs in the sudden luxuriousness of vegetation and the steamy breezes blowing from the distance-misted peaks, so he remembered things heard from other adventurers who perhaps trod this road before us. Phata himself had never wandered this way, and now he told me the reason:

Rumour had it, he said, that at the foot of the mountains where they climbed sheer to the sky, in a place where volcanic vents drove jets of steam and boiling mud high into the air, there one could find a marsh and a jungle of tropical aspect. More green and luxuriant than the coastal forests of the south, that region, whose fringes housed a pigmy race of men at once curious and terrible. Their weapons were blowpipes whose darts were dipped in orchid-extracted poisons, and their gods—

Their gods were monsters of the marsh, great slugs as big as mammoths, whose nocturnal habits had awed the pigmies since time immemorial, elevating the monstrosities to the plane of deity. Of the worshippers of these loathsome beasts, Phata had also heard it said that they were shy. Normally they would keep their distance and only intervene when strangers pressed too closely upon their preserves: their settlements and the marshes where dwelled their slug-gods, which were *taboo*, forbidden to any outsider.

A little more than this my partner knew, but not much. The pigmies respected strength, but if a man was a coward . . . then let him not go into their jungles or anywhere near their marshes. Their darts were swift and certain and their cruelties toward their enemies enormous. They had filed teeth and they ate the flesh of any that wronged them; either that, or they fed them to their slug-gods.

And so Phata's warnings should have been deterrent enough, and perhaps would have been but for his final word: that he had also heard it said of these little men that they all wore great bangles and necklets and earrings—aye, and massive noserings, too—and all of purest shining gold! Which seemed to me to hint that the mother lode might well lie central within their domain. So be it; we would befriend them, if indeed they existed at all . . .

Well, they did exist and we found them—or rather they found us—but not for a good many days.

In between we panned and pocketed, and ever the fruits of our labours were richer, until our yaks were heavy burdened with the weight of our wealth. And the forest grew up around us as we followed the stream toward its source, so that we walked in rich leaf-mold through sun-dappled groves of exotic blooms; and ever the way became more lush and steamy. The foliage grew more tropical in appearance, and the raucous cries of beasts and birds more frequent and more clamorous, until it became hard to believe that we were on the mainland at all but must surely, miraculously have been transported to orchid-wreathed Shadarabar across the Straits of Yhem.

By now our beasts had had enough. Their hooves were not made for this sort of terrain and they grew more rebellious by the hour. We put them on long tethers in an open if somewhat bushy pasture close to the stream and left them there, at the same time relieving the yaks of their golden burden, which we buried in an unmarked cache pending our return. Then we pressed on.

Now it was not our intention to avail ourselves of more gold, not at this time, but simply to see if Phata's myths and legends had any truth in them. In any case, we had neither the strength nor the facilities for handling more of that weighty stuff; but our curiosity was aroused in respect of the pigmies and we wanted to know more about them, to see them for ourselves and perhaps strike up a trading relationship with them. Of course, being prospectors, we still greatly desired to know the *location* of the mother lode—that mighty deposit whose merest traces had been washed downstream over long centuries—but only as a prelude to future and better equipped expeditions.

After three more days of penetration into the now dense jungle, always following the stream—though this was now much more difficult due to the generally swampy nature of the region—Phata Um and I arrived at a blue lake whose central island seemed feathered with a village of tiny houses on shivery stilts, above which drifted the blue and grey smoke of cooking fires. Small brown men in hollow-log canoes fished in the lake with nets weighted with nuggets of gold, and their appearance was in accordance with Phata Um's earlier description. His informants had not lied.

At this point we might have turned back, or perhaps negotiated the lake until we discovered once more the course of the stream on its farther shore, except that any such decision was taken completely out of our hands. For two days and nights now we had suspected that we were observed, that secret watchers lurked behind the hanging vines, in the thickly clustered ferns and wide-leaved foliage, and on several occasions slight movements had been noted on our flanks which had a stealth not normally apparent in common animals. We had felt intelligent eyes upon us where we walked the stream's bank, and there had been whistled calls which had not the ring of ordinary birds but hinted of the conveyance of certain secret messages.

Nevertheless, and for all that we were prepared for the confrontation and had indeed expected it sooner or later, we started horribly when the flared snouts of long blowpipes emerged suddenly from the lakeside's fringing foliage; and without conscious volition both Phata and I reached for our knives. With ferocious warning hisses—filling their cheeks with air as they came into view and gripping the stems of their deadly weapons with their teeth—the pigmy party emerged from hiding and we saw that we were surrounded.

"Well," said I, placing hands on hips and smiling, however nervously, "this is what we expected, Phata . . . but what do we do now?"

II

My partner said nothing but having recovered from his initial shock he merely held out his great hands before him at arm's length, his fists open and palms uppermost. Lying in the cup of his left palm, in clear view, was a tiny golden whistle with which I had heard him imitate certain birdcalls. Deliberately and very slowly he placed the whistle in his mouth and blew a mellow, throaty warble, somehow managing to smile the while. The pigmies immediately lowered their weapons and clustered to him, their brown eyes aboggle, their mouths brimming with a strange and primitive language beyond our ken. Encouraged, Phata broke into a piercing trill which trailed off into a series of sharp, piping chirrups of inquiry.

The pigmies were enthralled. One of them, stepping forward, pointed excitedly at his own mouth and said something utterly unintelligible. When Phata frowned and shook his head, the little man looked momentarily frustrated and began to hop up and down; but then he grinned, stopped dancing and handed Phata his blowpipe. This was done with a spontaneous naivete which could in no way be construed as acknowledgement of subservience; but it did have the effect of leaving the pigmy's hands free. The smallest fingers of these he now placed in the corners of his wide mouth, and using fingers and mouth together he delivered a sustained blast of a whistle which was very nearly deafening. Phata and I made loud noises of approval and I ventured so far as to pat the performer upon his brown back.

It was now my turn to show my talents, and being something of a sharp (that is to say, I have a certain knack at sleight of hand), I confounded the small folk by pulling nuggets of gold from their ears and noses, by making my thumbs disappear and reappear momently, and by use of my speciality, which was to toss a nugget into the air—only to have it fall back to earth as a shower of fragrant flower petals. Child's play for sure, but effective beyond all expectations. We had mighty *juju* indeed, Phata and I, and the N'dola—for so they called themselves—made us most welcome from that time forward. Alas, this happy state of affairs was not to last; but of course we were not to know that.

In no time at all we found ourselves seated in a hollowed-out log canoe and paddled out to the isle of the N'dolas, where immediately we were taken to see the chief, An'noona. An'noona's hut was taller and bigger than any other, and its stilts correspondingly stronger; but they nevertheless trembled and swayed a little as the chief himself—a tiny, ancient, wizened pigmy—descended fragile looking ladders to meet us.

Close by was a large open space with a dais and throne, upon which the chief seated himself with a pair of pigmy councillors standing behind him. Phata and I were led to the space in front of the dais, where once again we performed our repertoire of tricks. Thankfully, An'noona was no less appreciative than his subjects, and each phase of our performance was greeted with hand-clapping and a great deal of chatter and grinning. And my partner and I kept smiling, but we exchanged meaningful glances at sight of all the sharply pointed teeth which the concerted grinning so amply displayed.

Just as we were reaching the end of our show, a disturbance at the rear of the pigmy crowd (for by this time the entire village had turned out to see us) drew our eyes. And now, as the milling ranks of tiny people grew silent and shrank back from the place of the disturbance, so for the first time we saw the tribal witch-doctor, Ow-n-ow. At first glance we knew we had an enemy in this evil looking midget; the way his hooded eyes met ours, the way he pointed with his feathered wand and shook his bone rattle in imitation of a deadly snake told us so.

And now he approached, with many a leap and bound, gyrating wildly as the crowd gave him room and his naked feet sent the dust flying. Right up to us he came, leaping high in the air to point his gold-tipped wand first at me, then at Phata Um. And now he paused before us, arms akimbo, his wicked monkey face contemptuous as he silently defied us to do our worst.

"What now?" asked Phata Um from the side of his mouth. "They hate cowards."

"Then we must show them what we're made of," I countered. "Now is not the time for faint hearts. Let's see if we can deflate this little dung-beetle." So saying, I stooped and pretended to snatch up a handful of sand, which I hurled straight into the witch-doctor's face!

Instinctively, he threw up his hands before his eyes—but instead of stinging dust and grit he found himself surrounded by a settling shower of tiny, rose-tinted petals. Before he could recover, Phata Um took hold of his shoulders and lifted him up bodily until he stared directly into his startled, frightened eyes. The little man knew that my partner could crush him there and then, if he so desired. Phata did no such thing but merely blew a deafening blast on his whistle, already secreted in his mouth. Then he put the shrieking, wildly kicking little man back down on his feet again.

Backing off in confusion, Ow-n-ow tripped and sat down hard in the dust, and the momentarily silent crowd at once burst out afresh with hoots of derision and raucous catcalls, until the witch-doctor scrambled to his feet and fled. Then for some little time the clearing was full of tiny mimics who replayed over and over Ow-n-ow's downfall and less than graceful exit, until the chief clapped his hands sharply and brought the assemblage back under control.

Briefly, in a voice wizened as its owner, which yet carried across the clearing, An'noona then spoke to his subjects, the while pointing at Phata and me where we patiently stood; and in the next instant the entire crowd prostrated itself before us, then quickly jumped up and danced all about us. We had been accepted—which did not say a lot for Ow-n-ow's popularity!

After a moment or two An'noona stood up and came

forward on the log dais until his eyes met ours on a level. He lifted a heavy golden chain from his neck and placed it over Phata's head, unclasped from his own krinkly hair a massive brooch of gold crusted with gems and pinned it to my jacket, then stood back and admired us. Not to be outdone, Phata handed the chief his golden whistle, and for my part I gave to him a jewelled northstone set on a pivot in a little silver box. Delighted with this exchange of gifts, An'noona went back to his hut and Phata and I were left in the care of his councillors.

One of the latter pair—little more than a youth but with a great head of almost acromegalic proportions, which bore a livid scar running from his left temple to his chin—astounded us by speaking to us in our own tongue, however distorted by a twanging barbarian influence and accent. His name was Atmaas (the Knowing One) and he stumblingly explained his familiarity with our language by telling us the following story:

As a boy Atmaas had been constantly mocked by the other children of the tribe because of his cranial deformity. Eventually, unable to bear any more of these jibes and taunts and general cruelties, one day the dam broke within Atmaas and he fled the village into the Great Circle Mountains. There he was befriended (in however harsh and brusque a manner) by a dozen wandering, outcast barbarians from the north-west. They took from him his golden bangles, nose-ring and other trinkets, but in return gave him food and taught him their tongue.

Atmaas was quick to learn—which argued for a sound brain in that large, ugly skull of his—and soon his proficiency was such that he was able to converse freely with the longmaned outcasts from the north. Now they were able to question him about his golden ornaments, which had been divided between them, and they asked him to lead them to his homeland where they might find more of the precious yellow metal. At first he attempted to dissuade them, and such were his warnings that three of the barbarians did in fact split off from the main body; but the rest were not cowed by the lad's tales of great slug-gods and poisoned darts, and they pressed him to show them the way to his swampy homeland.

Fearing for what they might do to him if he refused them (and perhaps relishing a little the thought of sweet revenge for miseries his tribe had heaped upon him in the past), Atmaas at last agreed and brought the barbarians down out of the mountains, through treacherous swamps and reptile-infested forests to the lake of the N'dolas.

They arrived by night, and silently the barbarians paddled out to the island and stole into the village. Their intention was to fire the village and raze it down, killing any pigmies who might escape the holocaust; and perhaps they might have succeeded, for certainly the village was at that time tinder dry and the element of surprise was on the side of the northmen.

But by now Atmaas was beginning to feel pangs of guilt and remorse; and so, as the barbarians ran silently here and there in the night, setting fire to stilts, ladders, animal pens and the logs of the perimeter walls, so he stole away to the great golden gong whose voice was only ever heard in times of danger. As the fires began to take hold, he beat upon the gong and cried out in a loud voice to tell the men of the tribe to bring out their weapons and defend themselves and their families.

One of the startled barbarians came upon him as he thus

thundered, and in a berserker rage sought to cut him down. The single blow from the northman's sword caused the hideous gash to Atmaas' face and hurled him down half-dead; and thus he remained while the tribesmen in their high windows picked off the barbarians one by one with their poisoned darts. And at last, when the fires were under control, then the villagers discovered Atmaas where his crumpled body lay; and now they knew of his bravery—knew Atmaas of the Ugly Head as a hero—and now too they set about nursing him back to health.

Indeed, the chief's wives were given that responsibility, so that during Atmaas' convalescence old An'noona spoke often with him and soon came to know of the pigmy lad's intelligence. And so impressed was the chief that he made an order that henceforth any child of particular brilliance or talent should be named Atmaas after the hero; and thus Atmaas himself became first among An'noona's advisors. This was the youth's story . . .

III

By now night was drawing in, and soon a waxing moon was riding high above a mist that seemed to settle from the sky. Lanterns were lighted and Atmaas led us to a small hut on short stilts, which he indicated was ours for as long as we cared to stay. Now was not a time for sleeping, however, but for rejoicing; and when Phata and I would have gladly climbed the short ladder to bed, Atmaas stopped us and pointed through tendrils of thin mist and wisps of fragrant fire smoke to where numerous lanterns were bobbing and gathering at a central place. There was to be a feast, Atmaas informed—a celebration, a gorging of choice gobbets, a great guzzling of mildly opiate and heavily intoxicant beverages— and all for us! For An'noona had found us pleasing and desired to honour us.

Already the night was a muted hubbub, the air filled with enticing, exotic smells and the sounds of strange instruments; so that Phata and I felt a rising excitement as we tossed our necessaries in through our hut's high doorway and followed Atmaas to the feast. And as we seated ourselves cross-legged before a vast, low log table, of which there were a dozen, so an endless stream of laden platters of gold began to appear. There were more than two hundred of them, all of thick, beaten gold, all heaped with every sort of meat and fish and fruit and nut, until the tables were a-groan with their weight. Finally, by the time it had grown totally dark beyond the circle of lantern light, when it seemed that the entire tribe must be seated in the central clearing, only then did An'noona appear, taking his place at the head of our table.

The chief smiled a toothy smile at us and made a sign with his hand; and the horde at the tables immediately began chattering and chewing, and the babble grew deafening as a pigmy band struck up on tomtoms, wind and string instruments. We too would have eaten, for the sight of all this food had made us hungry and it was impossible to stop our mouths from watering; but we held back, however reluctantly, until Atmaas who sat with us saw our hesitation and knew the source of our discomfort.

No, no, he informed us: there were no enemies of the N'dolas on the menu tonight. There were ribs of wild pig and steaks of water buffalo, moorhens and jungle quails, river

oysters and rainbow trout and smoked eels of a rare and delicate texture—but no man-flesh, no. Of course, there was
one who would dearly love to see *us* trussed up and simmer-
ing in the cooking pots, who even now stood to one side in
the shadows and kept his evil eyes glued upon us where we
sat. And Atmaas, inclining his great and misshapen head, indicated where we should look to see this would-be malefac-
tor.

Even before we turned our heads that way, Phata and I
knew who the silent watcher would be. None other but
Ow-n-ow, the witch-doctor himself. We would be well advised, Atmaas needlessly informed, to keep out of the way
of the *nganga*, lest he find a way to pay us back for the hu-
miliations we had heaped upon him. And all through the
celebrations which followed, from time to time as the night
wore on, we would feel Ow-n-ow's gaze burning upon us,
Phata Um and I, and so knew beyond any slightest doubt
that Atmaas' advice was well founded.

What with the gorging on marvellous gobbets, however,
and gulping down great two-handed jars of beer—and the
pigmies doing their intricate tribal dances, and the music
which grew, as the night progressed, more wild and rhythmic
and repetitive, so as to become almost hypnotic—Ow-n-ow
gradually slipped to the back of our reeling minds, becoming
less a threat than an annoyance. Until eventually, drunk as
lords, stepping carefully over the still forms of little men
where they had fallen in their excesses, as the sky to the east
began to lighten a little, we wove our weary way to our hut
and climbed, however teeteringly, to bed.

And even here the pigmies were not remiss in their hospi-
tality; for giggling coyly in the darkness of our tiny rooms

were a pair of pigmy girls, black as the night but not nearly so secretive, who had doubtless waited for us through all the long hours of revelry and who now set about to put the finishing touches to our welcome. Through the thin, woven wall of my room I heard Phata's puzzled, boozy query: "Well, little one, and just what am I supposed to do with you?" And I smiled at the silence which then ensued, being certain that just like her sister who now pleasured me, Phata's visitor had doubtless taken the initiative . . .

FOR THE NEXT three days and nights we did very little. Indeed, two whole days were required merely to recover from the festive excesses of our welcoming celebration, so that our condition was only very shaky as we went about the village and took note of the tribe's way of life, its customs, habits, its social structure in general, and particularly its utensils, even the commonest or most mundane of which were of gold. It was a source of constant astonishment to us to see boys fishing in the lake with hooks of pure gold, and gardeners at work with forks and hoes of that same precious metal, and girls washing their scraps of clothing in great basins of the stuff!

Then, on the fourth day, Atmaas came to us and told us that An'noona had decided to honour us above all others. For no other outsiders had ever entered the fane of the slug-gods or seen the treasures therein, and this was the invitation which the chief now extended to us. Moreover, we were also to be his guests at the quarterly propitiation of the gods themselves; when with our own eyes we might gaze upon those monsters as Ow-n-ow called them out of their deep swamps to accept burnt sacrifices of buffaloes and pigs. For in two more days the moon would be at its full, and then it was that the ceremony must take place; and for a further three-month the slug-gods would be appeased and the village would prosper. First, however, we were to visit the fane of the gods and offer up our prayers to those gigantic gastropod deities; for it was only right that we who had found favour in the eyes of An'noona should now ask it of his gods.

That same afternoon, as Phata and I finished a simple meal prepared and served by our pigmy paramours, An'noona and his councillors, accompanied by the *nganga* Ow-n-ow, came to where we sat in the shade of our hut. Atmaas explained that we were to go with them to the fane of the slug-gods, and so we followed the party to the lake's edge where the chief's royal barge—a trimaran built of terrific tree trunks—lay waiting with its crew of smooth-muscled paddlers. With the chief seated centrally and in the prow, his retinue close behind him, and with Phata and me each in an outrigger, we soon were on our way.

Long that journey and tiring, so that the team of twenty paddlers was obliged to work in shifts of ten; but soon our craft had entered the wide body of the river where it came down from the central mountains and then, against the steady but gentle flow of water, we made good headway between banks strewn with orchids and overgrown with dense foliage and huge trees whose vines hung down to the river itself. And again we felt ourselves transported as if by magick to jungled Shadarabar.

As the hours passed so the night drew in, and great moths came to investigate the lanterns with which the trimaran's crew lighted its watery way; and as the full moon rose up into the sky, so we were able to discern ahead the rising cliffs of a great canyon. Only then did Phata and I know the real source of the river, which could be nowhere else but the mighty Inner Sea itself. For this was one of those outlets by which that imposing inland ocean emptied itself through the Great Circle Mountains.

And so, by light of moon and lantern, we proceeded until, deep within the defile, the canyon opened out to form a sort of small valley within the range. Here, on the nothern bank of the river, the land was a rank swamp a-crawl with lizards, crocodiles and great frogs which ran, slithered or hopped through rotting foliage and creeping vines of an unnatural, venomous black and green. And away in the dark distance, where the great cliffs rose up once more against the starry night, there we could see the glowing, smoky red fires of volcanic blowholes, which we knew for such by a sulphurous taint in the warm, clinging air of the place.

To the south there was neither bank nor marsh, only great cliffs rising into darkness, whose feet the river followed from that mighty Inner Ocean of legend. Here the current was a little stronger, the water deeper, and our craft hugged the sheer rock as it moved slowly forward.

Now Atmaas called to us from his position to the rear of the chief, pointing to the sprawling swamps of the northern aspect. That was forbidden territory, he told us, *taboo*, the domain of the slug-gods, where two nights from now we would see them called forth by Ow-n-ow to accept the tribe's tribute. But no sooner had he finished speaking than Ow-n-ow himself, whose seat was in the stern of the central hull, gave a great howling laugh that echoed back from the rock walls like the lunatic chorus of a pack of hyenas!

White in the near-darkness, I saw Phata's face as he turned it to stare at the *nganga* where he sat in the rear, rocking in crazed glee, his glowing eyes first on me, then on Phata, as if he knew some marvellously malicious joke about us and would love to tell it. But at that very moment, taking our minds off the evil witch-doctor, there came the cry of a pigmy who stood and leaned forward in the prow of the larboard outrigger, drawing all eyes to where he swung his lantern in darkness. For here the cliffs had been washed away to form a vast cave like the yawning mouth of some monster, into whose inky shadow our craft now slid as we stared about in lantern-flickered gloom.

Here the water was calm and still, and as torches were lit to augment the light of the lanterns, so we found ourselves in a high-domed natural cavern whose branching throat went back into untold labyrinths of rock. Huge stalactites hung from the bat-clustered ceiling. Between those needle points the paddlers now guided the royal vessel unerringly toward one dark canal whose walls seemed all agleam with winking, luminous green eyes. Since the channel was narrow, however, and since Phata and I occupied the outriggers, we were soon able to discern that these winking points were not eyes but the facets of fabulous emeralds in their natural state, imbedded in the glassy walls and polished by untold centuries of flooding waters! Moreover, the walls themselves were yellow with thick branching veins of raw gold! The place was nothing less than a vast, natural treasure cave; and I admit that my throat grew dry, as Phata's must have done, at the thought of the untold wealth mere inches from our itching fingers.

In a few moments more the channel widened out and we

saw to our left a wide shelf of rock which reached back toward the cave's shadow-hidden wall. And I knew at once that this was the fane of the slug-gods, for the sight that greeted my unbelieving eyes in that secret place was of such magnitude that it utterly dwarfed all which had gone before.

Can you picture endless ranks of great gastropods—giant slugs fashioned in precious yellow metal, with stalked eyes of uncut emeralds big as a man's fists—marching away into the gloom of the place; and the flames of the torches and lanterns reflected into our eyes from the nearest sculptures, until it seemed that the whole cavern flowed with molten gold, through which auric effulgence the emerald-eyed monsters seemed silently to glide on carpets of golden nuggets, imbued with an awe-inspiring sentience all their own? You cannot, nor could any man who has not seen it with his own eyes!

IV

As our eyes grew accustomed to the yellow dazzle, so we noted that upon rock-cut ledges to the rear of the temple stood dozens of smaller slug replicas, some large as dogs and others no bigger than small rats—but all of solid gold. We were given no great time to consider the vastness of the wealth here amassed, however, for no sooner had we disembarked to stand upon the great shelf than the members of An'noona's party prostrated themselves and Atmaas indicated that we should do likewise.

All of us, with the sole exception of Ow-n-ow, went down on our knees, heads bowed; and now, without more ado, the tiny *nganga* began his dance of propitiation. As he danced—a weird, gliding dance, hands held at the sides of his head, index fingers extended in imitation of horns—so one by one, beginning with the chief himself, each member of An'noona's party stood up, took out from his ceremonial robes a miniature golden slug and went to place it in its chosen niche, returning immediately and once more prostrating himself.

Even with bowed heads Phata and I managed to keep track of all this, until we were the only ones who had not paid tribute to the gods of this grotto fane. We need not have felt dismayed, however, for Atmaas had not forgotten us. Where he kneeled beside us, he produced two tiny miniatures from his red robe, giving one each to my colleague and me. Phata rose first, went to the wall and found a tiny niche for his effigy. As he returned so I rose up and did likewise—at which the chief and his retinue stood up as a man and solemnly applauded.

And all of this time Ow-n-ow kept up his eerie, gliding dance in imitation of the great slugs. Then, of a sudden, the witch-doctor hurled himself down amidst ankle-deep golden nuggets, wriggled on his belly to the base of the largest effigy and kissed its yellow bulk in a sort of frenzied fervor; following which he slowly stood up. Again the chief's party applauded, we two outsiders also, and with that the ritual was over.

We all returned to the trimaran, Ow-n-ow bringing up the rear, and in a solemn silence broken only by the dip of paddles and the grunts of the paddlers, we returned through the great cave to the river. Thus, in the dead of night, Phata Um and I were brought weary but full of wonder back to the pigmy village; and thus, all unbeknown to us, Ow-n-ow had set in motion that monstrous plot with which he intended to destroy us . . .

THE FOLLOWING MORNING I sought out Atmaas and took him to one side. If tomorrow night, at the full of the moon, Phata and I were to witness the calling forth of the actual slug-gods to accept burnt offerings, we would not want to be caught short (as might well have happened in the cavern fane) by being unprepared. Thus I begged Atmaas that he tell me whatever he could of the great creatures and explain the nature of the imminent ceremony. Would it be in any way similar to the proceedings of the previous night?

No, the pigmy youth informed, last night had merely been preparatory to the main event. What we had done last night was a prayer for the increase of the giant gastropods by increasing the number of their effigies. What we would do tomorrow would be an appeasement, that the slug-gods might look favourably upon the N'dolas and the tribe itself prosper. And in answer to my further questions he told me more about the "gods" themselves, though I suspected he was clever enough to realise that I had little or no faith in the creatures as true gods; in which deduction he would have been absolutely correct.

Why (I wanted to know) did the pigmies sacrifice cooked flesh to their gods, when it seemed to me that in the wild the diet of the creatures must surely be raw, be it flora, fauna or whatever? In answer to which Atmaas told me a very strange tale indeed.

The slug-gods (he said) were of a most capricious nature, with moods often as transient as the phases of the moon. Normally they fed on the vegetation of their swamps, though certainly they were omnivorous and could happily consume whatever presented itself. Indeed, it had more than once been apparent that their moods went hand in hand with their diet, which was the main reason that the sacrifice would be of sweet, cooked meats: to sweeten their tempers, as it were, and guide them to beneficent thoughts in respect of their worshippers.

But what in the world did Atmaas mean (I pressed) by his statement about the moods of the gastropods? In what way might their diet possibly determine their actions, beneficent or otherwise? Here the great-headed youth was at a loss. He did not know *how* it could be so, he said, only that it *was* so. Three years ago, for instance, there had been a plague of crocodiles. The rivers, swamps and forests had been alive with them. In the swamps particularly, the creatures were so numerous that the morass heaved with their movements. And so of course a great many were eaten by the slug-gods, being simply ingested before they could get out of the way.

This precipitated a period of nightmarish activity in the gastropods, which only ended when the crocodiles themselves died from lack of food or were killed off by the pigmies, who organised massive hunts specifically for that purpose; to decimate the reptiles and thus deny them as food for the slugs, which in turn should curb the wholly unprecedented— *activities* of those deities.

When I further pressed Atmaas in respect of these activities he was at first loth to answer. But eventually he told me that I must try to understand: the actions of gods were invariably hard for mere mortals to fathom. Who, for instance, might follow the whims of the moon-god in his continuous waxing and waning? Who could say when it would or would not rain? Or when the sun-god would choose to dry up the river? Or why the gods did these things at all? And if the great elemental gods were hard to understand, how then these purely mundane but utterly strange gods of the swamp?

As to what the slug-gods had done to terrorize the pigmy tribe: that was simple. They had adopted the sly, voracious, murderous ways of the crocodiles themselves. That is to say they had become *like* the unfortunate reptiles upon which they had fed, developing despicable habits and growing vile in their attitudes even toward the N'dolas. Aye, and some of them had even made their way through the canyon to the pigmy village; and that had been a very terrible time indeed!

But a slug big as a mammoth is not a crocodile, for all that it adopts the other's ways; and however sly it may be, still it may not come upon a man unobserved. As soon as the villagers knew their danger they called on Ow-n-ow to do something about it; and he, using knowledge passed down from past generations of *ngangas* before him, knew exactly what he must do. Having crocodile appetites without crocodile stealth—which with their bulk would be quite impossible—those few gastropods which made the journey to the village were quite ravenous. They no longer required vegetation but flesh, which for the most part their great size denied them. Ow-n-ow's answer to the problem was therefore simplicity itself. He merely *fed* the great beasts—on rabbits.

At this point I might have fancied that the pigmy youth was pulling my leg, but Atmaas assured me it was so and that he told only the truth. Following the destruction of part of the village wall by the slug-gods as they foraged for meat, on the very next night Ow-n-ow put out a great number of live rabbits tethered to small shrubs. The gastropods, when with the fall of night they returned, immediately took the bait and retreated into the forest shade to digest their victims—and they never returned.

In the early hours of the next morning they were seen making their way back along the river toward the canyon, all atremble and furtive—if that may be imagined—as if anxious now to be gone from the tribe's territory back to their own domain. And it was noted that they were now as timid as—as rabbits! And when Atmaas told me this last, finally I began to understand.

Over all the long, dim centuries since the Beginning, Nature had endowed the gastropods with a unique talent: the short-term ability to assume certain of the characteristics of whichever species they chanced to feed upon in their browsing. How or why this was so was a mystery, but so are so many things in Nature. Perhaps the talent had been a guard against great predators, when by eating the flesh of one such—perhaps accidentally fallen—the slugs would "inherit" its knowledge and so be able to combat or at least avoid the unwanted attentions of others of its sort. Whichever, the puzzle was too great for my fathoming.

Having talked with Atmaas for well over an hour, I wandered freely through the village, amused myself for a little while watching the pigmy children at play, and was thus engaged when Phata found me. He had borrowed a large canoe, he said, and a fishing net. Having watched the village fishermen, he now wished to try their methods for himself. Would I care to join him? Having little else to do, I agreed.

But down at the lakeside, as I dragged Phata's borrowed craft into the water and while he was busy folding his net thus and so, I noticed in the tall reeds close by a grinning, evil face which gazed intently upon our activities. Then the face was gone, but not before I had recognised it as the poisonous visage of Ow-n-ow. He was not done with us, that little man, not by a long shot. And all through the rest of the day that fleeting glimpse of his face, framed by reeds, kept returning to the eye of my memory, so that on several occasions Phata was moved to inquire if aught were amiss . . .

THAT AFTERNOON IT WAS very hot and so we slept in hammocks slung in the shade of our hut; but as evening came on we were up and about to greet our pigmy paramours as they came, all giggles and flashing white pointed teeth, to serve our evening meal. They ate with us, as usual, but no sooner had we begun to eat than there came a surprising diversion. Ow-n-ow, coming upon us from somewhere close at hand, clapped first myself then Phata Um upon our shoulders where we sat, chucked our concubines under their chins, and chuckling (benevolently?) went on his way.

"What in the name of Great Black Yib—?" I began.

"Perhaps the *nganga*'s mother-in-law died!" Phata grinned. "Or maybe he's just unwell, eh?"

"Let's hope so!" I answered. And laughing, however wonderingly, we finished our meal—which act, apart from climbing in a sort of drunken and totally inexplicable stupor to our beds, was all that we were ever able to remember of that entire evening and night!

V

That we had been drugged—the girls, too—did not become apparent until late the next morning, when rising haggard and in great misery from our beds we discovered An'noona, his councillors, a triumphant Ow-n-ow, and several other tribal dignitaries waiting for us to put in an appearance. And once Atmaas had made clear just what was going on—why, then we also knew just whose hand had done the deed! For now we found ourselves accused of an infamy far and away above all others; and of course it was Ow-n-ow who brought the charge against us, and his glib tongue which condemned us as Atmaas stumblingly did his best to translate the *nganga*'s accusations.

Oh!—and how that little monster had excelled himself in his deviltry!

He had noticed (as he now explained to a rapidly growing crowd of silent pigmies) a certain furtiveness about us in the fane of the slug-gods; and he had also observed the way our fingers lingered over the golden nuggets and effigies in that holy place. Then, because he had not wished to believe that we were capable of such evil thoughts and unnatural avaricious urges, he had put the matter to the back of his mind, telling himself that he—even Ow-n-ow, a *nganga* of the greatest power and perception—must be mistaken.

But then, later, he had seen us with a canoe out on the lake. What had we been doing, he had wondered? We had seemed to be fishing, and yet . . . could we have been practising the art of canoeing? If so, why?

Finally, last night, we had retired early, very early indeed, and this too had puzzled the witch-doctor (or so he said).

Indeed his suspicions were such that he waited until dusk to see us stealing through the quiet village to the lakeside, where we boarded our canoe and paddled away up river into the evening mist. He had then returned to our hut, intending to waken our sleeping-partners and question them as to our mysterious activities. He was unable to waken them, however, for they were in a deep, drugged sleep and would remain so until the drug had burned itself out of their systems. We (quite obviously) had drugged them in order to hide our absence from them.

Thoroughly alarmed now, Ow-n-ow had waited all through the night; and finally we had returned through the early morning mists, mooring our canoe and stealing back to our hut in a most suspicous and secretive manner. Then the *nganga* went to our canoe and discovered, within its hollowed interior where doubtless it had fallen from one of our pockets, a golden, thumb-sized miniature of a slug-god! So saying, and as Atmaas continued to translate, Ow-n-ow held up the alleged proof of our guilt for all to see.

And now the pigmies had drawn back from us, their mouths open in shock; even Atmaas (though I could see he was torn two ways) staring up at us in a sort of astonished disbelief; aye, and our pigmy paramours too. Frankly, I was too stunned to make a move, but Phata Um suffered no such restriction. He strode forward, his great hands reaching down and toward Ow-n-ow's scrawny neck. And certainly he would have killed the treacherous, lying little dog there and then— had he not found himself staring down the flaring snouts of half-a-dozen blowpipes, appearing almost magically in the hands of pigmies whose services had doubtless been acquired by the *nganga* against just such an eventuality.

Now we were ringed about by the tiny warriors, and quick as a flash our accuser had climbed like a monkey to our hut and disappeared within. A moment passed and we could hear the witch-doctor rummaging about—then another moment in complete silence—and finally, dramatically, the small fiend reappeared at the top of the ladder, his hands weighted with a pair of golden miniatures large as babies' skulls.

That was enough, the dog had done for us!

Oh, I suppose we might have argued, but I doubt that we could have won. The "evidence" against us was far too strong. We were haggard-looking, as well we would be after a night of furtive canoeing and temple desecrating; the girls we slept with could neither confirm nor deny our presence through the night, for of course "we" had drugged them; and most damning of all, Ow-n-ow had produced those golden miniatures, proof positive that we had indeed robbed the fane of the slug-gods.

And in our favour—nothing! We had no proof at all of our innocence, not a shred of it, and any denials or counter-accusations we might make must be through Atmaas, who would surely be seen as biased in our favour. And so, un-protesting, still a little dumb-founded by it all, we were taken away, bound hand and foot and locked in a tiny bamboo stockade or cage; and there we spent the day, working at the thongs that bound us and dreaming of sweet revenge against the little black devil whose evil wiles had brought us to this pass.

Toward late afternoon Atmaas came to see us, and just a single glance at the long and doleful face beneath that heavy, bulbous head of his was sufficient to tell us the worst. The pigmy council had met; we were guilty; our punishment would be . . . would be—

But he did not need to say any more; even a blind man could have seen our futures . . .

How would it be done? I asked the youth. When? But before he could answer I went on to tell him of our innocence, of Own-ow's treachery. I may even have started to babble a little (for certainly I was afraid for my life) but Phata Um's elbow in my ribs warned me to be quiet. And of course he was right for the N'dolas despised cowards, and Atmaas was a N'dola after all.

Finally, after sitting in a sort of sad silence for many minutes, at last the lad told us the worst, the how and the when of it. Which did nothing at all to calm us or allay our burgeoning fears.

It would be tonight! Oh, and there would be sweeter meat than pig and buffalo on the menu of the slug-gods this night. As to how: we would be staked out at the edge of the swamp, amidst the slaughtered, roasted beast carcasses; and when the great gastropods came in answer to Ow-n-ow's calling, then we would be put quickly out of our misery by a fusillade of poisoned darts. We would see the slug-gods, aye—and at very close quarters indeed—but mercifully we would never know the slow, deadly burn of their digestive juices.

Only one more thing I asked of Atmaas before he left us: that he ensure the poisons would be quick. In answer he told me that I need have no fear. One or two darts would merely paralyse, but five or six would certainly kill. Since we would be feathered by at least a dozen darts each . . . and he shrugged, however sadly, and left us to the speeding hours.

When the river mists were beginning to curl and the sun

was sinking toward the high horizon of stirless trees, then they came for us. We were bundled without ceremony into a log canoe which took the tail position in a large procession of these crude craft, being paddled round the island and along the tree-shaded river toward the great canyon. And if our single previous trip along that way had seemed a long one, this present journey passed in a flash.

For to my mind it was only a very short time indeed before our craft beached on a loamy, swampy shore; and there we were lifted from the canoe and carried to an area of comparatively dry ground, and propped with our backs to the boles of trees so rotten that they were close to falling. Now that we could gaze all about, we saw that this was none other than that great swamp where the canyon widened into a sunken valley; and that apart from this small clearing at the edge of the river, the swamp pressed close, dark and ominous on all sides.

Never in my life had I looked upon a region of grimmer aspect than the one which presented itself in that swamp. Huge humps of nameless, rotting vegetable debris rose everywhere, between which the mud bubbled up with a yellow froth of sulphur. Massy leaves, green and black and glossy, lay low to the surface, cloaking the movements of things which wriggled, crawled or swam through the quaggy morass beneath. And occasionally there would come a commotion of foliage and flesh, a thrashing of leathery limbs and clashing of jaws as battle was joined or prey snapped up; and in a little while the eerie silence would once again descend, only to be broken by the distant screams of predators or the noisy emission of pockets of gas bursting in great bubbles which oozed up from the depths of the bog.

"A great place for gods!" said Phata, his voice full of a doleful sarcasm. "But better by far for demons . . ."

By now the pigmies had built fires in the clearing close to the water's edge, where they proceeded to roast the many carcasses which they had brought with them from the village. And as the light quickly faded so the aroma of cooked flesh began to mingle with the fetors of the marsh, and the figures of the pigmies where they worked and moved became as grey ghosts in that awful twilight.

"Phata," I said, my voice a whisper, "this looks like the end. Man, I'm frightened!"

"Aye, me too," growled my friend, "but the end is not yet—not quite. I've been working on these bonds of mine, and I believe—*uh!*" And for a moment he fell silent and peered about with lowered brows, making sure that his actions went unobserved. "My hands," he finally continued, "are free—but I'll keep them behind my back a while longer. What of the thongs that bind you?"

"No good," I shook my head. "I haven't your strength, Phata. But listen, if you can move your feet a little, get them tucked in behind my back—"

Gloomier still the glade as I got my stiff fingers to work on the knots which bound Phata's feet, and as the fires burned lower so the golden edge of the moon appeared above the forest and distant cliffs. When Ow-n-ow saw that first moonbeam come stealing into the darkening clearing, then he laughed hysterically—like a maniac where he stood at the water's edge—and in another moment he laid back his head and gave a great baying howl which echoed all through the horror-laden swamp.

VI

Frantically now I worked on Phata's knots, for the fires were turned to embers, the sacrifices all prepared and the night closing in like a great black fist. And away in the swamp there were flickering blue ghosts, faint as foxfire but mobile and monstrous. The pigmies had seen these lights too, and the bulk of them soon retreated to their canoes. Some were left, however, who beat around the edge of the clearing with clubs and long, sharp knives, keeping away the crocodiles and other creatures attracted by the far-drifted aroma of cooked flesh.

Aye, and others of the pigmies there were too, who simply stood in a group with their blowpipes and waited. And then there was An'noona, seated in a sort of open, bamboo sedan, with his bearers close to hand; and finally Ow-n-ow, the grinning black devil, who now commenced that gliding, twin-horned dance of his, that impersonation of a slug as he moved about the clearing. Every few minutes he would pause, cup his hands to his mouth and utter a strange, coughing bark, the snort of a wild, alien thing. And in answer to this calling—

The blue fires came closer, glowing through the rotting, creeper-festooned swamp, moving less aimlessly now and with a sort of terrible purpose. And suddenly it dawned on me that this must be the sign of the slug-gods; that they glowed with that same luminosity as their lesser, aquatic cousins cast up on Theem'hdra's shores. In the instant of re-alisation, the last knot binding Phata's feet came loose in my fumbling fingers—and in that self-same moment the blow-pipe marksmen formed themselves into a line.

Ow-n-ow's dance was no longer a dance so much as a darting here and there in the darkness and a crazed snuffling and snorting; but worse by far were the answering calls which now issued from out the swamp itself! The slug-gods were closing with the clearing; it would not be very long before Ow-n-ow ordered that we be killed, following which the rest of the pigmies would flee the clearing and doubtless watch the spectacle of their deities feasting from the safety of the river.

No sooner had this last thought come to me than An'noona's bearers picked up his litter and bore the chief swiftly away toward the river. The beaters at the edge of the clearing likewise took their departure, their actions made hurried and clumsy through a shivery terror which was now clearly apparent in their every move. Until only Ow-n-ow and the marksmen remained, and they too fearsomely a-tremble as they cast all about in the night with bulging, staring eyes.

By now the bluely luminescent slug-gods were close indeed and their coughing calls loud in the darkness; and lesser predators must surely have left the immediate vicinity as they sensed the approach of those Lords of the Morass, for apart from the aforementioned calls and the continual bursting of gassy bubbles, all was now silent. Even Ow-n-ow had ceased his dancing and calling, and he stood with the marksmen where they awaited his command. Then—

Suddenly, with a great rupturing of squelchy, rotten toadstools, one of the towering vegetable humps at the far side of the clearing was shoved aside; and in the next instant a great shape moved slowly into the glade. We saw it—outlined in its own blue glow, silhouetted against the night—that vast slugshape whose eyestalks stood out like horns from its head, whose *motion* was a slow contraction and expansion which was yet sufficient to glide the thing along at a not inconsiderable speed.

Even as the great gastropod appeared, a second creature's head and waving eyestalks slid into view at the edge of the clearing close by; and now Ow-n-ow gave his near-hysterical word of command, and at once the pigmy marksmen lifted their blowpipes to their lips. This was what Phata had waited for. As the pigmies moved, so he moved.

In one motion he turned to me, ripped away the thongs that bound me to my tree and scooped me to his shoulder. No time to work on my actual bonds, however, those bindings which yet held my feet and hands fast; for even now a great head swayed out of the darkness, bluely-illumined eyestalks turning this way and that, and a corrugated grey-blue bulk loomed close.

Then I heard Phata's grunt as a dart struck him, and almost simultaneously I felt a swift stab at my own shoulder where another poisoned missile found its mark. In another moment we were away, Phata plunging into the swamp, wading chest-deep through slime and weed and vilely smelling rot, and me over his shoulder, head down, my face brushing the very skin of that quaggy, scummy surface.

Screams of fury behind us and harshly gabbled orders— and the *hiss* of darts cleaving the noxious air—and a second sharp pain in my back—and Phata grunting three, four times in rapid succession as his broad back and shoulder took the brunt of the fusillade. But then the clearing was behind us, lost in a boggy mist, through which the many blue-glowing forms of the slug-gods were seen faint as ghost-lights receding in our fetid wake.

For a little while longer Phata ploughed through nameless mire, where at any moment we may well have disappeared for ever beneath its surface, but then at last he
stumbled up on to a sort of island and dumped me against
the broad bole of a squat, stunted tree. It was the work of
mere seconds then for my mighty friend to tear away my
bonds, and at last I was free—but free to face what fearsome
future?

For already I could feel the poison from the darts working
in my system, numbing my mind and body and blurring my
vision, though the darts themselves had been shaken loose
during our flight through the swamp. Phata, having taken
perhaps half-a-dozen darts—a lethal dose according to
Atmaas—must have been in an even worse condition, but so
far his enormous vitality was buoying him up. Even he was
beginning to succumb, however, and as he swayed before me
where I sat with my back to the tree I could see that it would
soon be all up with him.

"Well, old friend," I said in a gasping voice which surprised
me with its faintness. "Is this the end for us, then?"

"For me, most likely," he answered, "for I took too many of
their damned darts. And you?"

"Just two—but enough to stretch me out for a while, I
fancy. The swamp will do the rest."

"At least you have a chance—" Phata began, but I angrily
cut him off with:

"You would have had a far better chance, great fool—all
the chance in the world—if you'd just looked after yourself!
A man like you, why!—it would take more than this measly
swamp to stop you!"

"I've no regrets, my friend," he grunted, "except perhaps I

would dearly have loved to snap Ow-n-ow's twiggy neck!
Also, it's a bit of a disappointment to die rich . . ."

I tried to stand, to embrace him, to weep in my frustration,
but no longer had the strength for any of these things. Instead
I merely collapsed against my tree, shivering in a poison-
induced fever, barely aware that Phata had broken off a stout
branch for a weapon and now stood over me, legs spread, club
dangling from his great hand.

When he spoke again his voice seemed to come to me
from a thousand miles away, but even so it carried hope. He
was never one to give in easily, Phata Um.

"If you can make it through the night, perhaps you'll get
out of here yet. And if I can stay active long enough—who
knows? Maybe the poison is less potent than Atmaas be-
lieves. I may yet work it out of my system."

"Phata," I managed to mumble, "you could be right. I pray
that you are . . ." And after that, all else was a drugged nightmare.

A nightmare, yes, for the things I seem to remember of
that night were never meant to be in any ordered, sane or
waking world. How best to describe it?

I became for the most part unconscious, but every now
and then I would stir up from the grip of the drug, usually
to discover that I had been awakened by the sounds or com-
motions of combat! Combat, aye, for Phata had not succumbed (though I shall never be able to comprehend the
sheer, raw power of will and physical energy which kept
him on his feet) and now he had the swamp's predators to
deal with.

Up they came out of that near-luminous murk; the sliding
things, the snapping things, and always Phata there to greet

them with his club. And oh the snarls of crocodiles with broken jaws and shattered skulls, the hissing of snakes split asunder, the squelching of crushed leech-things fat as a man's thigh, and the squeal of great bats knocked clean out of the misty, reeking air before they could make clear their intent! And never a one of them allowed to touch me, not while Phata Um retained what little must now remain of his strength and senses.

But in the end he was done, even Phata, and I felt his hands on my numb face and heard his whisper in my weirdly singing ears:

"Eythor," he said, kneeling beside me, his huge shoulder to the bole of the squat tree, his arms hanging limp. "The night is near spent and a dull glow lights the eastern sky. I too am spent, however, and I know it. It is the heart, the lungs, the organs which the pigmy poisons attack, and I have not worked them out of my system but into it . . ." And he paused for long moments, his breathing ragged where he slumped against me.

"I have noted," he finally continued, "how in this last hour the swamp's lesser monsters have moved away—and I know why. The great slugs, in their nocturnal foraging, are headed this way. The sacrifices were doubtless succulent and welcome, but not enough. The slugs are night-feeders, Eythor, and as dawn approaches they feed all the more rapidly, taking their fill before returning to some secret place to sleep out the day.

"Now, I am finished and I know it—but you can survive. You may live—but not if the slugs find you. So I have split my club to give it a sharp point, and now I go to do what I can to keep the great beasts at bay. I think they are simple creatures, like their lesser cousins, and if so they may fear me and my stick more than I fear them.

"You may not see me again, Eythor, for which reason I now say farewell!" Then I felt his cold lips on my brow, and somehow I forced open my eyes to see him lurch to his feet and stagger away into swirling, misty mire. I would have called him back, but my paralysis was now almost complete, my fever at its peak.

The last I saw of him, his silhouette was limned against an oh so faint, uncertain light—that of the coming dawn. But there were other lights, and far less friendly: gliding blue ghosts that told of the rapid encroachment of the swamp's giant gastropods. Then, for what seemed a very long time, I knew no more . . .

VII

. . . When next I recovered consciousness I was very weak, but I knew that I had survived the ordeal. The dullness had passed from my senses and though my body and limbs felt like lead, still they were mine once more—and at least they *had* feelings! So it may be imagined the degree of my shock and horror when, upon opening my eyes, I found myself staring up into the brown orbs of a grimacing pigmy face!

For a single instant my heart almost stopped—but in the next moment I knew that this was Atmaas, that the grimace was no more than a concerned, questioning smile distorted in my eyes by the abnormal bulge of his head, and that somehow Lady Fortune once more beamed upon me. I tried to smile in return—and immediately remembered Phata Um.

The joy occasioned by my awakening passed from Atmaas' face as a cloud passing over the face of the sun, and so I knew the worst. After that I quickly grew very tired—indeed, I believe a great deal of my spirit passed out of me—and I desired to know no more. Before I slept a pigmy girl, my own sweet concubine, fed me a warming broth (for certainly I could not feed myself), following which exhaustion overtook me . . .

MY RECOVERY FROM that time forward was slow but sure, and as time passed so I pieced together the story of what had happened—at least from Atmaas' point of view—during my long period of unconsciousness. Which leads me to the final and strangest part of my story.

All through that first long night, while I lay in a drugged coma at the foot of a tree on that small island in the mud, and while Phata Um stood over and protected me, the pigmies had waited to see what they might see. When we escaped and ran (rather, when Phata ran with me draped over his shoulder), Ow-n-ow had described our flight as a declaration of guilt, for rather than stay and face the justice of the slug-gods we had chosen the unknown terrors of the swamp. It would avail us naught; the pigmies would wait until morning and if we had not returned by then they would know for certain that we were finished.

Then they had sat in the safety of their canoes and watched the glowing gastropods as they glided through the glade of the sacrifice and took their burnt offerings. And the hours had slipped by and Gleeth the smiling moon-god walked the night sky of Theem'hdra, so that when the first glow of dawn was glimpsed down the river, then Ow-n-ow declared that we

must be dead and the slug-gods appeased. With the departure
of the great gastropods from the island, the chief and his councillors, the *nganga* too and certain of the tribal elders, returned
to make sure that indeed the sacrifice had been received.

And it was seen that all the offerings had been taken, to
the very last pig, and so for a further quarter the N'dolas
would surely prosper. Then, after clearing away the gory debris of that vast repast, lesser dishes were prepared and the
pigmies broke their fast and conjectured amongst themselves
upon the fate of the two who had dared profane the temple
of the slug-gods.

Most certainly we were dead and gone, they were all agreed,
devoured by the swamp's predators or sunken in its quick-
sand coils; for the marksmen with their blowpipes were certain that their fusillade had been utterly lethal. And so the
sun rose up higher in the sky and steamed away the mists,
and the N'dolas prepared to take their leave of the place.
Which was when, in broad daylight, the incredible and completely unbelievable took place before their very eyes.

Out from the swamp (where by now it should be resting in
some deep, shaded and secret grove), up on to the island of
the sacrifice, glided the lone shape of a great gastropod. And
beneath its waving eyestalks, held loosely in a mouth of
rough plates like giant rasps, the figure of a man was clearly
discernible, head down and limbs limply dangling. My figure,
as Atmaas was later to discover. As the pigmies on the island
fled before the gliding shape of this mighty Lord of the
Morass, so the creature proceeded to the centre of the clearing where I was deposited gently upon the sun-dried sward.

Safely out on the river once more and anchored to its bed,
the log craft of the pigmies bobbed gently as their boggling

crews followed in astonishment the actions of the slug-god where its slate-grey bulk stood over my crumpled form. And there they stayed as the day drew on and the sun rose to its highest, hottest point. And all the while they whispered about what it all meant, that this great slug-god should thus jeopardise its own life by standing out in the searing rays of the sun and giving shade to one who had robbed its temple.

Or could it perhaps be, the whisper began to be heard, that the outsiders had not been guilty after all?

Ow-n-ow heard the whisper, too, and grew wrathful. No, he protested, the man had been brought back by the great gastropod as a punishment. Plainly the man was not yet dead, for every now and then he would give a twitch, or move however fitfully. Patently the slug-god waited for him to awaken, when without a doubt it would straightway devour him—but not before he was made to see the end to which his iniquities had brought him.

But An'noona, who was growing more doubtful by the hour, could find little of any merit in Ow-n-ow's assessment of the situation; moreover, Atmaas was openly critical of the evil *nganga*'s explanation of this hitherto unheard of occurrence. Why, it could plainly be seen (Atmaas declared) that the slug-god *stood guard* over the outsider! It suffered the very rays of the sun upon its hide, which must in the end destroy it, simply to give him shade!

So the day wore on, and the sun beamed down as its orb moved across the sky, and the corrugated hide of the slug-god dried out and lost its greyish sheen. Occasionally a great croc would slide out of the swamp on its belly and make its way to where I lay—only to have the vast gastropod block its path with great grey body and cavernous grinding jaws . . .

By the time the shadows of afternoon began to lengthen the slug-god was plainly suffering. Its hide, completely dry now and beginning to turn a dull, sickly purple, had developed sores and cracks, and its movements had lost all of their previous co-ordination and rhythmic sinuosity. The creature was dying, which anyone but a fool must surely see.

And that could only mean that Ow-n-ow was a fool, for still he insisted—however blusteringly—that he was correct. A fool, aye . . . or a damned liar!

Finally An'noona lost his temper and put it to the *nganga* that if he was so well versed in the ways of the gods, perhaps he should go ashore on to the island and ask the great creature what it was about. Ow-n-ow, to give him his due, turned on the chief and demanded to know if An'noona had lost faith in his *nganga*? At which Atmaas had leaped to his feet in the chief's trimaran to confront the furious witch-doctor and curse him roundly for a liar and a blackguard.

And Ow-n-ow had no other choice but to do as the chief had suggested, for as a man the N'dolas were on their feet behind An'noona and his chief councillor, and the *nganga* could see that to refuse the challenge would be to lose face irretrievably and relinquish forever his power in the tribe of the N'dolas.

Nor was he given the chance to wriggle out of it; for while no order had been given, still the crew of the chief's craft brought the trimaran around until the tip of its larboard outrigger was touching the island, and all eyes were on the *nganga* when at last he stepped ashore. For a moment he stood there, seemingly undecided, with his back to the river and its flotilla of canoes; but then he squared up, stood erect, and finally he stepped forward. Right up to the rear of the slug-god he went, where its hide was cracked now like old leather, with some vile ichor oozing out of the cracks, and reaching out his hand he touched the purplish bulk of the thing.

At this a low, awed murmur went up from the pigmies in their massed canoes; but the gastropod moved not at all, though its great body pulsed as it had pulsed for many a long hour, listlessly and with no sign of cognition. Only the mighty head showed life, and even there the eyestalks drooped and were visibly a-tremble; and occasionally the great mouth would grind on nothing, in a sort of dumb agony.

Taking heart, Ow-n-ow moved slowly along the length of the slug's body until he approached its head. There he paused, and the eyes at the end of their rubbery stalks gazed dully upon him where he stood. At that very moment, even as the tiny witch-doctor and the massive gastropod came face to face, so I had chosen to move. With spastic jerks and twitches I changed my position on the ground where I lay; whereupon Ow-n-ow gave a cry of rage, snatched a long, curving knife from his belt and hurled himself upon me—or would have done but for the intervention of the mighty slug.

As if seeing Ow-n-ow for the first time—even as the *nganga* flew at me where I lay in a helpless heap—the slug-god was suddenly galvanised into action. The massive head swung down, the great jaws opened and snapped shut on Ow-n-ow's small black body, and the grinding plates moved with the in-exorable, utterly undeniable motion of glaciers. The *nganga* screamed—once—and then was still; and with a toss of its slaty head the huge beast hurled his mutilated doll corpse into the swamp.

Then the body of the beast stiffened and in another mo-ment it rolled slowly over on to its side. But even dying it was careful that I was not crushed. And finally all was still, and the gastropod lay beside me, its monstrous head close to my own.

For a long, long time then there were only the lapping of the river and the sounds of the swamp, and even these seemed muted. Then An'noona commanded that I be lifted up and taken aboard his trimaran; and finally, silently, overawed by all they had seen and with low-mouthed prayers on their lips, the pigmies departed from the swamp of the slug-gods and returned to their island village.

WHEN I WAS well again I went back to the swamp with Atmaas and together we ventured into the glade of the sacrifice. There the remains of the slug-god—its tremendous, cartilaginous skeleton and huge rough plates of vestigial shell—lay where the beast had fallen, picked clean by lesser monsters. There, too, was that which explained everything, at least to me.

Amidst shreds of corrugated hide and fragments of chalky bone I found a smaller skeleton, that of a man. The rings on its fingers were Phata's, and round the bony neck was the heavy golden chain given him in friendship by An'noona.

The Wine of the Wizard

Editorial Note:

Patently this penultimate tale *is* a fiction; but knowing what I do of Thelred Gustau's own disappearance, and something of the circumstances surrounding the disappearance of his nephew at that earlier time, I like to conjecture that its words fly perhaps not too wildly astray of the mark. As for the actual meat of the story, which commences proper with Chapter III: that is a direct translation from Teh Atht's writings.

MYLAKHRION'S POWDER, CONCOCTED AT GREAT EXPENSE FROM HIS OWN FORMULA & WITH *EXACT* REGARD TO MEASURES & INGREDIENTS, MUST I FEAR REMAIN AN UNKNOWN QUANTITY. THE MEREST PINCH, TAKEN AS SNUFF, PRODUCES MARVELS GALORE, WHOSE EFFECTS ARE SO WONDERFUL THAT THE POWDER COULD WELL PROVE ADDICTIVE. WHAT, THEN, ITS POTENCY WHEN BREWED UP IN A MEASURE OF WINE SUCH AS MY AWFUL ANCESTOR WAS WONT TO IMBIBE?

         . . . TEH ATHT.

I

"Do not drink it!" Thelred Gustau warned his nephew, Erik, as he passed him a tiny phial of greenish powder. "Merely prepare the wine—a sort of sherry, you say—and let me have it when the stuff is properly mature. I require it for certain tests, and of course I don't know exactly what this powder is or what it can do. Its mildest effect, I suspect, is to produce grotesque hallucinations. We shall see. But since Teh Atht specifies that it might be used in this wine of his 'awful ancestor,' and since you have a talent for producing these home-brewed concoctions—"

"Sherry," said Gustau's young visitor. "Quite definitely. But uncle, how old did you say this recipe is?" And he smiled, however wanly.

His uncle glanced up from his work-bench, where already he was absorbed once more in his work, and said, "Hmm?—its age?" The scientist frowned. "Why, no," he answered, "I can't really tell you how old it is—not with any measure of certainty—but I believe it predates the dinosaurs."

"That's what I thought you said." Erik managed another smile. "Very well, I'll brew your wine for you. Perhaps it will help take my mind off things."

Now his uncle suddenly grew concerned. He stood up and came round his oddly littered bench to lay a solicitous hand on the younger man's shoulder. "Listen, Erik. I know how bad things have been for you, and I don't want to sound cruel or uncaring, but you're not the first man who has had to face up to such a thing. Give yourself time. I know she meant everything to you and there's a place inside you that feels empty and dead, but it will pass. Believe your old uncle, it's not the end of the world."

Erik Gustau nodded. "I know, I know. But it feels like the end of my world. Uncle, she was so young! How do such things happen? If there's a God, how can He let such things happen?"

The older man could only shake his head.

ERIK GUSTAU WAS only twenty-three years of age. Tall, blond, handsome as all the Gustaus were, he was a young man in his physical prime. And yet now there was this air of total dejection about him. A great light had gone out of his life; out of his eyes, too, which had once been bright and piercing blue. Now they were dull, disinterested, only very rarely given to smiling. What good the money his grandfather had willed him, when the one he had built his world around was no more? Shoulders which had been strong and square drooped a little, and a walk once bounding and full of life seemed now the measured tread of an old man . . .

II

And now, with the tiny phial of greenish powder in his pocket, Erik Gustau made his way across the heart of London from his uncle's Woolwich address, and as he went he almost forgot the reason for his visit. Ever uppermost in his mind there loomed his lost love's face, and again and again he would find himself cursing the name of that incurable disease whose insidious tentacles had taken her from him and into an early tomb.

He knew of course that his uncle had only set him the task in hand to free him from the dreadful lassitude which sorrow had seemed to stamp into him; he knew also that there were greater talents to whom the task would have been better entrusted. Nevertheless he had decided to undertake its completion, if only to satisfy the other's curiosity and let the older man believe that in his way he had helped him recover from his bereavement.

Thus when he returned to the beautiful home he had readied for his lost love, and to the anxious servants who waited there, he set to work at once and brewed up a gallon of Mylakhrion's wine, applying himself diligently to the notes his uncle had prepared for him and adhering as best he could to the incredibly ancient formula or recipe. And so, some seven weeks later, the wine came into being . . .

IT CAME WITH a warning from Benson, Erik's gentleman's gentleman, who awakened him one morning from miserable, repetitious dreams with the ominous statement that something had "exploded" in the cellar! He at once remembered the wine, stored away in bottles for almost two months, and clad only in dressing-gown and slippers rushed downstairs.

In the cellar he found seven of his eight carefully labelled bottles shattered, their heady contents hurled to oblivion, and the eighth with its cork still bounding about the floor while a red fountain splashed the whitewashed ceiling. When at last he managed to ram the cork home again in the neck of the bottle, all that remained of a gallon of Mylakhrion's wine was an amount somewhat greater than a large glassful. This sole remaining bottle he carefully wiped down and reverently carried with him to his study on the ground floor.

There, sitting in an easy chair with the bottle on an occasional table before him, he dimly remembered something of his uncle's warning not to drink it, and something else of the tale accompanying it: of a time lost to man in the mists of predawn, where the first great civilisations of man were raised in a primal continent. And with the morning sun striking through his window and setting the wine to glowing a dull red, it suddenly seemed to him that he could smell the warm winds of that time-lost land and taste the salt of the mighty Unknown Ocean which washed its golden strand.

But then he shook his head. No, it was only the fumes from the escaped wine in the cellar that he could smell; his imagination had done the rest. Still, the red-glowing stuff looked remarkably palatable through the clear glass of the bottle. Almost unconsciously he removed the cork, poured a small glass half full, and set it upon the table close to the window. As he did so a heady fragrance rose from the bottle and seemed to hang round his head in an almost tangible cloud.

Now the sun caught the rim of the fine wineglass and set it a-sparkle, and mirrored through the wine Erik could see his garden, all umber-tinted and reversed by the wine and the curve of the glass. Reversed as he wished he might reverse his life—or end it altogether.

Almost without noticing it, he took the glass in his hand, raised it to his lips, and sipped a half-mouthful, washing his palate and allowing that nectar of primal origins first to cool, then to sear his astonished throat! Unsteadily he replaced the glass by the window, half-rose to his feet, and fell back in his chair as a wave of dizziness passed over him. And again his eyes went to the glass.

Ah! But this time he saw no umber garden reflected in its bowl. Instead he saw—or read, or heard, it really does not matter—the beginnings of a strange story from a world far distant and lost in the dim mists of time . . .

III

There had been a time when the sheer cliffs of Shildakor were a mile high, utterly impregnable and cursed by the long-dead wizard for whom they were named, so that no man might ever climb them. But that had been more than five hundred years ago in Theem'hdra's youth, when the Primal Land knew a strange era of half-barbaric civilisation and of sorcery, and when Bhur-Esh was a mighty city-state between the Unknown Ocean and Shildakor's sheltering cliffs.

Now those cliffs were great rounded nodding heads of pumice and volcanic rock, riddled with caves which stared blindly out over the Unknown Ocean, where the unruly waves were calmed even to this day by the olden, stony promontories whose twin arms once guarded the bay of Bhur-Esh. For spells and enchantments grow old even as continents and worlds, and Nature's own forces are at times more powerful than the builded walls of men or the mumbled runes of wizards.

Out in the Unknown Ocean, Ashtah the volcano isle still rumbled; but never so loudly as on that day, when rising up from the deeps, it had hurled molten death into the Vale of Bhur-Esh, forming a great roaring ramp between boiling sea and cliffs and removing forever the city and its rulers and the farmers who tended their beasts and crops outside the city's walls and beneath the sheer and mighty Ghost Cliffs. All of them gone, all but a handful of survivors, swept away by rivers of rock from Earth's heart; a proud people no more but a paragraph written upon a single scorched page of a planet's history. And in this Bhur-Esh was little different from other cities and civilisations which would follow down the aeons, though geologic ages would pass before Atlantis and Mu, and a handful of years more before Pompeii . . .

But after a time, when wind and weather began to work their ways—when the lava slopes grew green again and the great fishes came back to the warm seas, and when Ashtah settled down quietly to smoke and smoulder far out in the Unknown Ocean beyond the bay—then the descendants of the holocaust's survivors returned and made their homes in the lava caves, and they built stout doors and windows to guard against the inclement seasons. They floored their dwellings with planks cut from trees felled atop the now gentle cliffs, and the skins of animals were the rugs on their floors. They built garden walls, and brick chimneys for their fires, and fishing boats to go out in the bay for food; and as the years passed so the people prospered and grew in number. They became skilled at hollowing out or discovering new dwellings in the lava, and used the debris of their work as soil; and their terraces went down from the cliffs to the sea, laden with trellis-grown grapes rich and red from the fertile pumice.

So the people of New Bhur-Esh flourished, and where the former city and citizens had been utterly self-contained and -sufficient, they traded their wines with the wild, dark-haired

Northmen and the merchants of Thandopolis, who came in
their dragonships and merchantmen; and all in all they were
a happy people, even living in the constant shade of Ashtah,
which sometimes rumbled mightily or vented great columns
of smoke into the clear blue skies of Theem'hdra. Aye, even
in the shade of the volcano—and of the greater evil it
housed—they did their best to be happy.

As for that greater evil: it was a shadow fallen on New
Bhur-Esh out of the East, the necromantic shadow of a black
sorcerer from the coastal forests beyond the nameless river.
For even as the population of the lava valley grew and prospered, so rumours came from the East of a Yhemni Magus
whose ebon skin was never so black as his heart, which was
so steeped in sin as to be putrid.

Hurled forth from outraged Grypha of the Hrossaks,
spurned by the inhabitants of the jungle-hidden cities of his
native coastal forests, driven from beneath the walls of
Thinhla under threat of death by fire, the necromancer Arborass sought new lodgings—and rumour had it that he sought
them in New Bhur-Esh. Now when they heard this whispered abroad, the elders of the valley tribe (for they were
considered and thought of themselves as a tribe as opposed to
a nation) came together in meeting to decide what was to be
done about this Arborass, and this was their decision:

Just as Grypha and the Black Cities and Thinhla had turned
him and his acolytes back from their borders, so must they;
for it was of old renown that if ever a wizard made unop-
posed camp within a town, then that town was doomed by its
own slothfulness, and must soon dance to the wizard's tune.
Thus when the black, skull-prowed ship of Arborass sailed
out of the West to cleave the calm waters of the bay with

night-black oars, and when the necromancer himself stood up in the prow and gazed upon the valley's strand, he saw only the sharp weapons and fires of them that waited on his landing, and the sharper eyes of wise men who would not suffer a wizard to set foot upon their land.

And the necromancer Arborass swelled up in his rage, and his head was a great black shaven skull with eyes of fire, which towered above a billowing cloak of black velvet embroidered with silver runes. He stood in the prow of his devil's boat and raised his taloned arms as if to administer a great curse—then calmed himself and said:

"So, I am threatened with knives and fires, who have come these long sea-miles only to be your friend and protector. So be it . . . but before ten days are done, and before the setting of the tenth sun, you shall welcome me ashore. Even with open arms shall I be welcomed. Aye, and my weary rowers also, who tire of the sea's toil." And as the oars dipped and turned his ship seaward once more, so the people of New Bhur-Esh saw the necromancer's jest—for his rowers were sere mummies whose semblance of life was a blasphemy commanded by the necromancer himself!

IV

Now among them that gathered on the beach and saw this thing, and watched Arborass rowed out to sea once more by his mummied crew, was a lad of some thirteen years called Ayrish: which meant foundling. Learning the fisherman's trade, Ayrish lived with the poorest family of the cave-dwellers, for they had found him on their doorstep as a babe and had grudgingly taken him in. What were his origins no man could say, but it was thought a village girl had been his mother, and that in her shame she had lain him on a doorstep to be found.

Ayrish was big for his age and handsome, but ever he wore the marks of much toiling and the black bruises of beatings. The master of his house was a drunkard and bully; his three true sons were older than Ayrish, sullen and full of spite; so that in a word, his lot was not a happy one. Nevertheless he worked harder than the others for his keep and grew stronger each day, and without a mother's care waxed supple of limb and hard of will. And the three he called brothers, though they were not his brothers and dealt sorely with him, were a little afraid of him; for where they were dull and ran to idle fatness, the wit of Ayrish was sharp and his muscles firm, so that they thought one day he might turn on them.

Now, watching the necromancer Arborass rowing out to sea, and seeing that his course lay straight for the volcano isle Ashtah, Ayrish spoke up, saying: "You should have killed him, you men!"

"What do you know, boy?" an Elder at once rounded on him. "And who are you, a motherless chick not long hatched, to talk of killing? Arborass is a necromancer and wizard; aye, and a hard one to kill, be sure!"

"Nevertheless, you should have tried," answered the lad, undaunted. "The rumours say he is a fire-wizard. He commands the fires that rage."

Now another Elder grabbed Ayrish and shook him. "Boy, we did not let him land, you saw that. Why then should we fear him? And what fires may he command out on the bosom of the sea?"

All of them laughed then, and none louder than the louts Ayrish called brothers, until he said: "And what of Ashtah? Is not the volcano a raging fire, however much he seems to sleep? And what if Arborass wakes him? See, the wizard steers a steady course!" And all of them saw that the lad was right.

"He would not dare return," the Elders blustered. Ayrish, struggling free of them, said nothing. But to himself he said, *We shall see, in ten more days*!

THREE NIGHTS AND two days passed with never sight nor sound of Arborass and his magics; but on the third day, at noon, a mighty column of steam shot up from Ashtah and formed a leaden blanket in the sky. All through the afternoon the boiling continued, and an early, unseasonal night settled over New Bhur-Esh, and lightnings flashed and rumbled in the grey, rolling sky.

In the morning the Elders said that was that, and they brushed their hands together to dismiss Arborass, for surely he was boiled alive. But the next evening, at dusk, a great voice was heard echoing over the sea, and the ground trembled and shook, and rings of smoke went up from Ashtah as from some strange and sinister engine. On this occasion no one spoke of Arborass, for the great voice that had thundered was his, but magnified a thousand times.

In the afternoon of the eighth day a chanting was heard, rolling in on a breeze off the sea, and the voices were of those long dead, which had the reedy quality of flutes. And when the chanting was done, there came once more a great booming of laughter; and all the people of the lava valley knew that indeed Arborass lived and worked strange wonders.

On the ninth day Ashtah hurled a mighty cluster of lava-bombs aloft, which hissed down into the sea between the volcano and the bay, causing clouds of steam and waves which washed up fishes roasted in their thousands. This was early in the morning; but midway to noon a second eruption rained glowing rocks within the bay itself. At noon a third peppered the shallowest waters of the bay and sank a number of anchored craft; and three hours later a fourth devastated the beach. And the people of New Bhur-Esh saw that this regular vomiting of the volcano had clear design, for always the fires fell closer and closer to the vines and gardens and yards of the boat-builders; aye, and closer to their homes in the face of the old cliffs. And the stench of sulphur was everywhere, and the people cowered in their cavern houses.

Now, as the afternoon passed in troubled silence and night grew on, when it seemed that Ashtah's fearful game was at an end, there sounded again over the sea the chanting of Arborass' mummy acolytes, and the necromancer's mad laughter; so that all of the people feared what the morning would bring. For the next morning would be the tenth, when Arborass had prophesied his return . . .

V

The strange visions receded in Erik Gustau's mind like a frost steamed away by the morning sun, and his astonishment at finding himself awake and seated in his chair close to the window of his study knew no ends; for the thing had been so real that he had thought to find himself in his bed and dreaming. Especially since the boy Ayrish (had that been his

name?) had seemed so very familiar to him. But then, tasting
a lingering fragrance in his mouth and seeing the small wineglass glowing in the sunlight, he remembered; and filled with
an almost mesmeric amazement, he tilted the glass trem-
blingly to his lips once more . . .

TEN YEARS WERE passed away now, since the coming of Arborass the necromancer and wizard to New Bhur-Esh, and Ayrish was grown to a young man. None remembered the
youth's remark, uttered on that day when the wizard was
turned away from the strand and his tomb-looted rowers
bore him out to sea—that the men of the lava valley should
have killed Arborass—but all remembered the tenth day and
the wizard's return.

All the night before the ground had shivered while Ashtah
rumbled, and the dawn was a scarlet thing splashed by the
sun on volcanic clouds, and the beach afloat with rotting fish
and squids. Mist lapped thick and scummy on the dawn
ocean like curdled milk, through which—on oars which plied
with a soundless and soulless mechanism—Arborass' black
ship, sails furled up, came gliding in to beach with a hiss of
crushed gravel.

All the Elders were there together with the men of the valley tribe, holding a line as the wizard stood up in the skull-
carved prow. "And would you resist me?" he asked in a soft
voice as fires smoked behind his baleful eyes. "And who then
says me nay? Which is the spokesman, and what message has
he for me?"

At this the wisest and oldest of all the Elders came slowly
forward, frail in his years but with a strength of mind and will

which all knew and respected. "Turn back, Arborass," he warned in quavery voice. "We valley people would have naught of fire-wizards and necromancers. Aye, and if you step down from your ship, then be certain we shall kill you!"

And Arborass turned his back on the shore and them that stood there, raising his arms on high and calling on Ashtah which smoked in the sea. "Oh, do you hear this mischief, Ashtah?" his voice rolled on the undulant mist. "And what is your answer, Mighty One, to this threat against your true and faithful priest and servant?"

At that the volcano roared and hurled aloft a ball of fiery rock, which sped across the sky and rushed down upon the strand. All the Elders and men cowered back, except the old one whose age—and whose horror—bound him to the spot as were he chained there. And the rock fell on him and drove him into the sand and shingle of the beach, hissing and steaming and filled with the stench of roasted flesh. Aghast, the men were frozen for long seconds and held their eyes averted; and when they would have rushed upon the wizard in his ship, Arborass faced them once more and eyed them through heavy-lidded orbs. And in a very low voice he spoke again to the volcano, but every man of them heard his whispered words:

"Ashtah," he said. "O Mighty One, hear me. If I am harmed by these sinners who own you not—if a single stone be hurled or spear cast, if a tiny bruise or cut be made in me— then crush them to a man, and all that is theirs with them, and level this valley with the hot outpourings of thy inmost being! Do you hear me, Ashtah?" And the ground rumbled and shook until all of them that stood there were hurled down upon the wave-washed sands.

Then said Arborass, "It is good that you prostrate your miserable selves; Ashtah will preserve them that worship him and heed the words of his priest." And when the men of the valley looked up, they saw that the necromancer had stepped down from his ship, his ravaged rowers with him, and that indeed the wizard was come amongst them . . .

VI

But that was all of ten years ago, and much had come to pass in the years flown between. Of the wizard: at first his demands were not excessive, and his comings to New Bhur-Esh were never more than one in any month. Then, on the occasion of the twelfth visit—when the people had begun to grumble of this wizard-priest no one wanted, who must be kept in bread, meat, fish and wine—suddenly his needs were seen to be far more than the mere necessities of life.

For Arborass now demanded a girl, who must be of eighteen or nineteen summers but no more, and she was to be made ready for him to take back to Ashtah when next he came. The volcano-God demanded sacrifice, he said, to appease him in his merciful but ever restive slumbers; and to prove a point he asked Ashtah if he were satisfied with the worship of his people, to which the volcano answered in a rumbling and a spouting of fire, and a hail of blazing boulders which sank half of the fishing fleet at anchor in the bay. So that at last the valley-dwellers knew the price of the wizard, and perhaps a few of them remembered the words of a small boy who had said they should kill this curse come upon them from the sea.

On the day before Arborass was due, the Elders gathered in their meeting place to decide what might be done; but ere they could talk Ashtah belched a cloud of steam, which drifted in off the sea. And when it hung low in the sky over New Bhur-Esh, then lightning came out of it and wrote in molten fire on the ground, DOOM.

And so each girl of eighteen and nineteen summers was given a number, and a pebble marked with that number was placed in a leather sack, and each of the girls was made to put in a hand and draw out a pebble until only one remained. The number of the final stone would mark the identity of the unfortunate maid; and so was Ashtah's first sacrifice chosen from the girls of the valley tribe. And this was the awful custom which prevailed from that time on, twice in every year, so that Ashtah would be appeased and leave the people of New Bhur-Esh in peace . . .

VII

And so things had stood for ten long years while Ayrish grew to a man, and for the last three years he had given court to a girl of one of the valley's richest families; and this kept secret from her father, who wanted nothing of paupers and foundlings. Meanwhile the family Ayrish lodged with had prospered, mainly due to his prowess as a sailor and fisherman, but the youth had been kept in poverty while his so-called brothers grew more sluggish yet and their manners more swinish.

And Leela, the girl he loved, was past eighteen and already had stood once with the other maidens to draw pebbles from the leather sack, on which occasion she had been spared. Now, in some four months' time, she must undergo the ordeal once more, and if she again survived twice more, before her age took her beyond the limits set by the volcano-god's wizard priest. Except that each time there would be fewer girls, for many families with daughters had fled New Bhur-Esh forever and taken their girls with them.

Soon, too, it would be the day of the games, which took place only once in every three years, when the young men of the tribe sported for the hands of its maidens. Ayrish had already asked Leela to be his wife, and she had been pleased to answer yes. It was, however, the custom to sport for a girl; and so, as the day grew closer, Leela prayed to all the beneficent gods of Theem'hdra that Ayrish would do well. The day came and the three Ayrish called brothers were also at the games, mocking the foundling as usual and poking fun at his rags. Moreover, all three had set their hearts on Leela, who was the loveliest girl in all the lava valley.

Ayrish did well with the spear, average good at the lifting, and was fastest of all at the running; and so his points were better than average. Then came the wrestling. Now his brothers, being heavy and brutish, were good wrestlers. Also, because they were used to giving Ayrish the occasional clout, they did not worry that he would be in the circle with themselves and the best of the other young men. They were sure that they could beat him and all the others together, and so take their pick of the village girls. Aye, and the brother who was champion wrestler, he would then lay claim to Leela. So they thought . . .

The pebble circle was prepared and the contestants stepped within, and when the Elders clapped their hands, then the

youths were at it. And in a very little while, only four remained within the circle: Ayrish and his brothers.

Now they banded together and circled about Ayrish, intending to have done with him before fighting among themselves;
but where they were now weary, he was fresh and fast as ever.
As they came at him he tripped one and winded another, then
went to throw the weakest from the ring. But this one threw
sand in his eyes and near-blinded him, which was a foul. Mad-
dened, Ayrish lashed out and broke the other's jaw, so that
now only two brothers faced him.

Of this pair the winded one tried to get behind him while
the other came in like a bull, and the first grabbed him
round the neck to choke him while the other butted him;
and this too was foul fighting. Angered again, Ayrish kicked
one in the crotch and booted him from the circle, then
turned on the largest of the three who clung to his neck.
Aye, and he thrashed him soundly; but in the fighting, blind
with blood and passion, both men reeled from the ring together.

Now the points were counted and a draw declared, and
Ayrish was asked which maid he would claim. He claimed
Leela—but so did his brutish brother!

A tie-breaker was organised (spear-casting, at which Ayrish was reckoned the inferior of the two) and targets were
placed upright in the ground. But then, before the contest
could begin, the brutish one spoke up:

"Away with the targets! I have my target: it is the ill-
mannered, ill-clad ingrate who presumes to call me brother!
When I make my cast, it shall be directly at him—if he has
the stomach for it . . ."

"That will suit me very well," answered Ayrish.

Seeing the bad blood between them—and because they had chosen the same maid, which could only lead to later troubles; also because several of the Elders were the friends of Ayrish's foster-father, and knew that he favoured his true son—all were agreed that the twain should cast to the death: and this was the way of it. They would toss a coin, and the winner would make first cast from a distance of fifty yards while the loser stood blindfolded and motionless. If the cast missed its mark, then the other should throw, and so on, until such time as one was struck dead.

The swinish one won the toss and hurled his spear at Ayrish across the paced-out distance. Perhaps his aim was off, or perhaps Leela's prayers were answered, for the spear passed between the left arm and body of Ayrish, harming him not. Then it was his cast.

The other was blindfolded, the distance once more paced out and a marker set, and Ayrish began his run; but hearing the thudding of his feet, the brutish brother cried out in terror, snatched off his bandage and ran away. At the appointed mark, Ayrish let fly his shaft—which cut the other down in mid-flight and pinned him dead to the earth. Thus ended the games.

Now the victor turned to the two remaining brothers, one holding his jaw and the other holding his groin, and said: "So be it. Now are you satisfied, brothers mine? Or would you, too, challenge me?" Which offer both declined.

Then Ayrish went to Leela's father and asked for her, but her father said: "Not so fast, young man! Can you provide a house for her?"

"I shall make a home for her," Ayrish answered.

"Good!" said the other. "When you have done that, then

we shall talk again." And he laughed, for there was no cave left in all the valley, so that he was sure Ayrish would fail to make a home for Leela.

"Will you give me one year?" asked Ayrish.

"I will not!" replied the other. "Must my daughter wait a year for a man to provide a house for her? I will give you a six-month, and not a day more."

And Ayrish had to be satisfied with that . . .

VIII

The youth told Leela what he was about, said his farewells to the tearful girl and straightway went to his boat. Now the boat in fact belonged to his foster-father, a small vessel with oars and a sail; but the owner, tearing his hair and grieving the loss of a son, made no protest and let him take it; and the two remaining sons were likewise glad to be shot of him. All except Leela, who waved farewell to her man as he set sail out of the bay.

And for many days Ayrish sailed south, hugging the coast and searching for a likely spot whereon to build a house for Leela. At last he came upon a place much like the valley of New Bhur-Esh but smaller, where green-clad cliffs guarded a calm bay whose waters were shielded from the ocean's tumult by a low-lying reef; and at length he found a passage and sailed his fragile craft in to a safe harbour.

Now Ayrish walked upon a golden beach and stepped beneath the shade of cool trees where parrots perched amid clusters of great nuts, and he saw that the earth was fertile and its fruits plentiful. Wild pigs rooted in the bushes, curious of Ayrish and unafraid, and pigeons nested in the forest bowers and made soft song. The air was sweet here, with nothing of the stink of volcanoes, and a stream of fresh water sparkled and ran down from the cliffs to a pool, and from there to the sea. And Ayrish explored the forest and stream and entire valley, even to the foot of the tall, unscalable cliffs, and found no other person dwelling there; whereupon he knew that this was where he must build Leela's house.

He found a cave in the white cliffs where they were draped with ivy, and a series of caves within, all hollowed out long ages gone when the pounding ocean was deeper; and many of these lesser caves were like windows which gazed out upon the shore and the valley and forest. So Ayrish found his house, and now he set about to put it in order. He paved the floors with rose-tinted, curiously veined stones from the beach, and he built steps and stairs of felled trees and tough creepers. He painted many of the white walls with the delicate blue dye of sea-snails, which were plentiful on the shore, and he planted orchids from the forest in the cliff ledges about the ivy-hung windows. And all in all his house was finer than any house in all the wizard-haunted valley of the volcano.

Then, when all was done, he set sail for New Bhur-Esh; but not with so light a heart as might be reckoned. No, for he was troubled by recurring thoughts of the necromancer Arborass, and of the time of the sacrifice, which again approached. Aye, and he was anxious; for Leela must once more draw a numbered stone from the sack, and yet another maiden must go with Arborass to the isle of the volcano-god, rowed out to sea by his worm-ravaged crew and never seen again. These were the thoughts which troubled Ayrish as he set his sails north, but in his wily mind he had a plan.

Quite simply, he would return to New Bhur-Esh, speak to Leela's father, and before the day of the choosing of the sacrificial maid he would steal Leela away and return with her to their new home. Aye, and if her father and family had any sense at all, then would they give up their riches and belongings—which could provide little of pleasure in a place such as the lava-valley—and leave the tribe to its lot, returning with the lovers to a new and happier life and clime. So thought Ayrish . . .

Alas, a storm blew up one day that wrecked him on a wild shore of barren scrubland; and because his boat was broken, now Ayrish must journey on foot. Day after day he ran and rested, ran and rested, eating what he could find and drinking wherever he found fresh water. And when he slept, which was rarely, still it seemed that he was running; and in his nightmares a hissing river of smoky lava surged ever nearer.

Until at length he was come to New Bhur-Esh, and clambering and sliding down the lava crags went straight to Leela's house, even bearded and in his tatters, and there presented himself—at a door freshly painted with the thick black pitch of sorrow! And even thundering at the door, Ayrish knew what this foretokened.

His Leela was gone, taken that very hour and rowed out to Ashtah by Arborass' sere mummy servitors!

Now Ayrish waxed wroth, and taking Leela's father by the neck he shook him and cursed his name, saying: "Oh, you, who promised her to me: what madness is this, that you have let the necromancer take her? Why is Arborass not dead first—or you, dead?—but not her, taken!" And such was his grief and rage that he was like to throttle the man and murder all his household.

Then Leela's mother spoke up, crying, "It was not all his fault, Ayrish—though as much his as anyone's. He thought your brothers might save her."

"Them?" cried the agonised youth. "Why them?"

"When you were gone they paid her court, but she would have none of them. And they swore that if her number was on the last pebble in the sack, then that they would protect her with their own lives. And still she would have nothing of them. And the last pebble did have her number, and when the wizard came for her, because your brothers feared the wrath of the volcano-God, they did nothing!"

"They are not my brothers but men of this accursed valley!" cried Ayrish. "And you lava-lovers *never* do anything!" And he hurled the near-throttled master of the house aside like a rag doll.

Next he ran to the cave of his foster-father and battered down the door, and striding in he sought out that pair he once had called brothers. Drunk they were and swinish, but he rattled their heads together and tossed them forth, and dragged them down to the beach and doused them in the sea. And when they were sober he said to them:

"So, and would you steal my woman away in my absence? Aye, and then let Arborass take her without ever lifting a finger? Very well, *now* you shall lift a finger, and more than that if you value your lives. For if Leela dies, be sure your own lives are forfeit!"

Now the rest of that day Ayrish ate good meat and red, and he drank sweet water and a little wine; and all who saw him as he racked his desperate brain and stamped to and fro on the beach—bearded, ragged, wild and red-eyed—thought he must be mad. His once-called brothers thought so too, and grovelling in the sand as he cursed them, they made plans of their own.

Then, as the smoky sun sank down into the Unknown Ocean, limning Ashtah a black silhouette, and as the sea grew darkly green, Ayrish dragged the cowards aboard a boat and set sail for the volcano isle; and all who saw them go knew that they would never see them again . . .

IX

Now when their boat was out beyond the bay and half-way sailed toward its doleful destiny, then Ayrish and the brothers felt an unaccustomed swirl to the waters and a current which tugged them ever faster toward fire-crested Ashtah. There was only a crescent moon, and this half-hidden by sulphurous clouds, and something of a murky mist lay on the sea which gave them good cover. But the current which drew them un-erringly toward the volcano isle was strange, and with all of his sailor's craft Ayrish had no knowledge of it. He suspected, though, that it was more than merely the race of an ebbing tide.

As for the brothers: they sat sullen and silent while Ayrish handled the tiller; and the closer they got to Ashtah, the more sallow their faces and nervous their shifty eyes. And as they went so Ayrish whispered his plan to them, which was this: that they would seek out Arborass in the night and kill him, drive a stake through his heart, cut off his head and burn him; which is the proper way to deal with wizards. The broth-ers heard him and grew more afraid of Ayrish than of the isle now looming from the mist, for surely was he mad.

And as they ran on that strange and silent water, Ayrish lowered the sail and bade them take up the oars; and they closed with the black and craggy rocks of the place, and Ayrish jumped ashore and tied up the boat to a spur of lava. Then, while he was about this task, the brothers came up behind him and smote him with an oar, saying:

"*This* for our brother, whom you slew! And farewell to you, madman, who would kill a wizard! What? A wizard? A man with the power to command volcanoes and the art to raise up the very dead? Aye, and if we see you again, foundling, surely it were pulling on Arborass' oars with the rest of his tomb-risen crew!"

And they left him there on the rocks, and manning the oars drew away into the night. And only then did they learn of the watchdog Arborass had set over the nighted island, which was the sea itself! For row as they might and however zestfully, still they could not pull free of the place, and dawn found them exhausted and adrift a stone's throw from the lava crags of Ashtah's shore.

High in his eyrie—a corpse-constructed tower of black lava blocks and narrow windows, perched on the very rim of Ashtah's throat—Arborass saw them there in the sea and sent his minion mummies to deal with them. Down went the soulless ones and into the necromancer's boat, and out to sea where the brothers hauled on their oars once more in a useless frenzy. And the mummies cast spears through them where they sweated and toiled, and they fell into the sea.

"So perish all who would sail too close in the night!" cried Arborass from on high, and laughing he returned to his diversions.

Now Ayrish, who had awakened with the dawn and climbed

to the foot of Arborass' pile, heard the wizard's words and saw the death of the brothers in their boat; and so he knew that the necromancer's mummies were at sea and their master unprotected. Then he quickly found the tower's door and passed through into the wizard's lair; and he heard Arborass' laughter echoing up from unseen vaults beneath.

Following winding lava steps into the heart of the rock, Ayrish soundlessly descended and came upon the wizard in his inner sanctum. Now keeping silent and watching the doings of the man, he saw Arborass pass through a secret door, and in his turn he followed him. And in that innermost place, finally he saw Leela, all naked and lovely and a-swoon. She lay upon an altar-like slab which could be tilted by means of a lever, and the slab stood before a fiery blowhole whose rim was red with heat from Ashtah's heart. And Ayrish saw that when the slab was tilted, then would Leela plunge to her doom in the liquid rock of Ashtah's loins.

Now on that selfsame slab, close to Leela's head, were censers of smouldering opiates whose fumes subdued the girl; and as Arborass disrobed Ayrish saw that the necromancer would take first-fruits before feeding his god. And a red rage rose up in Ayrish as he thought of the misery of so many girls gone this way before. And such was his fury that he no longer owned his senses.

As Arborass went to the girl, so Ayrish leaped out upon him, a great knife uplifted in his hand. Arborass heard!—saw!—grasped the lever!—screamed as Ayrish's knife pierced him!

Now the youth swept the girl from the slowly tilting slab and made to carry her from the place; but the necromancer, dying, called upon his mummies to kill them. Down into that secret place the returning dead ones shuffled, and two of them snatched Leela from Ayrish's arms while the others sought to stab him with their spears. And he was struck, and the spear tore a wound in his side.

Then, in his pain and horror, Ayrish became filled with the strength of ten. Before the mummies could pierce him again, he snatched up two of their number like bales of straw and hurled them at the staggering necromancer. Now mummies, wizard and all fell atop the tilting slab, and all slid therefrom into Ashtah's fiery maw. In the next moment, even in the blinking of an eye, the rest of Arborass' tomb-spawn crumbled and fell to dust where they stood, and all the volcano isle shook itself as a man starting from evil dreams.

Then Ayrish took up the girl from where she had fallen, and he tottered from Arborass' tower even as it slid into ruins and toppled into Ashtah's furnace throat. And down the shuddery carven steps went Ayrish, and deliriously into his boat where it bumped against the rocky wharf and rolled on the choppy waters; and as Leela began to come awake he placed her in the middle of the boat, took up the oars and plied madly for the open sea.

Now, with Arborass dead, the island no longer exerted its magnet pull, and soon Ayrish was well clear of the volcano. But the sea grew rougher yet as Ashtah thundered, great waves rising and frothing in all directions; and the youth, weak from his scarlet wound, rose up from where he sat to attend to the sail. And at that very moment the boat tilting like a cockleshell, Ayrish was tossed overboard and dragged down in the wrack of ocean!

Up Leela sprang, recovered from her drug-induced swoon, and clinging to the boat's side she scanned the frothy deep and flying spume. And "Ayrish" she cried uselessly against the storm. "Ayrish! *Ayrish*!"

But only the volcano answered, with roar of steam and spouting lava flood. And splitting his sides in fissures of fire, Ashtah hurled his molten might aloft. God no more, he vented his fury upon the sky—and all the steamy bile of his belly fell in the valley of New Bhur-Esh.

"Ayrish! Ayrish!" the maid screamed again through the maelstrom of wind and water—and miracle of miracles, from somewhere close at hand, suddenly she thought to hear her lover's answer!

X

"Ayrish!" the maid's cry receded along with the rush and roar of the storm. "*Ayrish—*" it became the merest whisper. But to Erik Gustau, lolling in his chair, it seemed the name she cried was now his own! And her voice . . . *that* voice! The sweet, anguished voice he had thought never to hear again except in memory or later, God willing, in heaven. Could it be? A faint, far echo in a sounding shell: "Erik! Erik!"

Snatched awake, startled from his dream by hope and horror combined, the young man sprang up from his chair and reeled with a feverish vertigo. Rivered in sweat he clung to his table, glared at the spinning room, cursed the fickle god of fever-dreams whose spiteful hand had snatched him back.

Then he remembered the wine!

His glass stood empty, but wine enough in the bottle. "Lilly!" he cried after his dream, which suddenly he knew was more than any mere dream. "Lilly!" And tilting the bottle to his lips he drank it dry . . .

THE POST-MORTEM VERDICT was death by misadventure. But in fact Erik Gustau's lungs were found full of salt water. Indeed, upon hearing his master's cry and bursting in the door, Benson found him lying in a pool of water.

As for the deep gash in his side . . .

A mystery, the entire thing, which must forever go unexplained. And then there was that which even Benson dared not tell. For he must now seek a new master, and things were bad enough without making them worse. Who would employ a proven liar or madman?

Who would believe that upon entering his master's study and finding him stretched upon the floor, drenched and dead, Benson had thought to hear, as from a great distance in space and time, the glad, wondering cries of lovers reunited, the snap of sails filling in the wind, and the hiss and crash of a sundered island sinking in a primal sea? . . .

The Sorcerer's Dream

As translated by Thelred Gustau, from
Teh Atht's *Legends of the Olden Runes*

I TEH ATHT, have dreamed a dream; and now, before dawn's
light may steal it from my old mind—while yet Gleeth
the blind God of the Moon rides the skies over Klühn and the
stars of night peep and leer hideously—I write it down in the
pages of my rune-book, wherein all the olden runes are as
legends unfolded. For I have pondered the great mysteries of
time and space, have solved certain of the riddles of the Ancients themselves, and all such knowledge is writ in my rune-
book for the fathoming of sorcerers as yet unborn.

As to why I dreamed this dream, plumbing the Great Abyss
of future time to the very END itself, where only the gaunt
black Tomb of the Universe gapes wide and empty, my reasons were many. They were born in mummy-dust sifting
down to me through the centuries; in the writings of mages
ancient when the world was still young; in cipherless hieroglyphs graven in the stone of Geph's broken columns; aye,
and in the vilest nightmares of shrieking madmen, whose

visions had driven them mad. And such as these reasons were they drew me as the morning sun draws up the ocean mists on Theem'hdra's bright strand, for I cannot suffer a mystery to go undiscovered.

The mystery was this: that oft and again over the years I had heard whispers of a monstrous alien God who seeped down from the stars when the world was an inchoate infant—whose name, Cthulhu, was clouded with timeless legends and obscured in half-forgotten myths and nameless lore—and such whispers as I had heard troubled me greatly . . .

Concerning this Cthulhu a colleague in olden Chlangi, the warlock Nathor Tarqu, had been to the temple of the Elder Ones in Ulthar in the land of Earth's dreams to consult the Pnakotic Manuscript; and following that visit to Ulthar he had practiced exceedingly strange magicks before vanishing forever from the known world of men. Since that time Chlangi has become a fallen city, and close by in the Desert of Sheb the Lamia Orbiquita has builded her castle, so that now all men fear the region and call Chlangi the Shunned City.

I, too, have been to Ulthar, and I count it a blessing that on waking I could not recall what I read in the Pnakotic Manuscript—only such awful names as were writ therein, such as Cthulhu, Tsathoggua, and Ubbo-Sathla. And there was also mention of one Ghatanothoa, a son of Cthulhu to whom a dark temple even now towers in Theem'hdra, in a place that I shall not name. For I know the place is doomed, that there is a curse upon the temple and its priests, and that when they are no more their names shall be stricken from all records . . .

Even so, and for all this, I would never have entertained so long and unhealthy an interest in Loathly Lord Cthulhu had I not myself heard His call in uneasy slumbers; that call which turns men's minds, beckoning them on to vile worship and viler deeds. Such dreams visited themselves upon me after I had spoken with Zar-thule, a barbarian reaver—or rather, with the fumbling mushroom *thing* that had once been a reaver—locked away in Klühn's deepest dungeon to rot and gibber hideously of unearthly horrors. For Zar-thule had thought to rob the House of Cthulhu on Arlyeh the forbidden isle, as a result of which Arlyeh had gone down under the waves in a great storm . . . but not before Zar-thule gazed upon Cthulhu, whose treasures were garnets of green slime, red rubies of blood and moonstones of malignancy and madness!

And when dreams such as those conjured by Zar-thule's story came to sour the sweet embrace of Shoosh, Goddess of the Still Slumbers, I would rise from my couch and tremble, and pace the crystal floors of my rooms above the Bay of Klühn. For I was sorely troubled by this mystery; even I, Teh Atht, whose peer in the occult arts exists not in Theem'hdra, troubled most sorely.

SO I WENT up into the Mount of the Ancients where I smoked the Zha-weed and sought the advice of my wizard ancestor Mylakhrion of Tharamoon—dead eleven hundred years— who told me to look to the ORIGIN and the AFTERMATH, the BEGINNING and the END, that I might know. And that same night, in my secret vault, I sipped a rare and bitter distillation of mandrake and descended again into deepest dreams, even into dreams long dead and forgotten before ever human dreamers existed. Thus in my search for the

ORIGIN I dreamed myself into the dim and fabulous past.

And I saw that the Earth was hot and in places molten, and Gleeth was not yet born to sail the volcanic clouds of pre-dawn nights. Then, drawn by a force beyond my ken, I went out into the empty spaces of the primal void, where I saw, winging down through the vasty dark, shapes of uttermost lunacy. And first among them all was Cthulhu of the tentacled face, and among His followers came Yogg-Sothoth, Tsathoggua, and many others which were like unto Cthulhu but less than Him; and lo!—Cthulhu spoke the Name of Azathoth, whereupon stars blazed forth as He passed and all space gloried in His coming.

Down through the outer immensities they winged, alighting upon the steaming Earth and building great cities of a rare architecture, wherein singular angles confused the eye and mind until towers were as precipices and solid walls gateways! And there they dwelt for aeons, in their awful cities under leaden skies and strange stars. Aye, and they were mighty sorcerers, Cthulhu and His spawn, who plotted great evil against Others who were once their brethren. For they had not come to Earth of their own will but had fled from Elder Gods whose codes they had abused most terribly.

And such were their thaumaturgies in the great grey cities that those Elder Gods felt tremors in the very stuff of Existence itself, and they came in haste and great anger to set seals on the houses of Cthulhu, wherein He and many of His kin were prisoned for their sins. But others of these great old sorcerers, such as Yogg-Sothoth and Yib-Tstll, fled again into the stars, where they were followed by the Elder Gods who prisoned them wherever they were found. Then, when all was done, the great and just Gods of Eld returned whence they had come; and aeon upon aeon passed and the stars revolved through strange configurations, moving inexorably toward a time when Cthulhu would be set free . . .

SO IT WAS that I saw the ORIGIN whereof my ancestor Mylakhrion of Tharamoon had advised me, and awakening in my secret vault I shuddered and marvelled that this Loathly Lord Cthulhu had come down all the ages unaltered. For I knew that indeed He lived still in His city sunken under the sea, and I was mazed by His immortality. Then it came to me to dwell at length upon the latter, on Cthulhu's immortality, and to wonder if He was truly immortal . . . And of this also had Mylakhrion advised, saying, "Look to the ORIGIN and the AFTERMATH, the BEGINNING and the END."

Thus it was that last night I sipped again of mandrake fluid and went out in a dream to seek the END. And indeed I found it . . .

There at the end of time all was night, where all the universe was a great empty tomb and nothing stirred. And I stood upon a dead sea bottom and looked up to where Gleeth had once graced the skies; old Gleeth, long sundered now and drifted down to Earth as dust. And I turned my saddened eyes down again to gaze upon a gaunt, solitary spire of rock that rose and twisted and towered up from the bottom of the dusty ocean.

And because curiosity was ever the curse of sorcerers, it came to me to wonder why, since this was the END, time itself continued to exist. And it further came to me that time existed only because space, time's brother, had *not quite* ended, life was *not quite* extinct. With this thought, as if born of the thought itself, there came a mighty rumbling and the ground trembled and shook. All the world shuddered and the dead sea bottom split open in many places, creating chasms from which there at once rose up the awful spawn of Cthulhu!

And lo!—I knew now that indeed Cthulhu was immortal, for in Earth's final death spasm He was reborn! The great twisted spire of rock—all that was left of Arlyeh, Cthulhu's house—shattered and fell in ruins, laying open to my staggering gaze His sepulcher. And shortly thereafter, preceded by a nameless stench, He squeezed Himself out from the awful tomb into the gloom of the dead universe . . .

Then, when they saw Cthulhu, all of them that were risen up from their immemorial prisons rushed and flopped and floundered to His feet, making obeisance to Him. And He blinked great evil octopus eyes and gazed all about in wonderment, for His final sleep had endured for aeon upon aeon, and he had not known that the universe was now totally dead and time itself at an end.

And Cthulhu's anger was great! He cast His mind out into the void and gazed upon cinders that had been stars; He looked for light and warmth in the farthest corners of the universe and found only darkness and decay; He searched for life in the great seas of space and found only the tombs at time's end. And His anger waxed *awesome*!

Then He threw back His tentacled head and bellowed out the Name of Azathoth in a voice that sent all of the lesser Beings at His feet scurrying back to their chasm sepulchers, and lo! . . . nothing happened! The sands of time were run out, and even the greatest magicks had lost their potency.

And so Cthulhu raged and stormed and blasphemed as

only He might until, at the height of His anger, *suddenly He knew me!*

Dreaming as I was and far, far removed from my own age, nevertheless He sensed me and in an instant turned upon me, face tentacles writhing and reaching out for my dreaming spirit. And then, to my eternal damnation, before I fled shrieking back down the corridors of time to leap awake drenched in a chill perspiration in my secret vault, I gazed deep into the demon eyes of Cthulhu . . .

NOW IT IS dawn and I am almost done with the writing of this, and soon I will lay down my rune-book and set myself certain tasks for the days ahead. First I will see to it that the crystal dome of my workshop tower is covered with black lacquer, for I fear I can no longer bear to look out upon the stars . . . Where once they twinkled afar in chill but friendly fashion, now I know that they leer down in celestial horror as they move inexorably toward Cthulhu's next awakening. For surely He will rise up many times before that final awakening at the very END.

Aye, and if I had thought to escape the Lord of Arlyeh when I fled from him in my dream, then I was mistaken. Cthulhu was, He is, and He will always be; and I know now that this is the essence of that great mystery which so long perplexed me. For Cthulhu is a Master of Dreams, and now He knows me. And He will follow me through my slumbers all the days of my life, and evermore I shall hear His call . . . Even unto the END.